ONE
LAST TIME

THE KISSING BOOTH 3

ONE LAST TIME

BETH REEKLES

EMBER

Text copyright © 2021 by Beth Reekles
Netflix is a registered trademark of Netflix, Inc. and its affiliates.
Artwork used with permission of Netflix, Inc.

All rights reserved. Published in the United States by Ember, an imprint of
Random House Children's Books, a division of Penguin Random House LLC, New York.
Simultaneously published by Penguin Random House UK, London.

Ember and the E colophon are registered trademarks of Penguin Random House LLC.

Visit us on the web! GetUnderlined.com

Educators and librarians, for a variety of teaching tools,
visit us at RHTeachersLibrarians.com

Library of Congress Cataloging-in-Publication Data is available upon request.
ISBN 978-0-593-42565-7 (trade) — ISBN 978-0-593-42566-4 (ebook)

The text of this book is set in 11-point Palatino LT Pro.
Interior design by Andrea Lau

Printed in the United States of America
10 9 8 7 6 5 4 3 2 1
First Ember Edition 2021

For all the bookish fifteen-year-olds with a story to tell

ONE
LAST TIME

Author's Note

Hi, everybody!

Well, here we are. Five books, three movies, and ten years of the Kissing Booth, and Elle, Lee, and Noah's story is finally wrapping up! Can you believe it?

I wrote *The Kissing Booth* when I was fifteen, uploading it to Wattpad. I was astonished that *anybody* wanted to read it, and barely dared to dream I might publish something one day. (I also used to laugh at the comments saying it should be a movie—that seemed too brilliant and bizarre to even dream about. . . .) I always said back then that I never planned to write a sequel, or to carry on the story, but I had a hard time letting go of these characters. They've meant so much to me, and they've been such a huge part of my life. I'm glad I've had the opportunity to explore their story more, and to now wrap it all up in this novel.

I've always known how things would turn out for Elle and Noah—and Lee. I maybe didn't always know what the journey there would look like, but I knew the final destination. Which is exactly what you'll get to dive into now, in this installment of the Kissing Booth series.

This book was a really interesting challenge. Write a book based on the movie based on the movies based on my books. Er, simple, right? Maybe not quite simple, but a lot of fun. And while this book is a novelization of the third Netflix movie, you'll notice that it doesn't stick completely to the script. While it follows the same storyline, it does also follow from my sequel, *The Kissing Booth 2: Going the Distance*, so instead of Marco and Chloe, like in the movie, you'll be back with Levi and Amanda!

Plus, you'll get to see some scenes and interactions that aren't in the movie, and explore the characters differently. You won't need to see the movie to be able to follow this book. Maybe you're picking up this book having only seen the movies. Maybe you've been a fan since the early Wattpad days. Either way, thanks for being here, and I hope you enjoy this final chapter in Elle's story.

Beth X

Chapter One

Dad cleared his throat, tossing the mail onto the counter. A thick envelope slid its way over to me.

"What's that?" I asked, my mouth full of Cheerios.

Instead of answering me, he said, "Hey, Brad, why don't you go clean up your room, huh, before you head over to Benny's."

"But—"

There was no room for *buts*, though, because Dad just hauled Brad, my little brother, up from his stool at the breakfast bar with a grunt and set him on his feet. "Go on, bud, and I'll let you off doing the dishes with Elle this morning."

I was immediately suspicious. This summer, Dad had decided to give Brad more responsibility around the house. I'd already shown him how to fold laundry and how to make pasta. Dad had shown him how to mow the lawn properly on the weekend, and we'd just gotten into a routine where he helped one of us do the dishes. Dad said it was because Brad was in middle school now and getting old enough to help out, but we all knew the real reason: I'd be starting college in the fall and wouldn't be around to do all those kinds of things anymore.

My stomach twisted at the thought of it. In a few months, once I was in Berkeley, everything would change so much. It wasn't like the house totally fell apart without me—it was always fine when I spent a couple of weeks at the Flynns' beach house every summer. But still. I *was* kinda worried about leaving them to fend for themselves.

Just a few days ago, I'd been on top of the world, walking across that stage to get my high school diploma, tossing my cap into the air with everybody else. . . . I'd gotten into UC Berkeley with my best friend in the entire world, Lee Flynn, just like we'd always planned, ever since we were old enough to understand what college was. We'd spent our whole lives together, and we'd be starting this next chapter of life as college students together, too. It was so perfect. It was exactly the way it was meant to be.

We had said senior year was going to be *our* year—and sure, it had been . . . a little bumpy sometimes, but it had still been awesome. And college would be, too. As apprehensive as I was about how different everything would be, it was still exciting to think about.

"What's going on?" I asked, narrowing my eyes at the envelope and then at my dad. I shoveled down the last of my cereal, wiped the back of my hand across my mouth, and pushed aside the bowl.

Dad took Brad's empty stool, tapping the envelope near

me. "Maybe you'd like to tell me what's going on. This came for you."

"For me?"

I picked up the envelope and turned it over.

Ms. R. Evans

It was marked with the Harvard University logo.

Oh.

Oh shit.

My Cheerios threatened to make a reappearance and my heart was somewhere in my throat as I fumbled to open the envelope. This wasn't happening. This was not happening. A couple of months ago, I got a letter telling me I was waitlisted, and that was supposed to be the end of it. Except . . . apparently it wasn't.

I shook the letter out and laid it flat on the counter to read it.

. . . delighted to inform you . . .

My head snapped up, my mouth hanging open. "I . . . I . . ."

I could not get my words out.

Impatient, his eyes looking a little crazed behind his glasses, my dad snatched the letter up to read for himself. I watched his eyes dart over the words a few times before he let out a hoot of laughter and shook his head.

I winced, knowing what would come next, and headed him off with a groan, slumping forward to bury my face in my arms. "Please don't say it. Please don't say it."

"You got into Harvard! My little girl got into Harvard! You—" Then he cleared his throat again. "Honey, you didn't tell me you'd even applied. Is this . . . Is this because of Noah?"

I groaned again.

This was not supposed to happen.

The first college I'd applied to had been Berkeley—because, *duh,* of course it was. And then I'd applied to safety schools. Of course I had. That's what you did, right? That's what my guidance counselor told me to do. So, obviously, Lee and I had tried to pick all the same safety schools.

Lee had talked about applying to Brown when his girlfriend, Rachel, had applied there, and . . .

Maybe, sort of, in a moment of madness, I'd . . . sent off an application to Harvard. Where my boyfriend, Lee's older brother, Noah, had been for the last year.

It was madness, because I was not supposed to get in. I never thought I would. I mean, sure, I worked hard at school, and my grades were good, and I had a couple of extracurriculars, and I'd done well on the SATs . . . but . . . it was Harvard, you know? It wasn't supposed to be the kind of place you got into on a whim; it was the sort of place you spent your entire high school career working toward.

It was madness because they were never supposed to say yes.

"Kind of," I told my dad now. I lifted my head just a little, grimacing as I caught his eye. Ugh. He looked so damn *proud* of me. I wished he'd stop that. "I just . . . I dunno. I thought it might be nice. Like how Lee wanted to apply to Brown because that's where Rachel's going. I never mentioned it to anybody—"

"Wait—Lee doesn't know about this?"

Some of the pride started to dim in his expression. *Good,* I thought. A little parental disappointment was the least I deserved for keeping a secret from my best friend. The last time I'd done that was when I'd started dating Noah and I'd been worried about Lee finding out and taking it badly. And *that* hadn't exactly gone too great when he did find out, even if he forgave me in the end. . . .

"It's not like I was trying to hide it from him," I tried to explain. "This wasn't like . . . you know, when I started dating Noah. I just never thought I'd get in, so I didn't see the point in scaring him. I didn't think . . ." I let out a sigh. "I got wait-listed. Which I thought was kind of cool, you know? But people who get wait-listed for Harvard don't actually get in."

"Looks like they do."

"Yeah," I muttered.

A grin split my dad's face and he came around the counter to hug me. "Well, whatever you decide to do, I'm so proud of you, Elle. Harvard! I know I've had my reservations about you dating Noah, but, hey, if this is the kind of influence he's having on you . . ."

"I didn't *just* apply because of Noah, you know. I mean— it's Harvard. Who wouldn't want to get into Harvard?"

"He's just the reason you picked that over, say, Yale."

7

"Yeah," I admitted. "And I figured . . . I mean, I sort of . . . wanted to see if I could get in, you know?"

"Well, you kept it pretty quiet! Didn't even tell your old man!" He laughed as he sat back down opposite me, but then I watched his forehead crease and the smile slip from his face. He tapped the letter again. "So, uh . . . you didn't tell Lee. Or Noah either, I'm guessing?"

"No. Nobody knows about it. I didn't want to get Noah's hopes up, and I didn't want Lee to think . . . I didn't want to hurt him. Make him think I didn't want to go to Berkeley."

"Have you accepted your place there yet?"

I shook my head. I'd meant to. I just hadn't gotten around to it yet.

Maybe part of why I hadn't was because I'd held out some little, *tiny* piece of hope that I'd get off the wait-list at Harvard, but . . .

This was not supposed to happen.

One afternoon over the phone, Noah had mentioned, flippantly, that maybe I should apply—he'd said it'd be nice to have me around and to spend more time together and that he missed me so much. He hadn't meant for me to take it *seriously*, and I knew that, but . . .

It stuck. And I honestly had wanted to see if I could do it. *Harvard. I got a place at Harvard. Me—Elle Evans!*

My mouth was dry and my stomach had coiled itself into knots.

"Any idea what you're going to do?"

I stared at the letter from the admissions office, thinking of the one in my drawer upstairs that said much the same thing but had a Berkeley letterhead instead.

Lee and I had had our hearts set on Berkeley since what felt like forever. It wasn't out of state, and it was where our moms had met and become such good friends. It felt special.

And even if you took Noah and our relationship out of the equation . . . well, Harvard was Harvard. It was the kind of college you were supposed to dream about going to.

But, okay, the fact that Noah was there was a pretty strong pull, I had to admit.

I looked from the letter to my dad, who just looked so damn proud of me that he might burst.

"Please don't tell everyone about this," I said. "Especially not the Flynns. I need to . . . I need to think about this."

I couldn't bear it if Dad let it slip to Lee and Noah's parents first in a crazy proud-parent moment, and that was how Lee or Noah found out. I didn't even know how Noah would react to me getting into Harvard, or what he'd say if I decided to go—maybe him saying it'd be nice to have me there had been a throwaway comment, something he didn't actually mean. Maybe he wouldn't *really* want me there anyway.

And Lee . . .

Lee would be so hurt if I turned around and told him that, actually, despite all our promises, and despite how put out I'd been when I'd heard he'd applied to Brown, I'd done the same thing behind his back to be with Noah.

"Gonna have to decide soon, bud," Dad said. He reached over to squeeze my shoulder. "There's only so long Harvard will wait before they need an answer about this."

Before I told Noah and Lee, I had to figure this out for myself first. And fast.

Chapter Two

I spent the rest of my morning getting ready for lunch with the Flynns. Lee's mom had organized for us all to go out for a fancy meal to celebrate our graduation. I usually wasn't one for dressing up, so there had been a few outfit changes and a slightly desperate video call to Rachel, who was also going to be there. It had been enough to distract me from thinking too hard about the two admittance letters that now sat in my desk drawer. And then, of course, Noah had come by to pick me up and drive me to the restaurant, so it wasn't *really* like I'd had the time to think about it.

"So," Noah said, slinging his arm around my shoulder once we were out of the car. My hand moved up automatically, fingers locking with his. "I've been thinking."

"Careful. Don't wanna hurt yourself."

He rolled his eyes.

"About?" I prompted, jokes aside.

"I was thinking," he said again, "maybe this summer you could come with me to Boston. You can check out where I'm gonna be living. I can show you your dresser drawer."

"You saved a dresser drawer just for me? Awww," I cooed at him, turning my face up to his to bat my eyelashes. I pinched his cheek playfully. "Look at my boyfriend, the big ball of mush."

He was *such* a big ball of mush. At least compared to how he'd been when we first started dating. Noah had been our school's bad boy, with a reputation for hooking up with tons of girls (which he later told me was mostly untrue). He even had a motorcycle, and he used to smoke just to help him look the part. And here he was, talking about the dresser drawer he'd reserved for me.

I loved him so much.

"It would've been so awesome if you'd been in Boston with me. Even if it wasn't at Harvard. We'd have seen so much more of each other. Could've even, like, gotten an apartment together over the summer or something."

I stopped in my tracks, pulling my hand from his before he noticed how clammy it had become.

Noah stopped walking, too, turning around with a laugh. His face was stiff, though, and he couldn't quite meet my eyes, looking past me at the parking lot instead. "What, too mushy? I thought you wanted me to open up more, be more honest, not all macho-macho and never talking about anything emotional."

I opened my mouth, but nothing came out.

Noah's cheeks flushed pink. "I mean, like, you know. Elle." He cleared his throat, rubbing the back of his neck. "I wasn't serious. I mean." *Gulp*. "Moving in together'd be a big step. We're not there yet. I was just joking around."

This should be where I told him I got in. Hell, this should be where I told him I'd actually applied in the first place on the impossible chance that I might end up in Boston with him. He had no idea, but here he was talking about how nice it would be to have me around, how we could *live together*.

The idea of Noah wanting to make such a big commitment and live with me should have made my heart do somersaults. I should have been squealing and throwing my arms around him and shouting, *Surprise! We can! I can come to Boston!*

This was definitely where I should tell him.

Especially when he looked so mortified that he'd suggested we live together in what was almost a throwaway comment and thought I was horrified at the very idea.

"Elle?"

Crap. Come on, Elle, say something. Tell him!

I looked at Noah, focusing back on his face instead of staring right through him. And I said, "I think I left my curling iron on."

I didn't think he bought it, but he said, "Text your dad. He can check for you."

I quickly pulled out my phone and pretended to send my dad a text, typing it out and then deleting it straightaway.

"C'mon, we're already late," Noah said.

"Yeah," I said, shooting him a look, but a smile crept back onto my face. "And whose fault is that?"

"What, like it's *my* fault you look so damn good?"

I fell back in step beside him and he bent to press a kiss to my neck. I laughed and pushed him off. "Don't you dare! That's what made us late in the first place."

"You know, *technically*, we wouldn't be late if we didn't show up at all. . . ."

"Noah Flynn, don't even think about it. There is a big ol' ice cream sundae in there with my name on it, and not even you and your cute butt can get in the way of that."

"My cute butt, huh?"

I didn't know how, even after over a year of being together, he could still make me blush by saying something like that, but I blushed nonetheless. Noah chuckled, wrapping his arm around me as we walked inside.

• • •

Dining out with the Flynns was a pretty regular affair, but usually when we went out for a meal, my dad and brother were there, too. I'd thought it was a little weird that Lee and Noah's mom, June, had made a point of inviting only me out for brunch today, but maybe it was because she'd invited Rachel, too. Maybe it was less of an "Elle" thing and more of a "Noah's girlfriend" thing today.

Even after more than a year, me being Noah's girlfriend was still a new dynamic we were all getting used to.

The rooftop restaurant they'd picked out was gorgeous. I felt underdressed in my jeans, my gaze lingering on a group of women in their early twenties who were laughing and drinking mimosas. I was glad I'd let Rachel persuade me to leave my hoodie behind and put some effort into doing my hair.

We found the others easily enough, and as June got up to hug me hello, I said, "I'm so sorry we're late. Traffic was awful, and we didn't realize we'd have to stop for gas."

"It's fine," she said, smiling warmly as we took our seats.

I heard Lee mutter, "Traffic? Really? That's what she's going with?"

It was promptly followed by "Ouch!" as Noah stomped on his foot under the table.

Once we'd ordered, I looked out at the view of the skyline. "This place is so perfect."

"We wanted to finally take you guys out someplace special to celebrate your graduation properly," Matthew, Lee, and Noah's dad, said.

"Elle's right," Rachel gushed. "It's so amazing here. Thank you for inviting me."

"I can't believe we've actually graduated," Lee said, shaking his head. "It's so weird to think we won't be going back to school in the fall. Like, *that's it*. And now we've got the entire summer ahead of us—"

"It'll go quick," Noah told us. "Believe me."

"Yeah, you kids better make the most of it," Matthew said. "Any big plans for the summer?"

"You mean aside from the beach house?" Lee laughed. "Actually, we were talking about going up this weekend, if that's cool?"

I looked at his parents with an expectant smile, waiting for them to nod and say, "Of course!" Because why wouldn't they? Lee and I had been planning a long weekend at their family beach house for a couple weeks now. I'd gone there with the whole Flynn family every summer, but Lee and I had thought, now that graduation was out of the way, it would be cool to go just us guys, sneak some beers, blow off some steam after the craziness and intensity of senior year.

But instead of smiling back and saying we could go, no problem, Matthew and June just looked at each other. June pursed her lips, looking worried. I watched her husband nod back at her and got a sinking feeling in my stomach.

I wasn't the only one who'd noticed.

"What's that look?" Noah asked. "Is everything okay?"

"Everything's fine," June said with forced breeziness and a stiff, too-wide smile as she looked around at us.

Uh-oh, I thought. That wasn't a mom smile. That was more like the kind of smile she wore when she was taking a call from the office.

She drew a deep breath. "Actually, we have some news."

A creeping feeling of dread prickled over my skin.

"We've decided to sell the beach house."

No way.

This wasn't happening.

Today had already been a total roller coaster, but this was the worst part so far—and it wasn't even one o'clock yet.

"What? Why?" Noah burst out, while Lee shot to his feet, crying, "Hold on! What? Where's this coming from?"

"Lee, please, sit down," his dad said firmly.

Lee did, but gawped at his parents. "Wait a second—was this whole meal just to soften the blow and butter us up before you dropped that bomb?"

"No!" June sat up straighter, then fiddled with her napkin. "Not . . . really . . . Kind of. Did it work?"

"Using delicious meats and beverages to deliver bad news is wrong, Mom, just wrong. I thought we raised you better than that."

Noah elbowed him, to quit with the jokes. "You guys are serious about this? You're actually selling the beach house? We've had it forever!"

"We've been talking about it for a while now," June said. "It just doesn't make sense to hold on to it anymore, not with you kids going off to college. It's like you said last year, Noah. You guys are going to start getting jobs and summer internships, moving around the country for college or to meet up with friends. . . . A lot of things are changing, so it seems like the sensible thing to do."

"And we might as well tell you, because you kids will find out soon enough anyway," Matthew said with a sniff, "the whole area is being redeveloped. If we sell up now, we could get four, maybe five times what it's worth."

"You sound like a realtor," Lee grumbled, sinking in his seat.

"Honey," June said, "I *am* a realtor. We didn't make this decision lightly, you know. There are a lot of interested buyers, and that land is just too valuable to hold on to."

"The land?" Noah echoed. He leaned over the table, frowning. "They're not going to knock it down, are they?"

Matthew shrugged. "It's very likely. We didn't take you for the sentimental type, Noah."

He pouted, slouching in his seat. It made him look younger and was an entirely un-Noah-like look. In fact, he looked distinctly Lee-like in that moment. "We spent a lot of time at that place. It's . . . it's just weird to think it might not be there anymore," he added stiffly.

"Where are we meant to watch the Fourth of July fireworks now? Going to the beach house together is *tradition*. We swore we'd always go there every summer! You might as well cancel Christmas, Mom."

"Lee . . ."

"With the money we make from the sale, we could buy another," Matthew suggested, like that was anywhere *near* the point. "Some place where the paint isn't peeling and the pool filter doesn't break every year."

"No!" Lee cried. "I'm putting my foot down. You guys can't sell."

"Yeah," Noah piped up, shifting in his seat and crossing his arms just like Lee was doing. They'd always been so different, but right now, anyone could see they were brothers. They were a united front. "I've gotta go with Lee on this one. That house has been in the family for, what, eighty years? It was your grandma's place, Dad! You can't just *replace it*. You can't sell it!"

"If we're voting here, I'm a solid no, too," I said, raising my hand. The beach house felt like it was my place just as much as it was theirs. And Lee was right. It was tradition.

I shot Rachel a look, even though she'd only ever been to the beach house for a few days last year, and she waved a hand around awkwardly. "Me too."

June sighed. "I'm sorry, guys. It's already been decided."

The waitress chose that moment to appear with our plates of food.

"Like hell it has," Lee muttered to himself, but I heard him. He caught my eye and I didn't think I'd *ever* seen him look so determined.

If his parents thought we were going to let the beach house go without a fight, they were sadly mistaken.

Chapter Three

I'd thought the whole "Berkeley versus Harvard" thing was bad enough, but this?

Lee sulked through the rest of our main course—and, to my astonishment, so did Noah. They both pulled faces and scowled and grumbled under their breath, stabbed at their food, and cast the occasional glare at their parents.

They looked so alike in that moment that it was almost funny.

Almost.

Rachel, for her part, tried to keep the mood up. She tried to talk to Lee a few times, and when that didn't work, she talked to his parents with an enthusiasm that bordered on manic as she tried to beat past the silence that had settled.

I was still trying to get my head around it all.

Selling the beach house? I never thought that would ever be an option. It was *the beach house.* It was where we'd spent pretty much every summer of our lives. Some of my best memories had happened there. It was where Lee and I first swam without floaties! Where I got stung by a jellyfish when I was nine and made Noah give me a piggyback ride all the way back to the house. Where Lee got his first kiss, with a Latina lifeguard from upstate whose name *none* of us could remember now.

I glanced over at Noah, whose jaw was clenched. When we were growing up and Noah suddenly got too cool to hang out with us anymore, the beach house had been the one place where everything felt like it used to when we were still kids, where he'd hang out with us.

It was where we'd first drunk beer, snuck from a cooler one Fourth of July when we were thirteen—when Noah was starting to become a cool guy at school, breaking all the rules, but not so cool he couldn't include us in his little heist. (Although he had drawn the line at having us tag along to any parties he went to later that same summer.)

They couldn't just *sell*. That wasn't how it worked. Not for a place like the beach house.

It was so much more than just a piece of land, a bungalow with peeling paint and a dodgy pool filter.

My phone rang. A flash of guilt shot through me for not putting it on silent, but instead of apologizing and shoving the phone back into my purse, I took the excuse to leave the table. "I'm just gonna take this. I'll be right back."

I tried not to run away from the sour mood hanging over our table.

It was an unknown number, but I answered anyway. "Hello?"

"Hi. Is this Miss Evans?" a lady's voice asked curtly.

"Er, yes. Speaking."

"Miss Evans, this is Donna Washington from the Office of Undergraduate Admissions at Berkeley."

Oh crap. *Crap, crap, crap!*

"Uh . . ."

I gritted my teeth, my other hand coming up to clutch my cell phone. I cast a quick glance over my shoulder. Everyone was still sitting at the table, well out of earshot.

"I've tried to get ahold of you several times in the last few weeks."

My stomach clenched. I wondered if I was about to puke my overpriced, fancy meal all over the wall in front of me. Gulping, I said, "I'm sorry, I've . . . I've just been, like, insanely busy. You know, graduation and . . . and stuff."

Wow, Elle, great answer. It's easy to see how you got into places like Berkeley and Harvard with excuses like that.

"I'm sure you're already aware, if you've received my voice mails and our emails, that this call is to follow up on your decision regarding your attendance at Berkeley, starting in the fall."

"Well, I . . . I was wondering if maybe . . . maybe it's possible to have a little extension?"

Donna Washington sounded like she was not taking any of my petty, indecisive BS today. Her already-curt tone became even more clipped. "We've already granted you an extension beyond the usual deliberation period, Ms. Evans."

My hands began to sweat. "I . . . I know, and I really appreciate that, but please, I'm just . . . I just got off the wait-list somewhere else today, and I need the *teensiest* bit more time. Please—"

"Ms. Evans," Donna Washington interrupted, striking absolute *terror* in me for a second, "I need to inform you that you have until Monday to accept your offer. If we do not hear from you by then, we will have no choice but to offer your spot to a wait-listed student."

She waited for my answer. I was a little surprised; I half expected her to hang up the phone after that last piece.

"I understand," I told her in a small voice. "Thank you."

I stayed there for another minute after hanging up. My breathing was uneven and my palms were sweating. I wiped them on my jeans.

Until Monday. That only gave me three days, including today.

Just a couple of days to make a potentially life-changing decision. And fess up to Lee and Noah. Totally fine. I could absolutely handle that.

Maybe I could flip a coin?

Back at the table, I could see our desserts had arrived. Lee was waving a spoon around, talking agitatedly at his parents—undoubtedly arguing about the beach house again. Beside him, Noah was nodding, pitching in occasionally to back his little brother up.

Shoving my phone into my back pocket, I returned to the others.

"Back me up here, Elle," Lee said, interrupting himself midsentence to get me involved. "Berkeley isn't even *that far* from the beach house. It's not even in a different state! Even if we do get summer internships or whatever, they'd probably be around here somewhere. We could totally still make it to the beach house. Right, Elle?"

"R-right."

A pang of remorse tugged deep in my stomach.

It lessened slightly when I realized Lee had two sundaes in front of him that he'd been digging into in equal measure. He pushed the strawberry one back in front of me.

"Who was that on the phone?" June asked me instead of replying to Lee.

"Oh, uh, just my dad. You know, the usual. Needs me to babysit Brad."

"Mom, you can't—"

"Lee, please." His dad sighed, rubbing a knuckle between his eyes. "This isn't up for debate. You kids were saying you were thinking about going up to the beach house this weekend, right? How about we all go and start sorting some things out? We've gotta clear everything out, clean the place up. Might as well make a start sooner rather than later, huh? Rachel, Elle, we could do with your help, too, of course."

I bristled slightly at being lumped in with Rachel. Like I was just Noah's girlfriend. And not like I was part of this family and had spent a bunch of summers at the beach house with them, too. Like they hadn't said to me a thousand times, "It's just as much your home here as it is ours,

24

Elle!" and like I hadn't treated it *exactly* like that for basically my whole life.

"Happy to help," Rachel squeaked, sounding like she didn't have a lot of choice.

"Oh, I'm gonna be there," I heard myself snapping. June put a hand lightly over mine for a second.

"Fine," Noah barked.

"But just know," Lee declared, "we are not happy about this."

I glowered down at what he'd left of my dessert. *Yeah, that's not all we're not happy about.*

My cell was burning a hole in my pocket. *Forget the beach house,* I wanted to say. *What the hell am I going to do about college?*

My gaze slid between the Flynn brothers: Lee, grumbling to Rachel and pouting, looking more hurt than anything else, and Noah, who caught my eye and gave me a crooked smile.

Lee and Berkeley, or Noah and Harvard?

I had only three days to decide.

Chapter Four

After our fancy meal, Noah dropped me off back home. I'd been quiet the whole ride, stewing over this new development about the beach house and my college dilemma. Noah, luckily, had been too busy sulking, so he hadn't asked what was up with me.

I wanted to tell him so badly.

But how could I? How could I break Lee's heart like that? And part of me felt like I should make this decision without either of them—but *especially* without Noah. I didn't want to go to Harvard just so I could be with my boyfriend or because I let him persuade me into it for that very reason.

This was *college*. Wherever it was, it would send me down a new path, set me up for the rest of my life from here on out. Whether I picked Berkeley or Harvard, I couldn't base the decision solely on a *boy*.

Or, in this case, two boys.

Even though I didn't want his help to actually make the decision, I wished I could tell Noah. If only so he could hug me, offer some kind of advice, reassure me that it'd be okay, it'd all work out, that Lee would understand if I *did* ultimately decline my place at Berkeley.

Noah put the car in park while I fidgeted with my house key.

"So I'll pick you up tomorrow to head to the beach house?"

I almost rolled my eyes and said, *No, silly, I'll be riding with Lee,* before remembering that wasn't how this went anymore. Not because of Noah, but because Lee had a girlfriend to ride shotgun now, in my place.

As if reading my mind, Noah added, "My parents are gonna be driving Lee and Rachel. I was gonna take the bike."

I grimaced, but it was more playful than anything else. "Oh, come on, you know I hate that two-wheeled death trap."

"And you *really* hate having an excuse to cuddle up close to me . . . ," Noah murmured, the smirk I knew so well tugging at the corner of his mouth as he leaned across the center console toward me.

"Loathe it," I confirmed. "Utterly and completely."

He turned his head, his lips brushing over my jaw, making me gasp. My eyes fluttered at the sensation, my skin tingling where his mouth moved lightly up toward my ear. "So I'll pick you up at nine?"

I nodded, twisting to catch his mouth with mine. I'd never tire of this, I decided. *Never.* (And if I joined him at Harvard, I'd never have to be away from this feeling. . . .)

Reluctantly, I pulled away eventually. "Are you coming in?"

"Nah. I know Lee was heading home after taking Rachel back to her place, and I'd feel like a terrible son if I left my parents alone with him right now. Even if I'm on his side."

I couldn't resist a smirk of my own, and I pushed his shoulder lightly. "Look at you, Noah Flynn, all grown up, making these mature decisions."

Would I change this much after a year at college, too? Would Lee?

His cheeks turned a faint shade of pink. "Yeah, yeah, Shelly, get over it. Say hi to your dad and Brad for me."

"Will do."

We kissed again—this one not *quite* as long as the last—before I got out of the car.

I let myself in, Noah idling by the sidewalk in his car until I turned to wave him off, then called out that I was home.

"We're in here," I heard Dad call from the kitchen, where I found him and Brad playing a game of Uno.

"Room for one more?"

"Sure," Brad said, drawing the word out into about four syllables—making me immediately suspicious. "Come deal yourself in, Elle."

They waited patiently as I dropped my purse, joined them on the other side of the table, and picked up some cards from the pile in the center.

"It's my turn," Brad announced. "And then it'll be your go."

"Okay."

He slammed down a card. "Pick up four! Change to . . . green!"

I groaned, dropping my cards facedown. "Oh, man, come on! You've gotta be kidding me!"

"Them's the rules," Dad said. "Sorry, bud."

He didn't sound in the *least* bit sorry that I'd swanned in at just the right moment to spare him from picking up four more cards when he was down to three.

He high-fived Brad under the table, the two of them snickering as I collected another four cards and searched for a green card. Which I absolutely did not have. I had to pick up three more from the pile before I got one I could play.

"Today is not my day," I muttered, lamenting the sheer number of cards I now held.

"Something happen with the Flynns, kiddo?"

"Did you know they're selling the beach house?"

"Wait, what?" Brad cried. "But . . . but they can't! You promised I could come hang out there this summer!"

"Huh," Dad said, setting down a green card of his own. "June mentioned they were redeveloping the whole area. I guess I can't say I'm surprised. It makes sense, with all you kids at college."

"Uh, excuse me?" Brad protested. "*I'm* not in college."

"You'll be packing up your stuff and moving into a dorm,

too, before I can blink," Dad said, though it sounded like he was speaking more to himself than to Brad.

"But Elle's only going to be in Berkeley," Brad pointed out. "And Lee. So that doesn't count, right?"

I cringed.

"You still gotta make a call on that one, huh, bud?" Dad asked me quietly, rather than asking outright if I'd talked to Lee or Noah about it yet, while Brad was deciding his next move.

A literal call, I thought bitterly, remembering my conversation with Donna Washington.

It wasn't *fair.* This wasn't supposed to happen. If I had just stayed on the wait-list another day, I never would've put the decision off. Uptight Donna Washington would have called to ask about my decision, and I would have said yes, I accept, I'll see you guys in the fall, and everything would've happened the way it was supposed to, if only that damn letter from Harvard hadn't arrived this morning.

Maybe it was some kind of sign? That it had shown up when it did, just hours before Berkeley called, wanting to know if I was in or not? Maybe it was fate telling me where I should go. . . .

Dad seemed to be expecting me to answer, but I didn't want to dwell on college right now.

"We're heading up to the beach house tomorrow to start clearing the place out," I mumbled instead. Brad played yellow. Luckily, I had a bunch of those to pick from, including a +2 card, which I immediately inflicted on Dad before he got to call Uno. "But don't worry, I'll get back in time to babysit."

"I don't *need* a babysitter," Brad announced in a lofty voice, sticking his chin in the air. "I'm *eleven*."

I held up my hands, eyebrows shooting up. "My mistake."

Dad caught my eye and tried not to laugh.

"So how come you're out tomorrow night?" I asked him. I'd been forewarned this morning before the Harvard letter arrived that I was on babysitting duty tomorrow, but I never got the chance to ask why. Dad didn't really go out on the weekend, so I asked, "Is it something for work?"

"Actually," Dad said, almost mimicking Brad in the way he sat up straighter and cleared his throat. "No. I've . . . got a date."

I stared at him for a minute—long enough that Brad kicked me under the table and said, "Elle! Come on, your turn!"

I played the first blue card I saw in my hand and stared at Dad again.

A date?

Since when did Dad go on *dates*?

Come on, Elle, don't be weird about this. This was the first date Dad had been on in . . . ever. Since Mom. He was probably feeling weird enough about it without me adding to that.

So I said, "Okay, so . . . how do you know her? What's her name? Tell us about her. Where are you taking her on this first date? *Please* tell me you're not gonna do something dorky like bring her flowers. Actually, maybe you should—"

"Her name is Linda," Dad said. "I met her through work. And if you *must* know, Elle, we've actually had a couple of dates already, and I did in fact get her flowers, and she thought it was very sweet."

"Whoa, hold up," I blurted. "This *isn't* the first date? You've been out with her before and you didn't tell us about it?"

Dad shrugged, but I could see he looked a little guilty. I didn't want him to feel guilty. Or maybe I did. But I didn't want him to feel *bad* about it. It was just . . . weird.

And then he said, eyes focused on his cards, "I don't tell you guys about every date I go on, you know. But things have been going really well with Linda. I like her. And we're just gonna see how it goes."

Brad didn't even seem fazed. Did he know? Did Dad tell *him* that he was going on dates but didn't tell me? Did he not have anything to say about this?

"Do you not have anything to say about this?" I exclaimed, looking incredulously at Brad.

He glared back at me for a minute before sighing. "Is this the same Linda we met at that company picnic over spring break?"

"Yep, that's her, bud."

"Oh." He shrugged, studying his two cards again. "She was nice. She made good potato salad."

Dad played a card. Brad went next, yelling, "Uno!" and

Dad made some joke at him about how he must've cheated. I watched the exchange, fumbling to play a card of my own before Brad kicked me under the table again.

Seriously?

This was not the first date he's been on?

And I was only *just* hearing about this?

How long had this been going on, exactly, if Brad had met her? I'd spent spring break on a cross-country road trip with Lee, driving to visit Noah in Boston for a couple of days. Who knew I'd missed so much by not going to some boring company picnic? Had they been dating all this time or was this a recent development? Did Brad not *get* what was going on here, or did he simply not care?

Did I care too much?

Brad won the game seconds later. While he jumped up to perform a victory dance, Dad congratulated him and collected the cards before shuffling them. "Another round?"

"Duh!" Brad didn't need any convincing.

"Not for me. I've uh . . . I've got some stuff to do."

Worry creased Dad's face and he looked at me over the top of his glasses. I repressed a sigh; I didn't want to be weird about the date, but I obviously already *had* been or he wouldn't be looking at me like that.

Either that or I looked as exhausted as I felt. Today had been a lot. Actually, it had been way, way too much. I wanted to crawl into bed and pretend none of this was happening. It was way too much to deal with right now.

"You okay, bud?"

"Sure! It's just . . . this college thing, you know? I have to call Berkeley on Monday." I shot a quick glance at Brad, not wanting to say too much in case he accidentally let slip something to Lee before I could tell him myself. I made an effort to smile and keep my voice light when I added, "And I *promise* I'll be back in plenty of time for you to go on your date with the lovely Linda. And obviously I'm going to have to give you a curfew, mister."

He relaxed, smiling back at me. "Thanks, Elle."

"Anytime."

I kind of regretted making the offer as soon as the words were out of my mouth.

It wasn't that I didn't think Dad *should* date. It had been a long time since Mom died, and it wasn't like he didn't deserve to be happy or anything. It was just . . . Well, he'd been a single dad for this long. Dating wasn't something he *did* . . . except, evidently it *was*—he just didn't tell us about it.

I bit my tongue, thinking how dating in secret seemed to run in the family.

•　•　•

"Look," I said later while on the phone with Levi, after off-loading on him about the whole thing, "I kind of get why he wouldn't say anything. Maybe he was scared of how we'd react or thought it'd upset us, or he didn't want to say something and have us think it was all serious and get attached to some lady just for them to break up, but, well, what if that means this Linda is something special, and it *is* serious?"

"Elle," Levi told me, "in the immortal words of Taylor Swift, you need—"

"Do *not*. I am *very* calm. Okay? I'm calm. I'm just weirded out, that's all. Don't you think it's weird?"

He shrugged. Tonight Levi was on shift at the 7-Eleven where he worked, but now he was on break and FaceTiming me from out back. I used up *way* too many of his breaks calling him, but . . . well, we were friends, right?

After Lee, Levi was my best friend. He'd moved here last year, and since he was neighbors with our friend Cam, he'd become part of the gang. When Lee started senior year by throwing himself into the football team and his relationship with Rachel, and with Noah on the other side of the country, I'd been a little lonely. Levi and I had gotten pretty close; he'd even opened up to me about the ex-girlfriend who'd broken his heart and his dad being in remission following cancer treatment—things he'd taken months to tell any of the guys about.

(We had, maybe, kinda gotten a little *too* close.)

It shouldn't be weird that I called him a lot when he was at work. Although in my defense, he'd started the calling—it was easier for him to talk over the phone than catch up on texts while he was working, he'd said.

It shouldn't be weird, but it probably was—a little. Objectively speaking. You know, since I'd kissed him at

Thanksgiving last year and he'd made it obvious he was crushing on me.

But we were past that. We were friends. Levi knew that.

Noah knew it, too—which was equally important.

Definitely not weird, however, was me calling him up to rant about the new development that my dad was *dating* now.

"I can see why it's strange for you," Levi said, oh so diplomatically. I rolled my eyes. "But come on, Elle, you can't be that surprised, right?"

"I'm just . . ."

Surprised he didn't tell me before. Surprised this wasn't his first date with Linda. Surprised he was dating *at all*.

"It's not bad that I feel weird about it, right?"

"I guess not. But hey, Elle, try to see this as a good thing, you know? She obviously makes your dad happy or he wouldn't have mentioned her. And with you heading off to college next year, maybe it's not such a bad thing if he's got someone else around."

The words sent a shock through me, my brain juddering to a stop for a split second.

Someone else around?

I suddenly had images of this mystery woman cooking dinner in our house, sorting out Brad's muddy laundry after soccer practice on a rainy afternoon, sitting on our sofa and watching movies, eating dinner at our kitchen table. . . .

I could picture her with Dad and my brother, but it was hard to place me in that image. Off at college—wherever that was—and coming back home for the holidays to some new family I didn't recognize.

I didn't want to feel weird about it, but I *did*.

Levi could tell immediately he'd said something wrong, and he ran his hand awkwardly back and forth through his short brown curls. He changed tack: "But, you know, maybe it's not even gonna work out anyway. And your dad must be taking things really slow if he's only just mentioning her. It could be months before he even considers having her over to meet you and Brad."

"Yeah. Sure."

He tried again, putting on a bright smile. "How did it go earlier with the Flynn clan? Did you guys have a nice time?"

"Not really," I mumbled. "They're selling the beach house. We're all heading there tomorrow to start clearing the place out."

Levi groaned, head tipping back and his hand lowering the phone slightly. "Elle, I'm gonna go before I screw up any more and bring up something else that's gonna upset you, okay? I'm gonna hang up and send you a couple of memes instead."

I managed a laugh at that. "Thanks, Levi."

After we hung up and he, as promised, messaged me with a couple of screenshots of memes he'd saved to his phone, I wondered if I should've told him about my college dilemma.

No, I decided quickly. I didn't want Levi getting roped into that mess, too. He'd been tangled up in more than enough of my drama when it came to the Flynn brothers, I figured.

This was something I had to deal with by myself. And time was ticking.

Chapter Five

In the year that we'd been together, riding on the back of Noah's motorcycle had become a much less terrifying experience. I wasn't even shaking when I climbed off outside the beach house, but I *did* have some serious helmet hair going on.

I was convinced that those movies and commercials of women pulling off helmets and shaking out their flawless, bouncy, shiny hair was a total myth.

Noah smirked at me as I angled my head in the view of my cell phone camera, patting down my frizzy hair before giving up and pulling it all back into a ponytail.

He took off his own helmet. His hair was, predictably enough, shiny and flawless.

"Don't worry," he told me, "you still look cute."

"Wish I could say the same for you."

He got my purse out of the seat of the bike.

I always had trouble packing for the beach house.

Always.

But today, for the first time ever, it had been easy. I threw a bunch of empty canvas totes into my purse along with my wallet and phone charger, and that was that. We were only here to start clearing things out, and I was sure we'd come across stuff we wanted to keep and take home (hence all the empty tote bags).

Wrapping my hand around the handle of my purse, I was horrified to find my eyes prickling. We hadn't even *started* yet, I hadn't even gotten *inside*, and I was already getting emotional.

Today was going to be difficult, I knew. I'd barely slept last night, trying to work out what to do about everything—Dad suddenly having a dating life, college. . . . At least today I only had to deal with one thing: saying goodbye to the beach house.

So much for a fun final summer of freedom before college.

My hand found Noah's as we headed up the porch steps. The white paint peeled and the bench by the door looked even sorrier than it had last year. It always felt like it would break the second you sat on it—although it hadn't failed us yet. The sand on the worn floorboards crunched under our feet.

The beach house was, in all honesty, a little cramped and kind of old. In contrast to the Flynn house—with its classy furniture, the on-trend colors of the walls and kitchen cabinets, the spacious, sprawling rooms—the beach house was packed full of mismatched furniture, and everything was faded. Hinges creaked, hairline cracks ran through the paintwork . . .

But, just like the Flynn house, it felt like home.

I could already imagine, a little bitterly, how it would be described in the listing by the realtor: *charming, full of character, compact.*

Resentment bubbled through me as I imagined realtors combing through our beloved beach house, finding the flaws in this place we had all cherished for years.

"We're here," Noah called as we stepped inside.

His mom popped her head out of the kitchen. Her hair was piled up in a clip, untidy but practical, and she was wearing a pair of old jeans and a pink T-shirt. "Oh, great! Perfect. Noah, your dad's cleaning up outside. Go give him a hand, would you? Elle, Lee's made a start on your room. You should probably go help him out."

Instructions doled out, she vanished back into the kitchen. Pans clattered and cabinet doors banged shut.

Noah gave me a brief kiss on the cheek and sighed as he drew away. "Guess we'd better get to work."

"Guess so."

I walked down the hallway, my eyes skimming over the photos cluttering the walls. I was so used to them that I'd barely noticed them the last few years, but now I drank in every one. June always printed the photos she hung here in black-and-white—making them possibly the fanciest-looking things in the whole beach house.

It hurt to realize she hadn't hung up any new ones this

year, from our last summer at the beach house. Most of the photos were of me, Lee, and Noah, but there were a few of all five of us. I inched down the hallway, remembering the moment we'd taken every photograph. Every dinner outside, every day on the beach . . . that year we were fourteen and Lee got sunburned all over his arms, the first year Noah had tried to help his dad out with the barbecue and burned *everything* but we'd all eaten it anyway so he didn't feel bad. That first year I'd had *boobs* and had covered them up with a T-shirt the whole summer, but Lee had stuffed a bikini top with tissue and walked around the beach wearing it for an entire day, trying to make me feel better. The last summer before Noah started middle school, where he looked so scrawny and gangly he was almost unrecognizable.

I watched us get smaller and younger and no less crazy or fun.

There was a photo, near the top of the gallery wall at the far end, of me with my mom and dad on the beach. Mom was a few months pregnant in it.

She kinda looked like me, I thought. Darker skin, darker hair, rounder hips, and my brown eyes. Brad got her eyes, too. And her curls.

We looked so happy.

I suddenly felt grateful that I wouldn't have to see a picture of Dad and mystery woman Linda playing happy families on the wall one day.

Tearing myself away, I strode past Noah's bedroom door,

past the bathroom between our rooms, to the open door of mine and Lee's room.

Apparently I was not allowed to share a room with Noah here, but Lee and I had *always* shared a room at the beach house. It would've been weird not to share with him last summer.

I guessed it wouldn't even be a thing this year, since they were *selling the place.*

"Hey."

"Oh, hey," Lee replied from a pile of towels and clothes in front of his dresser, sounding dejected. His voice was small and flat and he peered up at me with wide eyes. That puppy-dog face that (almost) never worked on me. "I didn't hear you guys come in."

"Where's Rachel?"

"Helping Mom in the kitchen."

I crouched down on the floor next to Lee, in the pile of stuff. The dresser drawers were all pulled open, more things spilling out. "So what's the plan today?"

Lee looked down at the piece of fabric in his hands, reciting in a monotone, "Go through everything. Decide what to donate and what to throw in the trash. Decide what we're keeping. Clean up as we go."

Staring at Lee's side of the room and the carnage that had erupted around his dresser, I said, "That sounds like more than a day's work."

His mouth twitched. "Here's hoping. Hey, check these

out." He held up the thing in his hands—a teeny-tiny pair of swim shorts. "Age six to seven."

"Holy crap. When was the last time you cleared your shit out?"

"Me?" he scoffed. "I bet you five bucks you've got a training bra in your dresser."

"I'm gonna take that bet, because there is no way I've left stuff here that's that old."

He grabbed a towel from the pile, holding it up as I got to my feet. "And look! Remember this one?" The towel was covered in a giant picture of Mater from *Cars*. "We got it for Brad that year, but then I puked on it after I bet Noah I could eat more ice cream than him."

I laughed, remembering. "Didn't he eat, like, eight ice creams?"

"Nine," Lee corrected me. "Believe me, that memory is seared into my brain forever."

I laughed again, peeling myself away from Lee's stuff to go through my dresser. I opened the top drawer. A few T-shirts, a bikini I left here last year, a bottle of sunscreen, some tangled headphones, and a whole lot of sand.

I started going through the T-shirts. Most of them were old graphic tees—one was a hand-me-down from Noah that I'd definitely stolen from Lee at some point. Holding it up in front of me, it was still a little on the big side. I folded it back up and placed it carefully on my bed, starting the "keep" pile.

The second drawer was more T-shirts, some shorts, a sundress I didn't even remember but was *definitely* too small for me now. I found a snorkel and put it on to pull a face at Lee—and found him wearing the teeny-tiny swim shorts on his head and the Mater towel tied around his neck like a cape, sending me into a fit of giggles.

All of my drawers were half empty. I found a book, some earrings, old rope bracelets and anklets. A few odd playing cards and a Ping-Pong ball, which *really* baffled me because I didn't remember us ever having Ping-Pong here. A couple of towels I'd used for the last few years that, now that I was looking at them with a critical eye, were scratchy and starting to become threadbare. They smelled like summer: like sea salt and sand and lemonade.

I clung to them for a minute before adding them to the trash bag in the middle of the room.

When I finished sorting out the bottom drawer, I bent down to make sure I'd gotten everything and ran my hand around inside. Sand and bits of fluff brushed against my fingers, and then, right at the back, caught on the drawer, a piece of fabric.

Oh my God, I thought suddenly, *that* was why this drawer always jammed when I tried to open and close it— which, in turn, was why I'd just found so much crap in it that I'd never bothered to clean out before.

My fingers scrabbled at the fabric and I knelt down to tug on it, grunting as I felt it finally break free, and fell backward into my donation pile. (Which consisted of one dress and a pair of shorts that had never fitted me right but I'd always thought were cute.)

"Ha!" Lee crowed as I straightened back up to look at the offending garment. "I told you, Miss High-and-Mighty! 'I don't have anything old in my dresser'!"

I threw the now-broken training bra at him, knocking the swim shorts off his head. "That so doesn't count."

"Uh, yeah it does. Five bucks, Shelly."

I poked my tongue out at him—and then took a second to assess his progress. I didn't think I'd done too bad. The keep pile was pretty small—most of the stuff I'd gone through had only been good for the trash, but it hadn't taken me very long.

Lee, however, didn't seem to have made any progress.

"Is that all your trash pile?" I asked, although I had a sneaking suspicion I already knew the answer.

"None of this is trash, Shelly. You take that back."

"Those sweatpants have holes in them, Lee."

He held them up, examining them more closely. "They're artfully distressed. It's fashion. Something *you* wouldn't understand."

I rolled my eyes. "Lee, come on. I know this isn't fun, and the whole cleanup thing sucks, especially because of *why* we've gotta do it, but it's just some old clothes."

"They hold *memories*, Elle."

"Oh yeah? What memories does that pink polo shirt hold for you that makes it so hard to get rid of?"

"That time my mom trusted me to do the laundry and I messed up royally."

I shook my head. "Well, pick up the pace, okay? I don't wanna have to go through more of our stuff by myself. And if your mom comes here to find out what's taking so long, she's gonna put *all* of that in the trash."

Grumbling, Lee tugged the towel-cape from around his neck and bunched it angrily into a ball before shoving it into the already-pretty-full trash bag. I took a second to go get another one. Judging by the amount of stuff Lee had been hoarding in his dresser, we were going to need it.

In the kitchen, June and Rachel were sitting, drinking tea, laughing about something.

"Found this in the back of the cupboard," June told me, tapping her mug. "Lavender and orange. You want some?"

That would explain the funky smell hanging around here, I thought, and tried hard not to wrinkle my nose.

"Er, no thanks. Just came for another one of these." I waved the black trash bag I'd just torn off the roll, and my eyes fell on a plastic box and a roll of Bubble Wrap. "Are you packing up *everything* today?"

"Oh, no. I doubt we'll even really make a dent in it today, sweetie. We just thought it'd be a good idea to get started as soon as possible. Besides, we can't pack up the kitchen yet—not if we're going to be back and forth here all summer while we sort everything out and get this place ready to sell."

"Right."

It wasn't much consolation, but it was something, I guessed.

I slunk back to the bedroom before I got roped into a conversation about how much work the beach house needed. It didn't *need* any kind of work.

I mean, sure, every other summer Lee and I would paint the porch, just for it to peel off again a while later. And *yeah*, okay, maybe this place was always full of sand, and the bushes and scrub outside by our path to the beach were always overgrown, and maybe the kitchen window leaked when it rained sometimes. . . .

But it didn't *need* anything. This place was just perfect the way it was. It was *ours*.

Back in the bedroom, the piles of stuff I'd set aside drove the air from my lungs. Lee had even managed to separate out a couple of piles, although his keep pile was still pretty large. Wordlessly, I set down the new trash bag and then moved to the closet we shared.

A blown-up beach ball fell out, hitting me in the face and then collapsing on the floor with a wheeze, deflating slightly into a misshapen lump.

I kicked it to one side and Lee immediately piped up, fixing me with an accusatory look. "Hey, make sure you don't put that in the trash. That's a good ball."

"You want me to donate it?"

"*No.* Keep."

Well . . . I mean, it *was* a good ball. . . . It had been our most faithful volleyball and soccer ball, as required, for several summers—we'd had to switch out a real ball for this inflated one after everyone realized that whenever I tried to join in a game, I mostly just got hit by the ball instead.

But, nope, we had to be ruthless. I nudged it onto the trash pile, hoping Lee didn't notice and try to keep it.

I had more stuff than Lee in the closet. We both had windbreakers in there—and *another* one each right at the back of the closet, a clichéd pink and blue pair, which, judging by the tags, we'd gotten when we were ten. After rummaging through some of the clothes—everything going into the donation pile except for the jeans Lee had left here last summer that he thought he'd lost and a jacket of mine I'd forgotten all about that miraculously *still fit*—I went on my tiptoes to scout out the top shelf.

"Hey, Mr. Sentimental, come give me a boost. Put those football muscles to good use."

Lee sighed loudly, muttering about how I was interrupting his flow (he'd been looking at a bunch of receipts he'd just found and there was zero *flow* going on), but he didn't hesitate to crouch down as I stood on the bed. I climbed up onto his shoulders and he carried me the few steps back to the closet. Lee had spent last summer working out and beefing up a little, and after being on the football team throughout senior year, he'd built up some serious muscles—which were definitely coming in handy right now.

"Don't you dare drop me."

He swayed, and I smacked the top of his head, making him laugh.

"Anything good?"

"Um . . ." My face scrunched up at the layer of dust on the shelf—and how did sand even get all the way up here? I pulled out an old beach bag, another towel, a collapsed neon-green rubber ring, and some old floaties. I tossed them all onto the floor near the trash bag.

"Oh my God!" I cried, leaning forward and reaching in with both hands for a stuffed bear, gray with a tartan bow tie . . . and still fluffy! I gently brushed some of the dust off before nuzzling the bear against my face and then holding it down in front of Lee's. "Look! It's Bubba! I thought I'd lost him *years* ago."

Mom and Dad had gotten me Bubba when they'd brought Brad home from the hospital after he was born.

"He's gonna look great in your fancy-schmancy dorm room at Berkeley," Lee told me.

"Ha-ha. Right. Yeah."

Why was it suddenly so hard to picture the dorm room at Berkeley that I'd been dreaming of for years?

"So . . ." He took Bubba, his other hand gripping my knee to make sure I didn't fall. "Toss, right? Trash bag, meet Bubba. Bubba, meet trash bag."

"No, Lee!"

I made a grab for Bubba and Lee laughed as he held him just out of my reach. As I bent down, arms flailing for the bear, Lee started moving about the room. I shrieked, grabbing at his hair. "Put me down! *Put me dowwwwn!*"

Lee bent forward and tossed me onto the bed, my

stomach flipping as I fell. He gasped for breath between laughs. I grabbed the nearest thing—a floatie I'd just tossed out of the closet—to throw at him, but he just collapsed to the floor, laughing harder, holding his stomach.

"Looks like you two are working hard," a voice drawled from the doorway. I stopped mock-glaring at Lee to see Noah leaning against the door frame, his arms crossed, smirking at me.

"You two had better not be making sexy eyes at each other," Lee said, still breathless from laughing. He'd thrown one arm across his eyes, the other hand still on his stomach. "Not under *my* roof, no sir."

"Sexy? Me?" Noah scoffed, clutching a hand to his chest and then winking at me. "Always."

Lee faked a vomiting noise.

"Mom wants you guys to come help in the rumpus room when you're done in here. Which means she thinks you should be done in here by now."

The three of us looked at the piles of stuff—mostly Lee's, although we'd just trampled my donation pile and I was lying on my keep pile.

"Give us five minutes," Lee said. He got to his feet, shoved a bunch of stuff back in his dresser and the rest in a trash bag, and then looked at me. "Jeez, Shelly, it's like a clothes bomb went off over here. Keep your side of the room clean, huh?"

Chapter Six

Once we'd gotten our room cleaned up, hauled the trash bags to the front of the house, and added our donation items to a cardboard box Matthew had left out for us in the lounge, we took a break to sit outside. A can of Pepsi Max sweated in my hand, fresh from the refrigerator.

Lee's parents spent a good ten minutes trying to get us back inside.

Matthew eventually grabbed an old water gun he'd found somewhere, filling it at the pool and squirting us in the faces with it until we caved, shrieking and laughing and shouting in protest as we fled back inside.

"See." Lee sighed as we wiped our faces on our shirts and arms on the way to the rumpus room. "This is why it's so great here. Dad would *never* do something like that at home. We all need this place."

He was right. This place brought out the best in all of us. I didn't think June or Matthew had really thought about how *they'd* cope without the beach house.

We didn't make a lot of progress in the rumpus room, a

spare room at the back of the house we'd mainly treated as a playroom through the years.

There was a cabinet against one wall housing a bunch of Matthew's old vinyls and a record player. Lee made a beeline for it before we did anything else, setting up a Beach Boys album to play. A sagging sofa took up another wall, an ancient armchair beside it and a couple of beanbags that had lost any kind of comfort, like, a decade ago. I just *knew* the closet in the corner would be full of old toys and games. An outdated TV was on a stand near the windows.

How many rainy days had we spent playing Monopoly or Guess Who? or Battleship or a kid-friendly version of Trivial Pursuit? How many games had we played in here? And then there were the evenings Mr. and Mrs. Flynn just wanted some quiet time and would set the three of us up here with a movie and some popcorn.

Rachel wandered over to a cabinet and pulled one of the doors open. The handle broke off in her hand and she looked at us in alarm before Lee laughed, reaching for the handle. It was some tacky glass knob, smudged from years of use, that had probably been super modern at one point, the kind of thing everyone wanted. He polished it almost to a shine on his shirt before holding it up.

"Don't worry, Rach. It's been like that for years. Elle, remember we used to pretend it was a diamond?"

I grinned. "And we'd break in and steal it."

"The great jewel heist." Lee sighed, looking every bit as nostalgic as I felt. In all fairness, *we'd* probably been the ones to break the handle off the cabinet door just for an excuse to use it in our make-believe heist.

Good times.

Lee turned back to Rachel and placed the glass knob between her fingers like a ring. She giggled, blushing, and leaned forward to kiss him on the cheek.

I looked at Noah, who fake-vomited like Lee had just done a little while ago at us, but more quietly. I nudged him with my elbow. "I think it's sweet," I whispered.

"Sickly sweet."

Hmm, maybe a little.

Rachel wiggled the handle back into place and opened the cabinet. There was a stack of books inside and she pulled some out, putting them in the middle of our group. I picked one off the top, quickly realizing it was a photo album.

So, okay, maybe it was *my* fault we ended up making so little progress in the rumpus room, because I was the one who started combing through the photo albums. The boys didn't need any persuading to procrastinate by joining me, all of us sharing the best photos we came across and regaling each other with stories of how we remembered the moment. Rachel seemed to be having just as much fun listening to us and looking at the photos, too.

I paused when I came across a photo from when we were all really small. We were maybe eight or nine, the three of us standing on the beach. Lee was missing a tooth. My hair was short and wild, fluffy and sticking out at all kinds of angles.

Noah wasn't much bigger than us in the photo, and his hair was cut short, too, shorter than I ever remembered it being. He was holding a hot dog, and Lee was waving a little paper flag. I stood in the middle of them, my arms slung over both of their shoulders, eyes narrowed to a squint with how big I was smiling at the camera. The photo quality wasn't the best, but you could make out the colorful blur of fireworks in the background.

"Look at this," I said, scooting closer to Noah so our thighs pressed together, pushing the photo album halfway onto his lap. Lee bent over to look at the photo. I pointed to the writing beneath it I had just noticed. "Fourth of July. *Ten years ago.* Look how little we all were."

"It's weird how that doesn't even feel that long ago, huh?" Lee said, looking at both of us with a sad smile, eyes full and one corner of his mouth tilting upward. He pointed at the bright pink dungarees I was wearing in the picture. "I remember those. You wore them all summer."

"I think it was the girliest thing you wore for years," Noah agreed.

They probably weren't wrong, I thought, letting out a breath of laughter. I traced a finger over the picture. Me and my boys. Right where I belonged.

My phone buzzed. My eyes drifted a few feet away to where I'd left it on the floor before I snatched it up to shut off the reminder I'd set yesterday: CALL BERKELEY.

"Somewhere to be?" Rachel joked.

"Gotta take my pill," I lied, jumping up and going back

to where I'd left my purse near the front door, grateful they couldn't see me and that none of them had questioned me or followed me out. I stared at my phone for another few seconds before shoving it into my purse.

Out of sight, out of mind.

Right?

• • •

We made the mistake of opening the closet in the corner. The first game we pulled out was Hungry Hungry Hippos, which, of course, meant that we needed a winner-takes-all tournament, playing one-on-one. I lost to Rachel, and Lee lost to Noah; then Noah and Rachel played a fierce game for the final, with Rachel ultimately winning. Lee and I whooped at the top of our lungs, jumping up to do a victory dance—neither of us could remember the last time Noah had lost at that game, despite us not playing for years.

And Noah, unless I was very much mistaken, was *pouting*.

I ruffled his hair and wrapped my arms around his shoulders as he groaned in defeat, and I kissed the side of his head. "Aw, don't be a sore loser. She's a tough cookie. A worthy opponent."

"I think we should have a rematch. I'm just rusty, that's all."

"Mmm-hmm," Rachel scoffed, grinning.

"Your prize, O Hungriest of Hippos," Lee announced. He reached into the closet and pulled out a comically huge pair of pink heart-shaped glasses and a feather boa. Rachel laughed, letting him put them on her. She wore them for at least an hour—she still had them on when June and Matthew yelled that they'd ordered some pizzas for our lunch.

We found the pirate accessories and toys Lee and I had loved so much one summer. A pogo stick that I was shockingly okay at, but Lee fell off almost instantly. An old gaming console of Noah's, which he immediately set up, loaded a game into, and became utterly enraptured by, picking up right where he'd left off for a good twenty minutes until we dragged him away from it.

We found tennis rackets and balls for different games, a couple of footballs, and a brand-new baseball mitt that even my hand was too big for now. I put it in my keep pile, thinking Brad might like it. A sash covered in Boy Scouts badges that belonged to Noah, prompting us to tease him over each one. Lee found a box of magic tricks and we spent a while trying to understand how they worked and one-up each other with our showmanship skills until Rachel uncovered a crappy old karaoke machine that had been my mom's.

I'd thought Lee was bad at going through his dresser, but he was *way* worse when it came to our old toys; it was damn near impossible for any of us to persuade him to part with something when he discovered it, having not thought about it for maybe five years or more. He and Noah argued over a few things, until Noah sat on him while I took the pogo stick out to one of the donation boxes in the lounge. Rachel gently talked Lee into parting with a broken Nerf gun.

Using the old pirate swords, I challenged him to a duel over the magic set, and eventually wrestled him to the floor and wrenched his sword away when I saw he wasn't going to give up.

It was rough, and he *definitely* kept sneaking things back into the keep pile. It kept mysteriously growing. I saw the magic set there again now, even though I'd already moved it to the donation pile at least three times already.

Rachel had gone back to the lounge with a pile of our toys for donation, and she hadn't come back yet. I guessed June had roped her into helping with something else or another cup of weird floral tea.

"Hey, son, come hold the ladder. I'm gonna check these gutters," Matthew called down the hallway.

Lee looked up at Noah from his collection of Pokémon cards. "He means you."

"Maybe *I* wanna play Pokémon."

"Gloom used Petal Blizzard!" Lee exclaimed, slamming down a card at Noah's feet.

"Man, if I had Psyduck . . ." Noah shook his head, already heading to the doorway but turning and waving his arms in sharp motions, eyes narrowing. "There'd be a mean Cross Chop coming your way, buddy."

"Yeah, you *wish*."

Once Noah was gone, Lee sighed, shaking his head and gathering the cards back up. "See what I mean? Everything's different here. Imagine if the kids at school could see the infamous badass Noah Flynn, with his motorcycle and his cigarettes, the guy who got into all those fights, playing Pokémon. They can't sell this place, Elle, they just *can't.*"

I sighed, too, helping him to his feet before wrapping my arm around his side. "I know. But I think they've made up their minds, Lee. It's not like we could buy this place ourselves or anything. It's just . . ." I trailed off, having to swallow the lump in my throat. "Just another part of growing up, I guess."

A part I definitely didn't want to deal with either but that I'd take over picking a college right now.

Lee set down the pile of cards, his right arm coming up to hug me back, his left hand moving to the photo album we'd left out earlier. He flicked back to that Fourth of July photo I'd found and he sighed heavily, wearily, his head tilting sideways until it rested on mine. "I wish we could go back to this. When we were little kids and my parents weren't trying to sell this place and talking about us moving away and getting jobs and . . ."

"Click your heels three times," I joked, but we both did.

"I don't want to believe this is our last summer here, that we're not even going to get to enjoy it, you know? It feels like there's so much we never got to do here. And now we're never gonna get the chance."

I wasn't sure if it was Lee's words, or the photo, or all these old memories resurfacing, but it hit me suddenly and I gasped. I scrambled away from Lee, moved an end table and some boxes of games out of the way, and pulled the closet door open wider.

"What're you doing?"

"One . . . sec . . ."

My fingers danced along the floorboards, working on muscle memory as I looked for that one nick in the wood that . . . There! I bit my lip as I wedged my short nails around the edges of the floorboard until it sprang loose.

"Oh my God," Lee whispered, and I knew he remembered, too.

Our secret hiding spot. We both crouched over the open floorboard as I reached in and pulled out an old tin lunch box, cradling it in my hands like it was the damn Holy Grail.

Which, to us, it really was.

I popped the lunch box open and placed it on the floor between us. There was the necklace Lee had bought me with his own allowance when we were seven. A tooth I'd lost (and was now totally grossed out by, and even more grossed out that we'd thought it was awesome enough to keep at some point). There was a euro that Lee had found and we had just thought was cool and mysterious at the time. A few other trinkets we'd collected over the summers here when we were little, and . . .

From the bottom of the lunch box, I pulled out a wrinkled piece of notepad paper and smoothed it out over my thigh. The very buried treasure I'd been looking for.

"Wait," Lee breathed, his hand gripping my wrist. "Is that what I think it is?"

"Yep," I said, popping the *p*. "Lee and Elle's Epic Summer Bucket List."

"Whoa."

We sat there in reverent silence, reading over the list. The paper felt soft in my hands, the ink was faded, and our writing looked childish. Lee's looked messier and even more scrawled than it did now.

So many years ago—I couldn't even remember *how* long ago it was now—Lee and I had spent time one summer putting together a list of all the crazy things we wanted to do when we were bigger, before we went to college. When we were teenagers and so grown up and knew everything about the world.

Never mind the toys, the games, the training bras, and the deflated beach balls. This fragile piece of paper right here, this was the thing that held all our childhood dreams and fantasies in one place.

Lee and Elle's Epic Summer Bucket List

1. Pull off the Great Jewelry Heist
2. Dunk Noah in the pool!
3. Teach Brad to swim without floaties
4. Go dune-buggy racing (do not tell Mom and Dad)
5. Laser tag—STAR WARS STYLE! Elle calls dibs on Han Solo! (THEN LEE GETS TO BE PRINCESS LEIA!)

"Barbie rescue mission," I read off the list, smirking at Lee. "I distinctly remember that being your idea."

"Uh, duh. Cliff jumping was mine, too."

"Race day." Then I pointed at another one. "Dude! Helium karaoke!" I giggled at the memory of how much fun we'd had with the broken karaoke machine.

"Forget that," Lee said, laughing as he pointed at a different one. "We'd totally get arrested for this one."

We shared a grin.

"Damn, Shelly," he said quietly, looking back down at the list, wonder in his eyes. "We put together a solid bucket list back in the day. We thought we were gonna kick ass and rule the world."

I laughed, putting the list back on top of the lunch box. "Hey, maybe *you've* retired now you've graduated high school, but there's still plenty of time for *me* to kick ass and rule the world."

I said it with way more confidence than I really felt, and my stomach twisted again as I thought of my phone and the ignored reminder to call Berkeley back, but Lee didn't seem to notice. He just kept smiling at me.

Chapter Seven

"So did you guys make much progress?" June asked with a skeptical look at the cardboard boxes bound for charity shops and the meager few trash bags.

Rachel avoided June's sharp gaze, ducking her head and biting her lip. Noah scoffed, but Lee cut him off quickly. "Tons," he cried.

June looked at me, arms folded, one eyebrow arching.

"Yep. Definitely tons."

"Mmm-hmm." She turned her unimpressed look on Noah. "And I thought *you* were supposed to be supervising."

"I was busy supervising a ladder for Dad while he inspected the gutters and pretended he knew what he was looking at."

"Hey, watch it," Matthew warned, shaking a finger jokingly at his son.

Noah rolled his eyes, casting a quick smile our way. "You put them in a room full of toys, Mom. What did you expect?

When have you *ever* known these two to turn down a pogo stick?"

Matthew laughed. "Boy's got a point, honey."

"Kids, look," said June. "I know this is difficult, and I know you're going to find all these nice childhood memories and toys, but I really need you to pull together and come through for me on this, okay? We really need to get this place sorted."

I exchanged a look with Lee, both of us feeling just a *little* bit guilty under this wave of parental disappointment. Especially when June looked so *tired.* I had to wonder if it was the weight of selling the beach house or if it was being busy all day.

"How long does it usually take to sell a house out here?" Rachel asked, clearly making an effort to defuse the tension.

It didn't really work.

"We've still got to put it on the market," Matthew said, "but we've already had a few inquiries. By the time we pack up and get it on the market . . ."

June added, "Surveys, paperwork . . ."

"Probably two or three months." He nodded, sharing a small smile with his wife. "It's gonna be a real pain coming back out here all the time, though."

"Wait, what?" Lee asked, a frown tugging at his face.

"Well, we've gotta meet with the appraisers, surveyors, and contractors, obviously," his dad explained. "Plus we were gonna get a few things fixed around here, just in case."

Lee began to huff at the mere idea of it, but my brain had already kicked into gear.

A couple of months to sell the place . . . and we definitely weren't gonna get packed up in just one or two afternoons, judging by how today had gone.

And neither me, Lee, nor Noah were anywhere near ready to say goodbye to this place just yet.

I elbowed Lee to get him to look at me. After a second, he cottoned on. I saw his eyes brighten and we shared a moment of being absolutely in sync with each other—like when we'd decided to run the kissing booth at the school's Spring Carnival last year, where I'd first kissed Noah.

Because what better way to spend our last summer before college?

What better way to spend our last summer with the beach house?

"Wow," I said loudly, turning back to Lee's parents. "That sure does sound like a real pain."

"Especially with all the roadwork going on this summer," Lee added.

"And all that cleaning is gonna be *rough*."

"Gonna have to get at all those weeds . . ."

I saw Noah looking at us like we'd gone mad (which was a look he gave us relatively frequently, in fairness) before it dawned on him, too.

"Gonna have to patch up the driveway, too," Noah pitched in, giving his parents a probably-too-serious look and nodding when they turned to him.

"Constantly having to drive out here all the time, to check up on all that work." Lee sighed, brow furrowing. "Right, Rach?"

"Right," she said quickly. "Right. Totally. It's gonna take up a whole lot of time over the next two or three months. That's a lot of work."

"*So* much work," I added.

June and Matthew looked at each other for a long moment, half confused and half amused. She pursed her lips, obviously trying to hold back a smile; he gave a helpless shrug.

"All right," June said, clapping her hands and twisting to face us again, looking at each of us in turn for a long moment with a piercing mom stare. "Spill it. What are you kids getting at?"

Lee took the lead, declaring with a grand voice, "So glad you asked, Mother Dearest! Since this is going to be our final summer in the beach house, what with your hearts shrinking ten sizes and shriveling in your greed and old age, and since you've decided to *destroy* my delicate childhood memories, it seems to me you guys could use someone—or *someones*—here to help coordinate stuff. . . ."

"And we'd be happy to stay here for the summer and take care of things for you guys," Noah said, taking over. "We can do a bunch of the work, too. Except the gutters, obviously, since Dad's already done such a *stellar* job of those."

I could've smacked my hands over both their mouths.

Lee calling his parents greedy and old, Noah making fun of his dad's DIY abilities . . . *Yeah,* I thought. *Way to sell it, boys.*

"WOW, Noah!" I interrupted as Lee drew breath, putting on my best infomercial voice. "That sounds like a win-win for *everybody*! This summer, ladies and gents, for one summer only, a one-time exclusive offer! Get your beloved family beach house cleaned up for sale *and* have live-in supervisors to help manage the sale! Just call one-eight-hundred-US-GUYS to make sure you don't miss out!"

Matthew cracked a little smile, but June's face only turned stonier. "And I suppose it'll take *all four of you* here to supervise."

"A package deal, I'm afraid," Lee said. "No refunds, no exchanges."

"We'll take real good care of this place," I told them earnestly. "You know we will. I mean, who else could you trust to look after this place better than us?"

Lee added, "And we can all still be here for Fourth of July! Mom, you always say how important it is to keep traditions."

"It *would* be a great way to say goodbye to the place," Rachel said tentatively.

"And Lee will even take out the trash every Sunday," Noah promised, winking at his little brother and clapping him around the shoulders. Lee pulled a face back at him, but it was brief, before he turned a beaming face on his parents.

"So . . . Mom? Dad? What do you say?"

They exchanged another look, and I could hear the dramatic music playing out in my head, like we were on *The Voice* and waiting to hear who'd won the final vote. The seconds dragged on into eternity and I could've sworn not a single one of us was breathing. Even Noah looked tense, excited.

Matthew drew a long, deep breath, taking an *age* to let it out again.

June looked back at us once more.

"All right. You kids can stay here for the summer."

I shrieked, jumping into the air, my arms flailing, hands flapping. Lee crouched down before punching the air, jumping, too. Rachel let out an excited squeal.

Noah's arms wrapped around my waist and he lifted me up into the air, spinning me around. He set me back down quickly to wrestle Lee into a headlock, messing up his hair and then high-fiving Rachel.

"You guys are the best!" Lee shouted, bent over in the headlock. "Aside from selling our family summer home, which we'll never forgive you for, you're the best!"

A *whole summer*, here, with Lee and Noah and Rachel . . .

Last year we'd been worried that everything would change. We'd been worried that Noah wouldn't be around over the summer, and when Rachel had come for a few days it had created a weird, new dynamic.

But after this year, things really would change. Matthew

and June would sell the beach house and there really would be no more summers here, and *of course* things between us were going to change.

We needed this. This one final hurrah, a chance to properly say goodbye to the beach house—and to our childhoods.

Chapter Eight

It had been a long, exhausting day, but my mood was significantly improved now that Lee's parents had agreed to let us spend all summer at the beach house. I even kind of *enjoyed* the ride home on the back of Noah's bike.

Noah killed the engine, and I clung to him for a minute before pressing a kiss into his shoulder and peeling myself away. I handed the helmet back and waited for him to get my purse for me.

He took the hint, a smirk playing at the corners of his mouth.

"Not gonna invite me in?"

I shook my head. "I kinda want to spend some quality time with Brad tonight."

His eyebrows shot up. It wasn't that I didn't *like* my brother, or didn't spend time with him, but we didn't exactly do "quality time." And it wasn't a *total* lie . . .

"Everything okay?"

"Yeah. Yeah, it's good."

Noah knew me better, though, his hand coming up to

cup my cheek, his palm warm and rough against my skin. His blue eyes bored into mine. "You sure? You know you can talk to me—about anything."

Not about this.

I could do with a little alone time to consider what I was going to do about college—or at least, as "alone" as babysitting got. But I also didn't really feel like getting into the whole Linda thing with Noah right now either. Today had been consumed with the beach house, so I hadn't had a chance to talk to anybody about it.

And I couldn't just drop the bombshell *now* that I had to babysit this evening because Dad had a date.

So I took a breath and smiled and kissed him and said, "I know. Maybe tomorrow, okay?"

"Okay."

"Love you."

"Love you, too, Elle."

He caught my wrist as I made to leave, pulling me back into him. My hands braced against his chest, the familiar leather of his jacket under my fingers, and Noah's lips moved over mine—slowly, passionately, making me weak at the knees.

"I hate when you do that," I mumbled against his mouth.

I felt him smirk.

"Do what?" he asked, all innocence.

"Kiss me and make me want to spend the rest of my life kissing you and forget about everything else."

He chuckled, the sound vibrating through his chest,

against my hands, and kissed me once more, tender and light and lingering until finally, we broke apart.

Once I was inside, my dad called, "Elle? How'd it go today?"

I dumped my stuff and dug out the baseball glove I'd brought home for Brad.

Dad was in his office, and I poked my head in. "Yeah, it was, um . . . It was weird, actually. But, hey, I got this baseball glove for Brad!"

"I heard my name! I heard my name!"

Brad came barreling out of the lounge, right into my side, and made a grab for the glove. I automatically held it up above my head.

"Elle, come on! What other cool stuff did you bring me? Lee sent me a picture of a Nerf gun and a pogo stick. Did you bring those, too?"

I looked over at Dad, and we both rolled our eyes. Typical Lee—pawning his old toys off on Brad, just so he didn't have to feel like he was giving them up or giving them away.

"No, but you do get the baseball glove," I told him, finally handing it over. "And there is *no way* you're getting that pogo stick. I'm not looking after you when you break your arm falling off it."

"You have to look after me anyway."

"Listen to your sister," Dad said. "And, Elle, tell Lee no pogo sticks."

"Way ahead of you."

. . .

I was sort of expecting Dad to be all dressed up, doused in too much aftershave, looking dorky and like he was trying too hard, in too-fancy shoes and a tie and everything. But once he'd gotten ready, he was just wearing some jeans and a sweater and the shoes he wore pretty much all year-round.

He just looked like Dad.

"All ready for your big date?" I asked, plastering on a toothy smile.

"We're just getting dinner, Elle." He rolled his eyes, but looked excited. Happy. He looked like it was more than "just dinner."

I did my best to mimic how he looked whenever I went on dates with Noah: I planted my hands on my hips and narrowed my eyes, my chin jutting forward, and pretended I was looking at him over the top of glasses—a look I had seen *way* too many times and knew by heart. "I hope she remembers you've got a curfew, bud. Is she picking you up?"

He laughed. "I've ordered an Uber. We'll share a ride."

"Since *when* do you use Ubers?"

"Since I finally worked up the courage to tell my kids I'm going on a date, so I can leave my car here and share a bottle of wine with a beautiful lady."

I groaned, pulling a face and leaning back. "God, you're so cheesy. Does she know how cheesy you are?"

Dad only laughed, squeezing my shoulder when he

stopped. "Thanks for being so good about this, Elle. I know it's gotta be a little weird for you. It's weird for me, too."

I really didn't think I was being as good about this as he seemed to believe I was, but I wasn't about to correct him.

"So did you make a decision on college yet?"

I shook my head, a sinking feeling in my stomach at the mere mention of it. "Not really. I'm gonna try to decide tonight and talk to the guys about it tomorrow. But, um, speaking of Lee and Noah . . . before you go . . ."

I explained to him quickly about the plan for us to spend the summer at the beach house, helping get it shipshape and ready to sell, being there for the contractors and whoever the hell else needed to come by.

It wasn't that I'd *planned* to tell him when he only had a couple of minutes before his Uber arrived and he had to go, but I would've been lying if I said that wasn't extremely convenient.

"The whole summer?"

"Well, just till the house sells. And obviously I can come back here to help out with Brad and babysit, and go buy milk and run Brad to soccer practice. Please, Dad? I really need this summer with Lee, especially if I'm going to end up at Harvard."

It was a dirty trick and he knew it, but that didn't make it any less effective.

Dad sighed. "If I hear one *inkling* of trouble or crazy parties or—"

"Cross my heart. We'll be good."

"Brad's got soccer practice—"

"Thursdays and Mondays, I know. And you've got that conference coming up, and probably more dates with Linda. I *know*, Dad."

It wasn't like I hadn't been doing this for the last few years already.

Dad's cell pinged loudly and a car drew up outside. He smiled indulgently at me before sighing again and hugging me. "You get to stay at the beach house as long as I can count on you. Deal?"

"Deal. Deal, I swear. Thanks, Dad. You're the best."

I waited on the doorstep to wave him off on his not-first date. When I got back inside and locked the door, I turned around to find Brad lurking in the hallway.

"What's that about Harvard?"

Once Brad had been sworn to secrecy, and after we'd had dinner and sat down with a movie, I could tune out and spend a couple of hours mulling over what to do about college. I *hated* this pressure of having to choose—the sooner I made that call, the sooner this was all going to be over with.

On the one hand, there was Berkeley. My mom's alma mater, the college I'd always had my heart set on, the one close to home . . . the college I'd always planned to go to with Lee. Whenever I'd pictured college, it had involved Lee. We'd spent our entire lives together; I'd never expected this next chapter to be any different.

On the other hand . . .

Oh, man, I couldn't forget that look on my dad's face when he found out I'd actually gotten into Harvard.

I remembered sitting on a hilltop with Noah last year, when he was trying to make the same decision about whether to accept his offer. We'd gone out to his favorite spot to talk about everything, and our relationship, and I'd told him he'd be crazy to give up an opportunity like that.

Why was it so much harder to convince myself of that?

I *had* really liked Boston when I'd been there over spring break. . . .

Maybe it was awful, but I'd never really even looked into the program at Berkeley. I'd never felt like I *needed* to. So right now, balancing it up with Harvard, which I'd *actually* spent some time researching, it mostly just boiled down to . . .

Well, Lee.

And as much as I loved my best friend, he couldn't be the reason I chose a college.

The thought hit me like a truck. And in that moment, I realized I'd made my decision.

Chapter Nine

As I walked up to the front door of the Flynn house the next day, I felt incredibly queasy. I'd almost turned around, like, thirty times on the walk over.

I loved the Flynn house. I'd spent a lot of time here over the years; Lee and I were so close that it was practically a second home to me. I even had my own toothbrush in the bathroom. It was way fancier than my house; it even had its own pool. Even though that had made me just a little uncomfortable from time to time, it was still familiar, and I knew it as well as I knew my own home. But right now, it loomed large. Even the flowerbeds that June had recently had put in on either side of the path up the front lawn felt like they were closing in on me.

I could do this.

Lee would understand. He *had* to.

As for Noah . . . well, he'd been the one talking about how we could've gotten an apartment together, right?

I sighed. Who was I kidding? It wasn't Noah I was worried about telling.

Now that I was finally standing in front of the door, I gripped the handle and steeled myself. I could do this. It wasn't like I'd kept a *secret* . . . not like that time I'd been dating Noah behind Lee's back. It was just . . . a recent development. A surprise. And Lee would understand this was a decision I'd had to make on my own.

I just hoped he would understand it wasn't about me picking Noah over him.

I tried the door; as expected, it was open.

"It's just me," I yelled into the house. My voice echoed off the walls. Unlike the compact and joyfully messy beach house, *this* house was huge. A sprawling maze of rooms, one after the other, all clean lines and sharp corners and not a fleck of dust (or grain of sand) in sight. From the entryway, I could see all the way down the hallway, through the open-plan kitchen to the glass doors leading outside to the backyard and the pool.

"Elle! Hey." Noah popped up in the kitchen doorway, a mustard-smeared knife in his hand. "I didn't know you were coming over. Or are you looking for Lee?"

"Both of you, actually," I mumbled, heading over to him. Noah went back to making his sandwich. I shook my head for a moment at the mere sight of it. Noah and Lee always made the *biggest* sandwiches, and this was one of the most impressive I'd seen. It had to be at least four inches tall.

Noah caught me looking and smirked. "What? We had leftover beef."

"Yeah, and everything else." I squinted at the sandwich. Spinach, tomatoes, and turkey, too, by the looks of it. "That could feed a village."

Noah scrunched his nose up. "What, of My Little Ponies? You want some?"

I shook my head. I didn't think I could stomach *anything* right now, but I also wouldn't have been surprised if I took a bite and found anchovies or pineapple or something else totally wrong in there.

"So what's up?" he asked, grabbing the sandwich with both hands and wolfing down a huge bite. Unlike Lee, he chewed and swallowed before speaking again. "Or were you just missing me?"

I wrung my hands.

"I have to talk to you about something."

Noah paused, the sandwich halfway to his mouth. He set it back down slowly, eyebrows drawing together and forehead puckering. Those gorgeous, electric blue eyes pierced right through me as they searched mine, trying to understand.

I couldn't say I blamed him for looking so concerned: the whole "we need to talk" vibe was never a good one. Even if this time it maybe kinda was.

I took a few more deep breaths before squaring my shoulders and telling him, "I got into Harvard. And I've decided to go."

I had a whole speech prepared. About how I'd just

wanted to see if I could get in, how proud my dad was, how I'd been wait-listed, and how this had nothing to do with Noah or Lee . . . I didn't know what had happened to the speech, but now the news was out there, and there was no taking it back.

Noah stared at me.

I squirmed, but he stayed silent.

I sighed, caving. "Well, say something!"

In an instant, Noah was grabbing me by the waist and hoisting me into the air. I shrieked when my feet left the ground and he spun me, cheering, and set me back down to kiss me fiercely.

Noah's kisses were intoxicating. The taste of his lips was addictive; the feel of his tongue in my mouth and his hands on my skin could make me forget the rest of the world ever existed; the warmth of his body so close to mine and the familiar smell of him could make me melt.

But right now, none of that could ease the gnawing anxiety that I would need to tell Lee about college, too.

And then I heard, "Please tell me you guys aren't engaged or pregnant. But if you are, I'd better be the maid of honor or the godfather."

Noah broke our kiss, his face falling slightly as it dawned on him that my decision to go to Harvard might be something for him to celebrate, but it meant letting Lee down. He drew back from me, hands falling from my hips, and looked between us before clearing his throat and rubbing the back of his neck.

"I'll, uh, give you guys some . . . space."

He grabbed his sandwich and vanished from the kitchen.

Lee looked a little pale now, and I could hardly look him in the eye. He stepped over to me, hesitating before putting a hand on my arm. "Elle? What's . . . what's going on? Hey, come on," he said, his voice soft and gentle, a small smile on his face as he guided me to one of the stools at the breakfast bar. "Don't cry."

"I'm not crying," I insisted, but my voice wavered and my vision *had* gone a little misty. I blinked a few times and grabbed Lee's hands in both of mine. "It's about college."

"What about it?"

Oh God, I hated how peppy he sounded. How *optimistic*. How *excited*.

And I was about to break his heart.

I tried to remember my speech, what I'd thought over and planned to say to him last night, every word and turn of phrase I'd agonized over, but now I could only remember fractured snippets of it.

"I know we always planned to go to Berkeley. Since forever. Like our moms did and, you know, because of Brad, and . . . God, Lee, I didn't *mean* for this to happen. Okay? You've got to understand that. But it's . . . You didn't see the look on my dad's face. He was so goddamn proud. And . . . and I am, too, obviously. It's a huge deal. Not . . . not that Berkeley isn't or anything but . . . just think of all the doors it might open, being out in Boston! And I *swear*, I wasn't trying to keep secrets. Noah didn't know either, and my dad didn't know. I didn't even tell Levi about it either. I only just got the acceptance from Harvard and—"

"Acceptance?" Lee asked, chest heaving with a sigh. "You're not going to Berkeley, are you?"

Why did this feel so awful? I'd *made* my decision.

"Since when were you interested in going to Harvard?" Lee asked, and then he sighed again and took half a step back, running a hand over his face and then up through his hair. "Nope, don't answer that. Obviously since Noah went there."

"You were applying to Brown," I said meekly. "And—"

"Yeah, but my dad went to Brown. It wasn't just about Rachel."

No, but it was maybe 90 percent about Rachel.

"I got wait-listed," I told him, backtracking. "I didn't expect to get in. I never expected to even get wait-listed! I think I applied because I knew it'd never happen, but . . . now it has, and . . . and I had to make a choice."

"And you chose him," Lee mumbled. "Again."

I was still holding one of his hands, and I gripped it tighter, desperation seeping into my voice. I leaned into him. "It wasn't about that, Lee."

Except it was.

It was maybe 50 percent about that.

But how could I explain that while I'd actually looked into classes at Harvard, the campus, everything, I'd never really done that with Berkeley? Sure, I'd mostly done that because Noah was there, but . . . Well, I'd liked what I'd seen

82

enough to want to apply, hadn't I? I'd only picked Berkeley because Lee and I had picked it *together*. And how could I tell him that if I chose to go there, it would've felt like I was choosing it *only* because of Lee? I just knew he'd feel even more hurt and rejected if I told him that.

To my utter shock, Lee squeezed my hand back and gave me another one of those small smiles that I *really* did not deserve. "It's okay. I get it. It's Harvard. You have to go. Same way Noah did. You don't turn something like that down, right?"

I wanted to cry and bury my face in Lee's shoulder. I wanted to grab his face and scream at him in relief. I wanted to shove him back and tell him to stop being nice to me, stop being so sweet and understanding, because I'd hate me, too, if I were him.

All I could do, though, was sit there with my mouth clamped shut and stare down at our hands.

"And I bet your dad was crazy proud," Lee said, a little too brightly. I glanced up to find his smile bordering on manic, his jaw clenched tight. "There you were, panicking about getting into *any* college and spending all that time stressing over getting your application essay written, forcing me to get involved in school council and spend all those lunch breaks planning dances and charity events and . . . you did it! It all paid off! And now . . . now you . . ." He cleared his throat, shuffling in his seat. "And now you get to go to Harvard, Shelly."

His use of my old childhood nickname, the one only Lee

(and, more recently, Noah) was allowed to use, somehow made it infinitely worse.

Please stop being nice to me.

But wasn't this what I'd wanted? Wasn't this how I'd prayed he'd react?

"Yeah," I managed to mumble, "Dad's crazy proud. And it's not like I won't see you or anything. We'll have weekends and holidays and spring break. Hey, we could even do another road trip! And we can video chat and . . . and nothing has to change, you know? We can hang out every holiday."

Lee's face twitched. Flatly, he told me, "I'll be with Rachel over the holidays. I made us a schedule and everything."

"Well . . . well, that's okay, because Brown's not that far from Boston."

"So I get to go to the East Coast and see you *and* Noah *and* Rachel. Great."

Okay. This was what I'd been expecting.

Weirdly, it was almost a relief to see him losing his cool— even just a little. I hated the idea of Lee resenting me for this but not *telling* me. The thought that he would, and would go talk to Rachel about it but not me, brought that queasy feeling right back again. I couldn't have him start pushing me away already.

"Sure," he went on, striding across the kitchen and grabbing a carton of juice out of the refrigerator. "Yeah, the four of us can spend every holiday or long weekend together, and I don't get to spend quality time with you *or* Rachel. Or Noah!"

He tore open a cupboard, snatched out a glass, hammered it down on the counter, and slammed the door shut again.

"You'll get to spend quality time with us, Lee."

"I saw what long-distance did to you and Noah. Before Thanksgiving it screwed everything up for you guys. And *yeah*, I know, you worked it out, and you guys are good now, but I'm not gonna let that happen to me and Rachel."

"I'm sorry," I whispered. "Lee, I don't mean to make you feel like you have to choose between me and Rachel. We'll . . . we'll figure it out, right? We always do. We can make a schedule for the time we'll spend together, like you've got with Rachel."

Lee gave me a long, stern look, but I could tell it wasn't completely serious. I still found myself wishing he'd yell at me, that he'd *really* just *lose it*, the way he did when he discovered I was dating Noah behind his back. I could see it, bubbling away under the surface.

But Lee wasn't an angry guy. He never had been. Which was why he was narrowing his eyes at me now, tilting his head and telling me in a cool, offhand voice, "Rachel gets Labor Day. But I *guess* . . . I guess I can give you National Cupcake Day."

"I promise I will make you the best, most incredible, most unforgettable cupcakes you have ever dreamed of."

He raised his eyebrows at me, and we suddenly both cracked a smile. I've always been the *worst* at baking. Notably, one disastrous Home Ec class a few years ago.

"I promise I will get Levi to make you the best, most incredible, most unforgettable cupcakes you have ever dreamed of," I corrected myself. Levi loved baking so much that he'd actually gotten a job in a bakery, in addition to his shifts at 7-Eleven. If National Cupcake Day was Lee's and my new thing, I would absolutely be counting on Levi to make it killer. (Especially since there was a solid chance I might make it quite *literally* killer by accidentally giving us food poisoning.)

Lee's smile faded too quickly, but he still didn't shout, or even pull so much as a puppy-dog face. He fidgeted and paced a little, and I knew he was stewing over all of this and how *much* it changed everything.

"Say something, Lee," I mumbled. His silence was killing me.

"This was supposed to be *our year*, Elle, remember? We were going to take senior year by storm, have the best time ever before we went to college and everything started changing. But it's already changing, isn't it? And we did. And now this was going to be our best summer ever, our *last* summer. It's barely started and it's already ruined. It's not just our college plans. Mom and Dad are selling the beach house and . . . Nothing's turning out the way it was supposed to, you know?"

He flopped down again on the stool next to me. I snaked

my arms around him, grateful when he didn't push me away. Lee smooshed his face into my shoulder.

"I promise I'm pleased for you about Harvard," he said into my sweater.

"I know." I did. "I haven't . . . I mean, I haven't accepted my place yet. Or turned down Berkeley."

Lee drew back suddenly, shaking his head. "No. Elle, come on. Don't make me that guy. You're right, it's a great opportunity. How could you turn it down? And if it's what you want, I'm happy for you. Really! Even if I don't look it right now."

I bit my lip, feeling a little guilty.

I'd wanted to come and talk to him about it before I officially turned down Berkeley. It was *my* decision to make, but Lee meant the absolute world to me. He always had. If it had really broken his heart, if he'd *asked,* I knew I would've rethought it.

I felt guilty, because I knew he wouldn't ask me to do that. And Lee knew it, too. I was giving him an out we both knew he would never take, not in a million years.

Not sure how to apologize for that, I told him, "I promise I wasn't trying to keep secrets from you again. It wasn't like that. I just got the letter a couple days ago, and . . . I needed to decide. You know, everything was happening with the beach house, and I didn't want to make you *more* upset if I didn't need to, if I'd decided on Berkeley, but—"

"But you didn't."

"I'm sorry."

"What about Brad, though?"

That *was* something that I couldn't talk my way around or do anything about. But now I'd come clean about the college stuff, I told him, "About that. My dad's got a fancy lady."

Lee made a choking sound and pulled back to gawp at me, his face scrunched up and one eye squinting. "He's got a *what*?"

I explained about Linda, who Dad had been on a not-first date with last night, only just stopping myself from off-loading on him about how bizarre I found it all and how it felt like a lot to get my head around.

Lee gave a low whistle. "Mr. Evans, you sly dog. Who'da thunk it?"

"Ew. Don't call my dad a sly dog. That's gross."

"Do you know what this Linda looks like?"

"*No.*"

"Last name?"

"I'd have looked her up online if I had a last name."

"At least someone's having fun this summer," Lee muttered, his dark mood from a few moments ago returning in the blink of an eye. I could practically see the storm clouds gathering around his head again.

It was obvious that he wasn't going to argue with me about this, though. He was obviously going to make every effort to be happy for me, be proud of me, and I loved him for that.

I had to make it up to him somehow.

And as soon as the thought crossed my mind, I knew *exactly* what to do. He was devastated about the beach house and about me turning down Berkeley—even if he wouldn't show that quite so much. Lee wanted this to be our final hurrah, an amazing, unforgettable last summer before everything changed and we had to start growing up. And I was damn sure going to make that happen.

Years ago, when we were kids, Lee and I had dreamed of all the wonderful and wacky things we would spend our summers doing.

If he wanted things to stay the way they'd always been, even just for a few more weeks, well, I could give him that.

"Lee, I swear to you, *on our friendship*, we are going to have the best summer ever. This is still our year. Plus, if it's our last summer with the beach house before your parents sell it, we *have* to make the most of it."

"Yeah?" He gave me a half-hearted smile, his head tipping to one side as he looked at me. "You better have a foolproof plan, Shelly."

"Think about it," I blurted, trying to keep up with the way my mind was already racing ahead, spiraling out of control before I had a chance to second-guess anything. "We've scored the beach house for the *entire summer*. Yeah, we've gotta help out and do a little work on it, but so what? We're gonna be living there by ourselves—with Noah and Rachel, I mean—and no adult supervision! Talk about the makings of a great summer! How many people would kill for that? We have the key ingredients right there waiting for us, just a short drive away."

"I'm listening."

"And," I pressed on, "our younger selves have already written up the recipe for us."

I watched it register with Lee.

"You're not saying what I think you're saying."

"I absolutely am saying what you think I'm saying. Lee, back at that beach house, we have a bucket list that tells us exactly how we can make this the ultimate summer. Everything we always wanted to do before college, every fun and crazy thing we dreamed of when we were kids. And now we have the chance to do them!"

In a slow, measured voice, like he hardly dared believe it, Lee said, "You mean do the whole list, this summer?"

"I mean do the whole list, this summer."

His blue eyes narrowed suspiciously. They twinkled with that impish look I knew so well; he was fighting hard not to crack even the barest of smiles now, too. I knew right then that I'd won him over and that this might just be enough to bury any fight he wanted to put up about college. How could he ever resent me, after I made this dream summer come true? How could he ever be mad at me or say I picked my relationship with Noah over our friendship, when I'd do all of this for him?

"Even race day?"

I laughed, a smile spreading across my face. *"Especially* race day! So what do you say, buddy? You in?"

He had to say yes. He had to. And I knew he would, because I knew Lee almost better than I knew myself, and he would never be able to resist. But I still held my breath, apprehension prickling across my skin like a million tiny needles.

Ditching Berkeley was my choice. Ditching *Lee* after all our plans for years to go to college together was my choice. But this summer, I would make it up to him. I would do everything I could to give him this last perfect summer before everything had to change and we had to start the next chapter and grow up some more. He deserved that.

Lee stood up from the stool and peered down at me. "The best summer we've ever had. You promise?"

I echoed him one last time: "The best summer we've ever had. *I promise.*"

Chapter Ten

I thought that talking through the whole college thing with Lee would make me feel better. I thought that once I'd clicked those buttons on the websites, officially declining Berkeley and accepting my spot at Harvard, I would feel better. I thought that packing for our summer at the beach house would make me feel better.

I was so, so wrong.

I felt kinda sick when I turned down Berkeley—even if it *was* pretty exciting to be sitting at my desk with my dad hovering behind me, beaming, as I accepted Harvard, realizing just how much all my hard work at school had paid off.

Lee did a great job at not laying into me for ruining the college plans we'd had since we were kids. He was the one to tell his parents about it when I stayed over for dinner that night, but he was still a little *too* happy for me.

If he could pretend to be okay with it, I could pretend, too.

It always took me forever to pack for the beach house, but this time it seemed to be even harder than usual. My brain was stuck on worrying about how upset Lee was and how badly I needed to make it up to him this summer, making it impossible to work my way through my mental checklist for packing.

And I really *did* need to make it up to him. I'd need to pull out all the stops. The bucket list would be fun—it would be *amazing*, if we could make it happen—but it'd also involve a lot of planning and preparations.

And money.

Great, I thought, *one more thing to have to figure out.*

I hadn't even thought about how I'd afford to do all those bucket-list items when I'd suggested it to Lee. I mean, race day alone . . . I'd spent so much time last summer and during senior year applying for jobs and not getting any of them—mostly because I didn't have the "experience." Something told me this summer wouldn't be any different. Maybe we could set up some kind of crowd funder? Was that even legal?

I tossed a few pieces of makeup from my dresser into my open suitcase, then ran my hands over my face. It'd be fine. It'd have to be. College was sorted, so now I just had to pull off the bucket list, find some way to pay for it, help fix up the beach house per June and Matthew's instructions, come back to babysit Brad while my dad went on dates with the oh-so-perfect, oh-so-wonderful Linda. . . .

"Get it together," I muttered to myself.

One thing at a time. I could stress over babysitting whenever that came up, and the bucket list could wait a little while. Right now I just had to make it through packing—and I was already running late.

Eventually, though, it was done. I hauled my suitcase downstairs and said my goodbyes to Dad and Brad, who complained to me yet again about not spending summer with us at the beach house. He'd bickered with me over it pretty much nonstop for the last few days since I'd mentioned it, and I was sure, if we gave him the chance, he'd smuggle himself into the back of one of our cars.

But even that was done soon enough. I loaded my bag into the trunk of my car and headed over to Lee and Noah's—where I quickly discovered neither of them were actually ready to leave.

"I thought you guys were packed?"

Noah bit his lip for a moment, a slightly guilty look on his face as I appeared in his bedroom doorway. He caved quickly, though, and said, "We thought if we told you we weren't planning to leave until lunch, you'd still be packing."

I let out a scandalized gasp, swiping playfully at his arm as he laughed. I climbed onto an empty spot on his bed, around his bag and the piles of clothes he was packing, and crossed my legs. "You're a pair of dirty liars. Give me some credit. I'm ready now, aren't I?"

"Are you?"

He had a point. It was about two hours until we were due to leave, as I had just found out, and chances were I'd remember something I'd forgotten to pack. Which was stupid, I knew, because I'd be back home every couple of days to help look after Brad, so it wasn't like I couldn't pick anything up, but—

"Aw, crap." I smacked a palm against my forehead. "I didn't pack any bras."

Noah shot me a smirk, raising an eyebrow. "Doesn't sound like a problem to me."

I rolled my eyes. "Keep it in your pants, you. You've got packing to do."

We sat quietly for a minute while Noah pulled a shirt out of his closet to fold and I went through a mental checklist of what else I might have forgotten to pack.

"You know," he said with that suspicious, too-blasé tone that made it obvious he was ready to talk about something kind of serious, "I know this isn't perfect because we're selling the beach house, but I think this could be good for us. For me and you, I mean. Kind of like a . . . test 'living together' thing."

I stared at him as he refolded his shirt for the third time.

"Living together . . . like a couple."

"Why not, huh? We got through long-distance last year, right? So this should be a breeze."

"A breeze," I repeated. Long-distance hadn't exactly been what I'd call *a breeze*. We'd broken up once. And it wasn't like everything had been just peachy after that. It had been better, and good, but it hadn't been easy.

I didn't see how living together could be any harder, though.

And I couldn't deny that my heart gave a little flutter at the idea.

"You'd really wanna live with me? At Harvard?"

"Well, I was thinking about it." Noah sighed, finally looking at me. He was kind of shifty, and he chewed on the inside of his cheek. When we'd first gotten together, he'd been totally awful at any kind of emotional conversation, but he'd become more comfortable with it in the time I'd known him—and, more noticeably, since he'd gone to college. This, apparently, was not one of the conversations he was comfortable with. "Obviously you'll be in freshman dorms this year, but maybe . . . you know, if we stuck around in the summer for internships or maybe in your sophomore year . . . just, you know. You'll be at Harvard. I'll be at Harvard. We've already been together over a year. It's not like it'd be . . . I mean, there were kids in my class sophomore year of high school who got *married* after being together for a month."

"Have you been thinking about marrying me, Noah Flynn?" I teased, unable to help myself, reveling in the blush that colored his cheeks and feeling only a *little* bad about the way he shifted his weight from foot to foot.

"It's not like we'd be moving that quick. Unless you think we would. I . . . I just thought, you know, we could . . . save on rent."

"So your decision for us to maybe move in together next year is based on . . . financial acumen."

He met my gaze long enough to see me grinning at him, biting my tongue, and nodded gravely. "A hundred percent."

He tossed aside the pile of underwear he'd just grabbed out of his drawer to kneel on the bed, his body stretching toward me. His bright blue eyes crinkled slightly at the corners and I could see the dimple in his left cheek I thought was so goddamn adorable.

"Elle Evans, I'm in love with you. And I would love to live with you in Boston next year."

A quiet hum escaped my lips and I leaned toward him, too. "Say that again."

"I'm in love with you."

"Yeah, you are." I grabbed his face, pulling his lips toward mine. I could taste the coffee on them he'd been drinking when I arrived, and I kissed him deeper, my fingers threading through his hair.

I leaned back and Noah moved with me, falling on top of me and just about catching his weight on one elbow, chuckling as his head shifted so he could kiss my neck.

"I thought you said I had packing to do?" he murmured against my skin.

I laughed, dragging his mouth back to mine. "Shut up."

. . .

"Don't forget to pack these," I said, grabbing the pair of Superman underwear from the pile Noah had dumped on the bed earlier and throwing them at him. He caught them deftly in one hand just before they hit him in the face.

One day, I might stop finding it hilarious that badass Noah Flynn wore Superman undies, but that day wasn't coming up anytime soon.

"Okay, so I'm gonna run back home to pick up some bras

and then come back here so we can leave *on time*. I swear. Hand on heart."

"Yeah, yeah. Hey, don't forget this one."

He picked my bra up off the floor to toss at me.

"Shoot. Thanks. And don't you guys *dare* go without me."

"Elle, you're driving. And Lee won't have room because he's picking up Rachel, so I couldn't leave without you even if I wanted to."

He had a point, but we were still on a schedule—mainly enforced by Rachel. I gave him a brief kiss before hurrying home, where I shoved a handful of bras into my purse, relieved that my dad had taken Brad to a movie so I didn't have to say goodbye again.

Back at Lee and Noah's, I found them packing up the cars. Noah was loading our bags into the trunk of my beat-up old Ford. I joined him there, moving my stash of bras from my purse to my suitcase and pointedly ignoring the way they raised their eyebrows at each other.

"Told you she'd be late," Lee said.

"I'm not late," I objected. "You guys are just early."

Lee's phone pinged with a text and he waved his phone in our direction. "That's Rachel, wondering if I'm on my way yet. You sure you've got everything this time, Shelly?"

"Uh, pretty sure," I said, going back through my mental checklist. Wait—did I pack conditioner?

Lee must've known what I was doing, because he got quickly into his car and leaned out the window to say "We'll see you guys there, yeah?"

"See ya," we both called.

"Are you *sure* you don't want me to drive?" Noah asked as we got into my car.

"Oh, come on. I'm not that bad! And you just have to ignore that sputtering sound when I turn the engine on." I patted the dash affectionately and started the car, not missing Noah's uneasy grimace when the engine gave its trademark sputter.

My car's air-conditioning left a little something to be desired, so I rolled down the windows and put on my sunglasses, grinning at Noah. "Here's to the start of the best summer ever."

Earlier this year, Lee and I had driven cross-country to Harvard for spring break. It had all gone by too quickly and it was a little rushed, but it had been a lot of fun. And right now, with the wind in my hair and the sun on my face and the radio blaring, it felt like I was back there, crossing off the thing on everyone's bucket list and having the best damn time.

And speaking of bucket lists . . . I really, *really* had to make it up to Lee this summer.

I felt a pang of guilt that it was Noah here with me now, and it was starting to look like it was always going to be Noah over Lee. I couldn't imagine how my life would be without Lee in it so much—and honestly, I'd kind of gotten used to Noah not being around every day.

I was starting to think of all the ways Noah might start slotting into Lee's place in my life once this summer was over. Movie nights, trips to the mall . . . entire weekends spent beating our own high score on a video game.

Would it get to be too much?

What if living together made it all too much, for both of us?

What if we couldn't even make it through this *summer*? Being away from each other had driven a wedge between Noah and me before Thanksgiving, to the point where I'd broken up with him. What was to say that being so on top of each other all the time wouldn't do the exact same thing?

Come on, Elle, you're getting carried away. Chill out.

I did my best to shake it off and looked at Noah again, admiring the sunshine highlighting his cheekbones, the stubble lining his jaw, the striking bright blue of his eyes. He caught me staring, and his lips stretched into a grin, flashing the dimple on his left cheek.

"The best summer ever," he repeated, picking up my hand to kiss it.

Chapter Eleven

It didn't take us long to settle into the beach house, leaving pure chaos in our wake where just a couple of days before, we'd left everything so wonderfully neat and tidy.

So much for clearing the place out, I thought wryly.

After dumping our bags (and promptly wrecking the place), the four of us headed to the nearest Target.

"Don't you think this is a little too much food?" Rachel asked, inspecting the overflowing cart as we got to the checkout.

"Have you seen these guys eat? Lee will eat that entire box of doughnuts in five minutes."

"Please," Noah scoffed. "I could do it in four."

"Yeah?" Lee jabbed a finger in my direction. "Shelly could do it in three. That girl can *eat*. Rach, believe me, we'll be back here in a couple of days having to do this all again."

It was probably a *slight* exaggeration. Maybe in, like, four days.

Rachel placed herself in charge of putting away groceries.

Lee was blowing up a pool raft outside—where she could keep an eye on him and stop him from digging into the snacks before she could even get them out of the grocery bags. Noah had set up some speakers, and a playlist began blasting through the entire house.

Meanwhile, I had taken myself and my suitcase down the hallway, past the wall of photos, to . . . Noah's room. Well, I guessed it was *our* room now. Lee and Rachel were taking his parents' room, since ours only had two single beds in it. They'd get their own bathroom that way, too, we'd figured. It made sense.

But it was still weird as hell to be unpacking my things into Noah's room, not mine and Lee's.

When Noah came back into the bedroom, his task done, he looked at me strangely. His eyebrows began to knit together, and his lower lip stuck out like he was deciding whether to say something.

"What?"

"It's just . . . that's my side of the bed."

I looked back at the bedside cabinet I was filling up, frowning. "No, it's not."

"Uh, yeah, it is."

I stepped back, scrutinizing the bed and comparing it to his back home. Huh. I guessed he was right. It was his side, but—

"But I don't like to sleep by the window."

His mouth worked like he was debating arguing over it, but he shrugged. "Sure."

"Well, I . . . I can move, if—"

"No, no, it's cool. You take that side."

"You sure?"

He'd better be sure.

"Yeah." He smiled at me. "Definitely."

He didn't *sound* very definite, but I had my win, and I was going to take it. I had to compromise when Noah took almost every hanger in the closet and almost all the space, though, so it felt fair in the long run.

Even if he did huff and give me a look when I took the top drawer in the dresser. And even when he took up, like, all the bathroom space.

But that was what relationships were about, wasn't it? Compromise. It wasn't about being selfish. And we'd have to figure it out if we were going to live together over the summer in Boston, like Noah had suggested—and like I maybe wanted to.

Since we'd all skipped lunch, we made dinner early. Lee and I took charge and made tacos—although, admittedly, it was mostly Lee doing the cooking, while I chopped up vegetables and salad and laid the table outside.

We were just sitting down to dinner when Noah disappeared back into the house, before reappearing with four cups and a bottle of champagne—which the rest of us greeted with a loud chorus of cheers.

"I swiped it from Mom and Dad," he explained, undoing the metal twist around the cork. "They had, like, a dozen. They won't miss it."

He readjusted his hold on the bottle to remove the cork. *Pop!*

Excitement danced through me, like the bubbles in the champagne Noah was pouring into glasses for us. He set the bottle down and raised his glass in a toast.

"Here's to the summer!"

"Our last and best summer at the beach house!" Lee concurred, and the four of us cheered and whooped and clinked our glasses together.

We sat down to dinner, sipping champagne. I wasn't *entirely* sure I was really a fan of it, and Lee said he'd prefer a beer, if he was being totally honest, which I was relieved to hear.

Rachel laughed. "Well if you guys won't drink it, I will."

"Might want to save some for later," Noah said.

"What? Why?"

"Well, just as a heads-up . . . Lee and I might have told a *few* people to stop by tonight. Kind of a . . . housewarming thing."

I narrowed my eyes, looking between the two Flynn brothers, who had wide eyes and big, innocent smiles plastered on their faces. Rachel gave me an uneasy glance.

"How *few* are we talking?" I asked.

Lee sipped his champagne again, pulling a face as he swallowed it, and waved me off. "Just an intimate gathering . . ."

• • • •

Lee and Noah's "intimate gathering" quickly showed itself to be a full-fledged Flynn brothers party.

They'd thrown a few truly epic parties at their house the last couple of years. Noah was usually the mastermind behind it all, and even though he'd been too cool to hang out with us at school, he had always let us tag along and invite a bunch of our own friends. Their house was so big, it was the perfect place to throw parties.

But the beach house was always cozy, intimate.

Which, I guessed it was right now, too. The seven people crammed onto a single couch was pretty cozy. The butt that brushed against mine as someone scooted by was pretty intimate.

Music pumped through the house like a heartbeat. People had brought cases of beer, bottles of vodka and soda for a mixer, and sparkling cider for the designated drivers. People squashed into the lounge, the kitchen, the rumpus room. They spilled outside. A group of girls sat with their legs dangling in the pool. A couple of guys had stripped down to their boxers to jump in. I watched now as they splashed at the girls, who shrieked, giggling.

Rachel had started to stress out, so I had given her my second glass of champagne. She'd polished off the rest of the bottle by now and had moved on to a can of beer. Her cheeks were flushed, her hair a little frizzy, and she looked like she was having a great time.

Lee was in the rumpus room—I could hear him yelling

over a raucous game of Hungry Hungry Hippos. Noah was in the lounge catching up with some of his old football buddies. He caught my eye, winked, and shot me a smile. My heart skipped a beat as I smiled back at him.

Despite us being at the beach house, it felt just like old times. Noah had rounded up a bunch of people from his classes, who were back home for the summer, and he and Lee had forwarded the invite to a bunch of our friends, too. I spotted Ethan Jenkins and Kaitlin from school council, and Tyrone, who'd been head of school council and graduated a year before us. Rachel's drama club friends were here somewhere.

The doorbell rang, and I flitted from mopping up a spilled beer by the couch to the front door, wondering which idiot had flipped the latch so it locked.

Olivia and Faith, girls from my class, were on the other side of the door. They squealed and jumped to throw their arms around me—something that took me totally by surprise, considering we'd always been friendly but never, like, best friends or anything.

"Girl! We've missed you!"

"You saw me, like, *days* ago at graduation."

Olivia giggled, hiccupping, and I realized they were already a little tipsy—which probably explained the hugging.

Faith, meanwhile, was looking around with wide eyes and saying, "Oh my God, Elle, this place is . . . it's so . . . quaint?"

"Cozy," Olivia supplied.

Faith nodded. "Totally charming. But you guys have it all to yourselves! That's so killer."

"Yo, Liv, you want your shoes back or what?"

The three of us looked to see Jon Fletcher, a guy from the football team, climbing up the porch. He had someone with him I didn't recognize. He waved a pair of bright pink sandals with cork wedges from the end of his finger, a case of beer tucked under his other arm.

"Ooh! Oh yeah!" Olivia turned to take them off him, throwing herself onto the creaking porch bench to pull them back on. "They're cute as hell, but my *God* are they impossible to walk in," she told me, teetering as she got up and almost falling into Faith with another giggle.

"Hey, Elle." His hand now free, Jon greeted me with a high five and a grin. He glanced past me, raising his hand in a wave. "Lee! Hey, man!"

"Fletcher!" Lee yelled back. He slung his arm around my shoulders, and a little beer sloshed out of his open can. "Good to see you."

"Oh, hey, this"—Jon stepped back, nodding at the guy beside him—"this is our new buddy, Ashton. Hope you don't mind we brought him along."

"This place is packed," I said, smiling at the new guy. "What's one more?"

There was something *weird* about Ashton, though, and I couldn't put my finger on it until the four of them came inside and he ended up standing next to Lee.

They looked *freakishly* alike. Although, where Lee was dark-haired, Ashton was a sandy blond. He was skinnier, too.

He was wearing jeans, a green hoodie, and a Berkeley cap.

Which Lee had just noticed, too. He pointed at it and said, "Good to meet you, buddy. I'm Lee. So, you a Berkeley guy?"

"Just finished my freshman year," Ashton told him with a wide grin and bright eyes.

There was an uncanny resemblance when they smiled like that. They had the same kind of zeal in their expression.

"Dude! No way!" Lee exclaimed, grabbing his shoulder. "I start in the fall. I have, like, a million questions."

Immediately, I got a pang somewhere in my chest. Something horribly like jealousy. My own welcoming smile stiffened into a grimace.

Ashton laughed, oblivious to my reaction. "Fire away."

"C'mon, we'll get you a beer." Lee drew him to the kitchen and I stood there, stomach sinking, feeling forgotten. Just a little bit.

No. No, this was a good thing. If I was ditching Lee to give up on our joint dream of Berkeley to go to Harvard instead, it was good that Lee had found someone he'd know at Berkeley. This was a good thing. A brilliant thing. I was excited for him to make a new friend.

(Was this how Lee felt when I told him about Harvard?)

The door opened again, commotion outside, and it was a welcome distraction.

Oliver, Cam, Dixon, and Warren all piled indoors, laughing at some joke. They spotted me instantly, shouting my name. Cam pulled me into a hug and Warren proffered a bottle of wine.

"Compliments of my big sister," he said.

"Ooh! Classy! Thank you."

I moved to take it but he pulled it back. "No, no. It's not for you." He thought for a second, already working to get it open. "Okay, Evans. You can share it. But only because I like you. And because I need you to open it for me."

"So generous," I told him, taking the wine and twisting the cap off.

Dixon cuffed Warren on the head. "Stop being a dick. And, uh, Elle, message from Levi—he couldn't get someone to take his shift at work, so he's not gonna make it."

I groaned, mouth twisting in a frown. I'd been looking forward to seeing Levi, given that we hadn't hung out in a few days—not since graduation, really. It hadn't even occurred to me that this last-minute party might clash with his work schedule. I'd have to remember to text him later, or tomorrow. Maybe he could come out to the beach house later this week to hang out . . . if he and Noah were still okay with the idea of being in the same room.

Quickly, I put my best party-hostess smile back on. "Well, at least you guys made it!"

"It's a Flynn party," Olly laughed. "We couldn't miss it. Plus, no parents around to come barging in and breaking it up! I still can't believe you guys have this place to yourselves all summer."

"And you and Noah are living together," Cam added

with a disbelieving look. "Like actual, proper grown-ups. Talk about getting serious. How crazy is that?"

"Not," Warren declared, "*half* as crazy as this party. COME ON!" He threw one arm around me, the other around Olly, and herded us to where the rest of the party was happening.

Standing just by the doors to the pool with Ashton, Lee raised his can and yelled to the crowd both inside and out, "To our last summer at the beach house!"

Cam was glugging from the bottle of wine, and I took it off him to join the toast.

"Hey, Elle?" I turned around to find Jon Fletcher pointing a thumb over his shoulder and cringing. "You, uh . . . you might wanna . . . Um, Noah's kinda getting into it with some dude?"

I started to ask what exactly that meant, but someone called Jon's name and he turned around, grinning, for one of those slap-on-the-back guy-hugs, leaving me to brace myself and hurry outside by the pool, the guys following me eagerly.

We found Noah and some guy I vaguely recognized from a rival high school football team squaring off against each other. Noah's hands were scrunched tightly into fists, and a small group was hollering, jeering, egging them on. Through all the noise, I could just about hear them snapping at each other—and, unless I was hearing them wrong, it was about *me*.

". . . told everyone at that party senior year she was off-limits, what, just so you didn't have any competition?" the other guy jeered at Noah. "Bro, you know how *pathetic* that sounds? The only way you can get a girl is to threaten to beat up any guy that makes a move on her?"

"Or maybe," Noah growled back, "I just didn't want her having to put up with assholes like *you*. How many girls did you bring as your date to that homecoming game? Four?"

"Oh, man, I *love it* when Flynn loses his shit," Warren said near my ear, grabbing the wine off me to take a swig. He shoved the bottle at me to cup his hands around his mouth and yell, "Someone throw a punch already!"

The other dude tried to shove Noah, and Noah knocked his arm away and threw a punch—which was, predictably, met by a chorus of cheers. They both dived forward. A fist clipped Noah's jaw; his elbow caught the guy's shoulder.

I guessed I shouldn't have been so surprised, but I stepped forward, grabbed the back of Noah's shirt, and snapped, "Hey, meatheads, break it up!"

They stopped almost immediately, stepping back and settling for glaring at each other.

"I'm sorry, who invited you?" I asked the guy.

He mumbled, but got the message, cussing at Noah and marching out.

Noah looked at me uncomfortably, saying quietly, "Elle . . ."

"Save it, you big jerk. Just try not to beat anybody else up, huh? I'm your girlfriend, not your babysitter."

He flushed, and I made my way back inside. I *so* did not want to deal with his attitude right now—or an apology that was too little, too late. I really thought that going to college had made him grow out of that kinda stuff.

I heard a smash from the rumpus room and cringed. This could be a long night.

Or . . .

I took another gulp of wine.

I could worry about the state of the beach house, or I could make that tomorrow's problem, join in the fun, and be a real part of this "housewarming" party. Didn't I have enough on my plate already this week? Didn't I deserve one night of letting my hair down before everything got serious and stressful again?

It wasn't a difficult decision.

Although, honestly, when I dragged myself out of bed the next morning and picked my way through plastic cups and empty cans and bottles to the lounge and kitchen and saw what a disaster the place was, I kind of regretted not doing a little more to keep things under control.

(Maybe our parents were right. Maybe we really *were* growing up.)

My mood lifted when I found Lee passed out on the couch with a Cheeto stuck to his forehead and cat whiskers drawn on his face. I could hear Rachel pottering around in their bathroom, and Noah was using our shower, so I crouched down near Lee's head and called up an air-horn noise on YouTube on my phone, turned the volume right up, and blasted it in his ear.

He shot up so fast, limbs flailing, that he tumbled sideways. I backed away quickly as he fell onto the floor. The Cheeto was still stuck to him when he sat up, bleary-eyed, rubbing his face and pulling himself back onto the couch.

"What the hell, Shelly? Was the air horn really necessary?"

"Necessary? No. Fun? Absolutely."

Lee groaned, lying back on the sofa and throwing his arm over his head. "What time is it?"

"Early," I told him.

"You could've let me sleep in. On our, like, first official day of summer."

I rolled my eyes, nudging him and poking at him until he sat up so I could squash myself onto the couch beside him. "I could've but, my good buddy, my pal, we've got a schedule to keep."

"What're you talking about?"

"Well, while you and Noah spent your afternoon yesterday planning a party, I was creating a masterful plan for our bucket list. Starting with cliff jumping this afternoon. Well. Technically, starting with cleaning this place up, but that's not on the bucket list, so . . . up, up, up! We have no time to waste!"

And honestly, between looking after Brad, the bucket list, and spending time with Noah, we really didn't.

Chapter Twelve

13. Cliff jumping!

14. Be extras on a TV show!

15. ~~Get arrested (LEE WE ARE NOT GETTING ARRESTED)~~ ~~come on, shelly (I'M SERIOUS) fiiiiinnnnneee no getting~~ ~~arrested~~

15. Break a world record. Like, for REAL. Get the medal and everything.

After we went cliff jumping, Lee and I sat on the beach with our faded, treasured bucket list between us, trying to plan out the next few activities. There were so many to choose from, and the planning was a whole task in itself. I mean, we couldn't leave too many of the best ones until the *end* of summer, because it'd be here before we knew it; equally, we didn't want to do too many of them too quickly in the next couple of weeks and not have anything left to look forward to.

Plus, some of them (mainly race day) were going to

require a *lot* of work. The costumes alone were probably going to take hours to organize.

The further along we got in figuring out which items on the list we'd do when and what we might need to prepare, the more I was starting to realize just what a massive undertaking this was going to be.

I had *sorely* underestimated this when I'd proposed the bucket list to Lee.

"We'll have to make sure none of this gets in the way of all the stuff your mom and dad want us to do," I warned him, seeing the manic, delighted look on his face as he found an ad on his phone for a TV show looking for extras not too far away. "Your mom said she was going to email us all a list of her own, and it might be even worse than ours."

"You say that like any of *this* is going to be work"— he laughed, gesturing at the bucket list—"and not the absolute most fun you've ever had or ever will have in your entire life."

"I'm serious! Did you see the pictures she sent us of what she wants the backyard to look like? All the weeds and shrubs we'll have to get rid of, power-washing the backyard and the driveway . . . That might take us a whole weekend. And I promised I'd still be around to help look after Brad—"

"Shelly, I promise you, we will do all that stuff. Well, maybe not so much the power-washing, but definitely the babysitting. Besides, Noah and Rachel could *totally* help with that."

I grumbled quietly, uncertainly, but let him carry on

talking about this call for extras. I had to remind myself just *why* I was doing this. For Lee. For our friendship. Plus, he was right. It *was* going to be fun.

Fun, however, was going to come at a very steep price.

The more we talked about stuff on the list, the more I realized how much money this was going to cost. Even just renting the dune buggies was going to put a considerable dent in my savings account. . . .

I could ask Dad for the money. He'd pull a face and probably give me a small lecture on being responsible about spending it, but he'd help out. It just . . . didn't feel *right*. Not when I was going off to Harvard now, *on the other side of the country*, instead of a short drive to the Bay Area, to Berkeley. I already had no idea how I was going to cover my tuition fees—now, suddenly, I was tallying up the cost of a plane ticket to get there, and adding luggage to the flight, and then coming home for Thanksgiving, Christmas . . .

Oh man.

Maybe I hadn't thought this through. Maybe I'd gotten too excited, too carried away. And maybe Dad had, too.

Was it too late to change my mind?

(I could only imagine how Donna Washington at the Office of Undergraduate Admissions at Berkeley would take it if I called her up to say I wanted to take back the turning down of my offer.)

There were student loans I could take out to cover college, just like everyone else did, financial aid, provided Linda from the office didn't suddenly move in with us. But

I didn't think I could get any kind of loan to cover "completing my childhood bucket list with my best friend."

"Lee . . . ," I said apprehensively, biting my lip and looking up from the Facebook page for the place that hired out dune buggies on the beach. "I think we might have a problem."

"Don't tell me they closed shop and sold up like Mom and Dad are doing," he huffed, reaching to take my phone off me.

"No. No, it's . . . Lee, I know I promised you we were going to do *everything* on this list, and don't get me wrong, I'd love to, but I'm just thinking . . . we might . . . we might have to maybe scrap a couple of things. Just a couple. I can't afford to do all of this. I'll go broke before we get to number ten," I told him, only half joking.

Lee looked genuinely confused, and for once, I honestly felt *jealous* of him, that he never had to worry about this kind of stuff. Growing up, it had always been completely obvious that the Flynns had more money than us. I mean, they had a *pool*. They had fancy cars. June's clothes always looked like they cost more than our grocery bills.

But we were all so close, it had never mattered. It was *definitely* never a point of contention.

Until, I guess, now.

"I can ask my parents to cover it," he said, like it was that easy. "It's no big deal."

It was a huge deal, I wanted to tell him, but he was already on my phone and looking at the dune-buggy page, enthusiastically saying we could get a better deal if we hired for a group and got some of the guys involved, too. Warren and Dixon would be all over it, he said.

It was a huge deal, because it didn't feel right for me to ask my dad for the money, so how could I ask June and Matthew? I got that money wasn't really an object for Lee, for his family, like it was for us, but . . .

My stomach in knots, I looked at the huge smile on his face, the way his blue eyes sparkled in the sunshine, his hair still damp from our jump into the sea. He looked so freaking *happy*.

I couldn't let him down.

Maybe just this once, I thought, it wouldn't hurt.

•　•　•

On our way back to the beach house from our afternoon cliff jumping, Lee and I had the job of picking up something for dinner—which, of course, meant Dunes.

Dunes was a permanent fixture of our summers at the beach house. It had always been there, as long as I could remember, and we were frequent visitors. A cute white building set just off the sand with a faded blue roof, it was a pretty typical family-friendly restaurant.

They did *the best* fries.

Lee and I were practically drooling just talking about the fries as we parked and walked in—and I stopped dead in my tracks. Lee didn't notice and let the door go; it swung back and smacked me on the arm.

"Ouch!"

"Sorry. What's up?" Lee turned to look at me, following my gaze. "What're you staring at?"

Speechless, my mouth suddenly dry, all I could do was point at the sign in the window with huge red lettering that read HELP WANTED.

This had to be—like, literally—a sign.

All that worrying about how I'd pay for the bucket list or wanting to put a little money aside for college? This was *meant to be*. Right?

We'd be at the beach house all summer. And, sure, we were helping fix it up for sale, but how much time would that take, really? And I'd be able to work shifts around any commitments with Brad. . . .

And I'd totally still have time to spend with Noah and do the bucket-list stuff with Lee.

Totally.

"Be with you in just a sec," a lady in a green apron said, walking past us in the entryway. She placed some empty glasses on the bar and then turned to greet us. A smile lit up her face. "Elle! Lee! Well, hey! I didn't expect to see you guys up here so soon."

"Hi, May."

May was maybe a little younger than my dad. Her hair was dyed an orange shade of red, same as it had been every summer we'd been here. She hardly ever seemed to age.

"Where's the rest of the clan?"

Lee told her, "My parents are planning to sell the beach house, so us kids are up here to, you know, fix it up and stuff."

"They are?" she exclaimed in dismay, her face falling. She clicked her tongue, crossing her arms. "That's such a shame. Seems everyone's starting to sell now they're redeveloping. It's just not gonna be the same around here. But, hey, I guess we'll be seeing more of you kids this summer, huh? I'll have to make sure we've got an endless supply of fries."

Lee and I exchanged a glance, grinning. May had always given us extra portions of fries.

It was definitely part of what made them taste so good.

"So, what can I do you for? You guys want a table for dinner?"

"Hoping to get something to take out, if that's okay, May," Lee said, already wandering over to the serving station to pick up a menu, someone's notebook, and a pen. "I'll just pass the order straight over to Gary."

"Oh, honey, Gary retired last Christmas. It's Kenny on shift today anyway."

May looked ready to admonish Lee then, tell him that he couldn't just swan around like he owned the place, but she only rolled her eyes and let him carry on.

Before she could walk off, I blurted, "May?"

"Yeah, sweetie?"

"Can I, um . . ." I frowned, letting out a wobbly breath. My palms were sweating. *Come on, Elle, you can do this.* "I wanted to ask you about the job. The help wanted sign."

May let out a startled noise and blinked, mouth forming a small circle. "You want to apply?"

Immediately, I launched into a sales pitch of Why She Should Hire Elle Evans, despite my absolute lack of experience in any kind of job but least of all the service industry, despite me not having a résumé with me, despite knowing nothing about what the job actually was.

". . . and I'm really responsible, and I'll work so hard, May, I promise, and I could start as soon as you need, and—"

"Okay, okay." She laughed, raising her hands. "Slow down, kiddo. Look, honestly, the help wanted sign—it was for someone in the kitchen, and we filled that position yesterday."

My heart sank. So much for it being a (literal) sign.

I felt like a total idiot.

May drew a breath. "But . . ."

But! There was a but!

"I guess I could use an extra pair of hands around here. We always seem to get so rushed off our feet this time of year. And I know you," she added with a wink. "I can trust you. So, all right, little Elle Evans. You've got yourself a job."

She stuck out her hand as I jumped, squealing, to punch the air before quickly composing myself to shake her hand solemnly. She kept her face straight for about a second longer before breaking into an affectionate smile.

May pulled a notepad from her apron and a pen from behind her ear and handed them over. "Here. Jot down your name and your email. I'll send you over a contract and get in touch about a start date. Chances are it'll be in just a couple days."

"That'd be amazing," I gushed. "Thank you so much, May, thank you. You won't regret this."

"Hmm, I'd better not."

"Yes! Yes, absolutely. Thanks again, May!"

After giving May my details, I joined Lee to double-check we'd included everything on our order for the kitchen, and we counted out our cash and tip. I felt on top of the world.

I practically floated back to the car. I slammed the door behind me and wrapped my fingers around the steering wheel, beaming.

All the stress, all the hassle trying to get a job last year, all that worrying about money earlier, and just like that. It was that easy.

Maybe I'd been wrong earlier. It wasn't that I'd rushed into the choice between colleges or didn't think it through, and it wasn't that I'd been too eager to suggest the bucket list. Maybe this was all *exactly* how it should be. Maybe everything was working out perfectly.

I felt weightless. Exhilarated. Exactly like I'd felt when I launched myself into the air from the cliffs a few hours ago. Everything *was* working out perfectly. And I would make sure it stayed that way.

Chapter Thirteen

Noah caught me doing Wonder Woman poses in the bathroom later that evening.

"What are you doing?" he asked, a smirk creeping onto his face to find me standing there in my pajamas, legs planted shoulder width apart, hands firmly on my hips, shoulders back, chin up, and, to top it off, a confident "you got this" stare at my reflection.

I kept the pose but broke into a smile and caught his eye in the mirror. "I'm power-posing."

"Riiiiiiight . . ."

"Amanda told me about it," I said, twisting now to face him. "She sent me all these videos on Instagram about it. She said she was going through, like, a phase or something, so I thought I'd try it. See, you do this"—I demonstrated for him, re-creating the pose with deliberate actions—"and it makes you feel like your best self, like you could take on anything."

Noah raised an eyebrow at me. His lips pressed into a

thin line and a muscle jumped in his jaw—but not because he was annoyed; he was trying not to *laugh*.

"I'm serious!" I said. I grabbed each of his hands in turn and placed them on his hips, then used my feet to nudge his legs apart. I pressed on his shoulders and tilted his chin up. "Noah Flynn, *tell me* you do not feel more confident."

Once I stepped back to admire the effect and prove my point, I immediately cracked up. The sight of my tall, broad-shouldered boyfriend, with his shirt off, showing a set of defined abs (although, admittedly, rather less well-defined since his freshman year of college) and his muscled arms . . .

Yeah, it was pretty hilarious.

"You're right," he told me, deadly serious. "I am a confident, independent young woman who got into Harvard. I'm basically Legally Blonde."

I laughed, swatting at his arm as he dropped the pose. "Her *name* was Elle Woods, which I know you know, because your mom *loves* that movie, so don't pretend you don't."

"Guilty." He held up his hands and then leaned in the doorway, crossing his arms. "You looked totally confident, for the record. Especially in that Mickey Mouse shirt I'm pretty sure you've had since you were, like, thirteen."

He probably wasn't wrong. It used to be a nightie, once upon a time.

"So why are you power-posing in the bathroom mirror?"

"Because I *can* take on anything. I mean, I got a *job* today. An actual job. Do you know how many jobs I applied for last year? And then I just walk into Dunes and, bam, May gives me one, just like that. This is *my summer.* I mean—it's *our* summer. Plus, you know, the whole 'getting into Harvard, making my dad proud' thing. It just feels like everything's coming together, you know?"

Noah wasn't an easy guy to read, but I liked to think I knew him better than most people, and I got the distinct impression that he was doing his best not to tell me that May only gave me the job because she liked me or felt bad for me or something.

"You're right," he told me instead after a moment, his voice soft. "Everything's coming together."

Noah straightened up from the doorway to pull me into his arms. I loved the way his arms wrapped around me, the way he smelled—always like that citrus bodywash he used. My heart fluttered and I was already moving onto my tiptoes to kiss him, my lips finding his so easily.

The first time we kissed, Noah had sent me spinning. The second time we'd kissed, back at his house in the kitchen, it had been clumsy and awkward and our teeth had knocked together. The first time we had sex, it was fumbling and eager and sweet.

There was a familiarity to being with Noah now. I knew the feel of his arms around me, of his tongue running across my lower lip, of his skin against mine. He knew the spot on my neck that made me melt, and the one that tickled and made me squirm and giggle. I knew he liked it when I stood behind him and hooked my arms around him, because he secretly kinda liked being the little spoon sometimes; he thought it was funny and cute.

There was a familiarity to it, but my pulse still raced and the rest of the world still disappeared around us, just like that first time we kissed.

We stumbled out of the bathroom, back toward the bed, tangled up in each other and barely even breaking apart long enough to catch our breath.

I would *never* get tired of this, I thought.

I would never get tired of lying snuggled into his side either. My head nestled into the crook of his neck, my hand tracing patterns on his chest. Noah's fingers dragged slowly through my hair.

"This is nice," I told him. It was only day two of our summer at the beach house, but: "I could do this all summer. Or longer. No going home in the morning to get a change of clothes or do chores, no 'only for the weekend' while you're home from college, just . . ."

I trailed off with a sigh.

"I guess it is longer than only this summer, though," I carried on. "You know, like you said about us maybe living together next year."

Noah was quiet.

Maybe a little too quiet.

My hand stilled against his chest. Hadn't he been talking about us maybe living together just a couple of days ago? Had I gotten it completely wrong somehow? Was it because I'd taken his side of the bed?

"Elle?"

"Yeah?"

"You didn't . . . I mean, you didn't pick Harvard just because of me, right?"

"*Someone's* full of himself," I said, trying to joke and desperately trying to ignore the uneasiness gnawing at the back of my mind. "Don't get me wrong, it's obviously an added bonus that you're there, but . . . no, Noah. I maybe *applied* because you were there, but I didn't pick it because of you."

He let out a long, deep sigh. "Okay. Yeah. I mean, obviously. Sure."

"Let me guess," I said, tilting my head back to raise my eyebrows at him. "Amanda?"

"Rachel, actually. We were talking about you and Lee doing this whole bucket-list thing and you not going to Berkeley, and . . . I don't know, I guess she just got me thinking that . . ."

"That my life revolves around you?"

"That maybe you put me and Lee and your brother and your dad in front of yourself sometimes," he said quietly, unusually serious, sounding so at odds with my chilled-out mood from a moment ago.

Now it was my turn to be quiet for a little too long.

"I don't do that."

"Well, yeah, I . . . I know, and I'm not trying to say . . ."

"So what *are* you trying to say, Noah?" I snapped, sitting up now, resting back on my ankles and fixing him with a hard look.

Noah sighed again, but this time he was more exasperated. He kept his eyes on the opposite wall, and I saw him clench his jaw before taking a deep, quiet breath and looking back at me again. He reached to squeeze my hand, and even though he smiled, it looked a little forced. "Nothing, Elle. It doesn't matter."

It felt like it so obviously *did* matter, but . . .

Honestly, I didn't want to fight with him right now.

So I let it go and snuggled back into his side, and he kissed the top of my head.

"I was thinking we could go to the beach tomorrow," he said softly, almost cautiously. "Hang out for a couple hours before we have to get started on some of Mom and Dad's chores. Have you seen the list my mom emailed us? And I thought this summer was gonna be relaxing."

"Yeah, tell me about it. And sure, beach sounds good."

I knew it was an olive branch, but I was willing to take it. After all, we were only on day two of our summer living together at the beach house. No *way* was I going to pick a fight so soon, especially when it sounded like he was just trying to look out for me—in his own weird way.

"I really am looking forward to you being at Harvard, Elle," he told me.

"You'd better be, jerk."

But I turned around and leaned up to kiss him.

Chapter Fourteen

A couple days later, I had my first shift at Dunes. I got a uniform and May started me off slow. It wasn't too tricky to get the hang of being a server—and it helped that I knew their menu inside and out. I spilled a couple drinks onto trays, but May didn't seem to mind.

"Happens to everyone at first," she told me. "And, hey, at least you didn't spill one on a customer! I did that when I first started waitressing."

"The day is young, May, the day is young. Please don't jinx me."

I had to go back home on Friday to look after Brad—and Levi was away with his family for a long weekend, so we didn't get to hang out, which sucked. It was a little weird to be going back home but not staying.

I wondered if this was how it would feel after I left for college, whenever I'd visit home. This feeling of home being so temporary all of a sudden.

We were only halfway through our first week living at the beach house, and Lee and I had already managed to tick a couple things off the Lee and Elle's Epic Summer Bucket List. We'd gone cliff jumping, and Levi had sent us a picture of some flyer he'd seen at the 7-Eleven for a hot-air-ballooning experience. Plus, Brad could already swim without floaties, so we were off to a great start.

We'd also managed to go dirt biking thanks to a Groupon his mom had found, and we joined in a Saturday-afternoon pie-eating contest—which we won, of course—between my shift at Dunes and a date night with Noah.

As great as it was to spend quality time with Lee and work through the bucket list, it was also amazing to be able to curl up next to Noah in bed each night and wake up next to him. It was a hot summer, but I still snuggled into the warmth of his body each morning for a few minutes before I had to get up and start the day.

And we'd only had a *couple* of arguments.

That was nothing new. Noah and I had always bickered, and these arguments were way less serious than the college talk we'd had in bed the other night. Now we just fought over whether the window stayed open or closed while we slept, or Noah finishing all the Cheerios, or when he stepped on one of my earrings and broke it. (Noah was mad because he'd stepped on the earring with a bare foot. I was mad because it wasn't like it was that hard to see and, you know, he'd broken it.) We'd fight over what to watch on TV, who got the last slice of pizza.

Right now he groaned as my third alarm went off and I

smashed my thumb at the screen to silence it, dropping my phone back onto the nightstand.

"What time is it?" he mumbled, dragging his face out of the pillow.

"Six thirty-six."

Noah's rough, husky morning voice and the way he smacked his lips together and wriggled his mouth around did way more to wake me up than any of my three alarms had done. His arm reached out, wrapping around my waist and tugging me in close. His hair was sticking up on one side and I giggled, brushing it flat with my fingers. Noah's lips found mine in a soft, lingering kiss and I melted against him. Our legs wrapped together and his nose nuzzled into mine.

"Are you sure you have to get up?"

"Mmm-hmm. I've gotta bake a bunch of cupcakes before my shift for a bake sale that Brad's baseball camp is having—"

"You're *baking*?"

"I picked up a couple tips, hanging out with Levi all the time."

Noah scoffed.

"*Fine*. Levi dropped a bunch off at the house last night and I have to decorate them. And then Lee and I have some bucket-list plans."

Noah sighed. "Of course you do."

"But I'll be back this evening. I was thinking maybe we

could go hang out on the beach for a little while? Take a picnic or something. And you can always come with us, you know."

Noah shook his head, pressed another kiss to the corner of my mouth. "Nah, I don't wanna interfere. The bucket list is your guys' thing. But a picnic sounds like a great idea. Maybe you can hold back a couple of those cupcakes for us?"

I grinned. My alarm began to sound again, so I gave Noah a brief last kiss before shutting it off and climbing out of bed. "Now, *that* I can do."

It didn't take me too long to get dressed, and I'd already packed my work uniform into a backpack for later. Noah had gone back to sleep but woke up enough to reach out, catch my hand, and pull me back for a kiss goodbye. "Have a good day. I love you."

"Love you too, lazybones."

The beach house was so quiet as I went into the kitchen that I could hear the sea. A breeze rustled through the trees outside. The pipes in the house creaked.

I'd never known it to be so quiet.

I tried to keep the noise down as I fixed myself some cereal and was so focused on planning the logistics of my day that I didn't even notice someone coming into the room until Lee waved his hand in my face and said, "Uh, hello? Earth to Elle?"

I jumped, my heart racing. "Jesus, Lee! Don't creep around like that!"

He gave me a sleepy grin and took the cereal from the

counter, shoving his hand in and eating it straight from the box. I realized then that he was dressed. Not that he'd combed his hair, though. It was in even more of a state than Noah's had been.

"What're you doing up?"

Lee gave me a flat look, still shoveling cereal into his mouth. "Shelly, those thirty million alarms you set probably woke up the whole goddamn beach. I figure if we rush the cupcakes, we might be able to have the brain freeze–off on your way to work. Besides, we both know you're the world's shittiest baker and you're gonna need help. Even if it's just the decorating."

"I like your style. But I thought you were gonna be here to deal with that guy who's redoing the driveway?"

"Noah can deal with that."

Lee was still sleepy, so we took my car. Dad was about to leave for work when we got to my house, so we didn't chat for long. He'd texted every day to check in and see how things were going, but he asked us again now anyway.

"It's great!" Lee enthused. "Having the place to ourselves is killer. Although Shelly and Noah seem to find something new to argue about every day," he added with a laugh.

Dad frowned at me. "You didn't say you and Noah had been fighting."

"We're not!" I told him, smacking my so-called best friend across the arm and shooting him a glare. "Well, I mean . . . kind of, but . . . but when haven't we argued about stuff? Everything's *great*. I promise."

"Hmm" was all my dad had to say about it. "Well, I've gotta head to work. Thanks again for helping out with Brad's bake sale, bud. And say thanks to Levi again. He's a good kid—wouldn't even take any money off me for them."

"I'll let him know."

"Well, have a good day at work. And don't forget I need you to pick Brad up tomorrow from—"

"Yeah, Dad, I know. I'm the one who put the Post-its on the refrigerator, remember?"

After he was gone, I shoved Lee's head before getting to work. A couple of Tupperware containers were stacked in the kitchen. Three were filled with cupcakes; the fourth had everything we'd need to decorate them. While I set up a workstation, Lee made us both some coffee.

That didn't stop me being mad at him, though, even just a little.

"Thanks for that," I huffed. "We don't *fight*."

"I have never known anyone to yell over a toothbrush," Lee told me, getting out a mixing bowl and some utensils. "A *toothbrush*, Shelly."

"It was over toothpaste," I corrected him, sticking my chin in the air. "And don't tell me you and Rachel don't argue about stupid stuff like that."

"Nope."

"What do you mean, *nope*? I've heard you guys . . ." I trailed off as I thought it over. Thinking about it, it wasn't so much arguing as . . . "Okay, well, you have disagreements."

"No, what we have is Rachel pointing out when I've done something stupid. Like leaving the toilet seat up or using her journal as a coaster."

"That's totally the same thing."

Lee scrunched up his face in a way that said, *Yeah, no, it's kind of not.*

"Shut up," I told him. "Okay, I'm going to frost these cupcakes here in blue, and you're going to do those ones in white."

"Remind me why you didn't just ask Levi to do this part, too? He *loves* this kinda thing, and you know his little sister would've loved to help out."

"Because," I snapped. I was still a little irritated at him for saying I'd been fighting with Noah—and for questioning me on this now.

Because I was trying to prove to myself that I could handle everything this summer. We'd graduated high school now and would be heading off to college soon. We were growing up and I *could handle this.* I had a job. I was pulling off the epic bucket list of our childhoods to create the perfect summer. I'd gotten into *Harvard,* dammit.

This was just a bake sale, that was all. A couple dozen cupcakes. No big deal.

Brad woke up just as we were adding sprinkles on top of the frosting. He gasped when he found us in the kitchen, then beamed and cried out, "Lee! I haven't seen you in forever!"

"Oh, charming," I scoffed, already abandoning the cup-cakes to start getting Brad's breakfast together.

He noticed. "I can pour my own juice, *Elle.*" And then: "No! That's too much milk! You're messing up the oatmeal!"

"You never complained about the way I made you oat-meal before," I muttered. He stomped over to scowl at the oatmeal I was making and pouted at me.

I *definitely* wasn't this difficult when I was his age.

When I put the milk back in the refrigerator, I noticed a mostly empty bottle of rosé wine chilling in there and my nose wrinkled. Since when did Dad drink rosé? And in the *middle of the week*? Dad's idea of a drink was two light beers on a Saturday night or maybe, if he was feeling fancy, a glass of red wine.

And then it hit me.

"Was Linda here this week?" I asked Brad.

"Yeah," he said, apparently not in the least bit bothered. "Hey, can you add some honey to my oatmeal? She did that the other morning and it was *great.*"

"Wait, she was here *in the morning*? Like, she *spent the night*?"

Brad pulled a face at me, like he didn't get why it was such a big deal, like I was acting crazy. "Uh, *yeah.* She, like, passed out on the couch watching a movie."

Lee hastily turned a chuckle into a cough and waggled his eyebrows at me. I glared back at him. Her wine was in the refrigerator, she was messing with the way we made oatmeal for Brad, she was staying overnight. . . . Wasn't this all moving way too fast for someone Dad had just been on a date with, like, a week ago?

(Except it wasn't just a week, was it? It had been going on since, like, spring break, by the sound of it.)

"Sure," I mumbled, slamming the refrigerator door closed. "I can put some honey in your oatmeal."

Brad ignored me completely after that, in favor of chatting with Lee (well, at him, really). He kept talking to Lee, barely stopping to say thanks, when I put his breakfast down in front of him.

I left them to it, finishing off the cupcakes and carefully packing them back into the Tupperware—setting a couple containers aside to take back to the beach house, obviously.

"Okay! Do *not* forget to bring the containers back, okay? They're Levi's. If you lose them, they're coming out of your allowance. Dad said so."

Brad pulled a box toward him to scrutinize the cupcakes. "You don't get the frosting as good as Levi," he grumbled.

"What's your problem?" I snapped. "Are you still jealous because Dad won't let you come to the beach house? I told you, maybe you can stay one night. If you're good."

Lee clapped Brad on the shoulder. "Psst. Hey, don't worry, little guy. I got this. We'll talk them around."

"Thanks, Lee."

A little while later, we took Brad to the baseball camp he was spending a few weeks at during the day, and it was still early enough that we decided to pull into the 7-Eleven for Slurpees.

"Howdy there, folks, what can I get you this fine morning?"

I spun around with a grin. "Levi!"

He was stacking boxes of tampons on a shelf and grinned back. Levi was tall and lean, with kind of gangly limbs and curly brown hair, a pointed chin, and warm eyes. He had a wide, friendly smile—the kind that made you feel like you'd just made his day.

Sometimes, though, I got the feeling that he didn't smile at *everybody* like that.

(It was still awkward to remember Thanksgiving, when I'd kissed him. But we'd both forgotten all about that by now—or at least put it *way* behind us.)

"Levi, my friend," Lee announced, clasping his hands behind his back and rocking on his heels, "put down the tampons! We require ten of your coldest Slurpees."

"T-ten? You bring the rest of the gang, too, or something?"

"It's from our bucket list," I explained as he put the last boxes on the shelf and walked us over to the cash register and the Slurpee machine. "And I want the blue one."

"Guess that means I'm red." Lee sighed.

Levi knew all about the bucket list. I'd obviously told him everything, but we'd also been posting a bunch of our escapades so far online so our friends could keep up with all the madness.

"Aah," he said, starting to pour the first one. "Is this for the great brain-freeze contest?"

"That it is," I told him with a grin.

"You don't think three each is enough?"

Lee gave a dramatic sigh, and we turned to each other, both leaning an elbow on the counter. "I thought you said this guy was cool."

"All this time," I agreed, shaking my head in dismay, "and he's still underestimating us."

"All right, all right. Ten ice-cold Slurpees it is. You guys know it's not even ten o'clock, right?"

"I feel like he's trying to make a point. What about you, Shelly?"

"Yeah, but I'm just . . . not . . . getting it."

Levi laughed. As he lined up our drinks, we told him about the successful cupcake decorating—even if Brad hadn't been too impressed with it.

"But look at that piping. Look!" I waved my cell phone in his face.

"Mary Berry and Paul Hollywood would be so proud," Levi deadpanned. Lee pulled a face, missing the joke, but I laughed. Lately, Levi had gotten *way* into *The Great British Baking Show* (or, as he insisted on calling it, *Bake Off*). "Let me just ring you guys up and then"—he looked around the store, which was empty save for his colleague mopping an aisle—"bottoms up, I guess."

Lee paid, Levi agreed to take some photos, and we stood facing each other, first Slurpee in hand.

"All right. You remember the rules?"

"No stopping or you're out."

"No time-outs."

"Three . . . two . . ."

The cold hit me in a heartbeat, sending a shock right up between my eyes. But I had this. Lee and I stared each other down as we guzzled the Slurpees. I gave him my best stink eye. He kept waggling his eyebrows and crossing his eyes in an effort to distract me.

It wasn't working, though. We moved on to the second Slurpee within a second or two of each other, but I made it to my fourth while Lee was still struggling through his second.

When he was halfway through his third and I was starting on my fifth, he gave up, dropping the mostly empty cup onto the counter and sinking against it with a groan. "You win, you win. I admit defeat. Uuuugh."

Just to make a point, I finished the last of my fifth Slurpee before raising my hands to the sky in victory.

"Don't gloat," Lee groaned, slumping melodramatically over the counter, his knees buckling. "I . . . I can't take it right now. Ugh."

Levi gave a long, low whistle. "Jeez, Elle. That was impressive."

I closed my eyes, the brain freeze pretty severe by this point. "If I puke while I'm at work, this is all your fault, Lee."

"You guys gonna be okay to drive?" Levi asked us, trying not to laugh.

"Sure we are. In, like, a little while," I admitted. I was definitely gonna need a few minutes to recover. Lee and I stayed at the checkout while we did so, groaning and holding our heads, Levi laughing and promising to send us all the photos.

Twentysomething minutes later, we were high-fiving and back on the road. Lee got out the crumpled, faded sheet of paper and unfolded it on his lap. He rooted through my glove box for a pen, then drew a neat line across the page with a grin.

20. Epic brain-freeze competition!!!

I pulled into the parking lot of Dunes, climbed out of the car, and handed the keys to Lee. "I'll text you at the end of my shift? Come pick me up and we can head for laser tag."

"You're only here a couple of hours," he said with a shrug. "I'll hang out with you. May won't mind."

I didn't have to say, "What about Rachel?" because she had plans to visit her grandparents today. But I did say, "What about the realtor? I thought she was supposed to be coming this afternoon. Your mom wanted you and Noah there."

Lee scowled, a dark look on his face. I felt a twinge of sympathy; any mention of selling the beach house seemed to bring his mood down.

"Noah can handle that himself. He's a big boy."

"Well, okay. But the costumes—"

"I put them in your trunk earlier. Ready to go when you are. Hey, do you think May will have any fries ready yet?"

May, it turned out, wasn't overly surprised to find Lee had tagged along. Although Dunes wasn't technically serving lunch for another thirty minutes, she got him a soda and a bowl of fries. She didn't ask why Lee was here, but she did ask why he had red smeared all around his mouth and why my tongue and teeth were bright blue.

We explained the bucket list to her, and Lee said, "And later we're doing laser tag."

"Oh! That's . . ." She gave us a curious look, her smile a little stiff. "No offense, but that sounds kind of . . . normal." Then she groaned melodramatically. "Why do I feel like there's a catch with you two?"

"It's *Star Wars* laser tag," I explained with a grin. "We've got Han Solo and Princess Leia costumes. We wore them for Halloween a couple years back. Lucky they still fit."

"Noah didn't feel like renting a Chewbacca outfit and joining in," Lee added.

May laughed. "You kids. I hope you bring in some pictures! Oh, hey, looks like we've got customers. Elle, time to get to work."

I was worried Lee would be a distraction, but it turned out I was so run off my feet once the lunch rush started that I barely had time to spare him a glance. I *did*, however, notice him taking a phone call, looking unusually serious. I walked over before dropping an order to the kitchen, long enough to hear him talking in a deep, gruff voice.

"Yes. Yes, of course. Next week is fine. Thank you *so much* for understanding about the short notice. Mmm-hmm. I'll be sure to let her know. Have a great day."

"What was that about?"

Lee jumped, and there was an unmistakably guilty expression on his face. He looked at me with wide, bulging eyes for a moment and then coughed, waving his phone at me. "Oh, nothing. Just, uh, just the realtor. Canceling. They double-booked us."

"And called you?"

"Mom gave them my number. Help organize things around the bucket list, you know?"

Huh. Well, I guessed that made sense.

"Now, don't you have tables to serve, missy? Those fries aren't gonna eat themselves."

Chapter Fifteen

"Lee?"

He looked up, and so did I. It was quiet—a lull after the last of the late-lunchers left and before the early dinner-goers arrived, something that, a couple of weeks into summer and several shifts into working at Dunes, I was getting familiar with. I was putting away glasses under the bar.

"Yeah, May?"

"What are you doing?"

Lee and I exchanged a confused glance. He looked down at the mop in his hand and the bucket. I could see him thinking the same thing as me: Was this a trick question? "Uh . . . mopping?"

May gave a long sigh, crossing her arms. "You don't work here. Stop mopping."

"But the floor was sticky."

May gave him a sharp look, a mom-type look that said, *Don't talk back to me, young man.* He gave her a bright, winning smile, even pulling out the puppy-dog eyes. May threw her hands in the air, waving them in front of her like she was trying to wave away bad juju.

"That boy," she told me with a sigh. She didn't add anything else, but I guessed there was nothing else *to* say. I knew exactly what she meant and smiled at my best friend.

"Tell me about it."

"Anyway," she said, taking a breath. "Elle, I've got you working a double today, don't forget, and I've put you down for those extra shifts you wanted next week."

"Oh. O-okay. Thanks."

She gave me an odd look. "Is that a problem?"

"No!" I blurted. "That's great. Thanks, May, I appreciate it."

She gave me a thumbs-up before going into the kitchen. Lee went back to mopping, humming to himself, his head bobbing as he cleaned.

I swallowed the lump in my throat. I'd asked for the extra shifts, so obviously I was happy to have them, and obviously it wasn't a problem or I wouldn't have asked for them in the first place.

I was trying to rack up as many hours as I could—more hours meant more money, and I could do with as much of that as possible right now. In the last couple of weeks, Lee and I had blown through a solid portion of the bucket list— from diving in one of those shark tanks to skydiving *and* taking a juggling class. The only one that hadn't cost me money had been the blanket fort we'd built (which Rachel and Noah got really exasperated by because we wouldn't let them in without a password and we'd stolen all the best snacks). Lee had footed the bill for a couple of them, which honestly only made me feel worse about the whole money situation.

We weren't exactly struggling to get by, but we didn't have the same kind of disposable income the Flynns did. The more money I could earn this summer, the better. I knew I'd need it once I got to college, and I'd rather not have to keep going to my dad to ask him for cash.

I definitely wanted the extra shifts.

But May reminding me about them just made me feel . . . kind of exhausted. It had only been a few weeks, but between all the bucket-list stuff, driving back and forth to help out with Brad . . . It was a lot.

And that wasn't even mentioning all the work we'd been doing around the beach house. So far we'd tidied up the backyard and painted the porch, Rachel had deep-cleaned the kitchen, and Noah was working on fixing the pool filter using several YouTube tutorials. Next up on the list: steam-cleaning the couches and painting the ceiling, which sounded like the kind of job we'd need all hands on deck for.

Just thinking about it all made me want to sleep for like a week.

"You know," Lee said, distracting me from myself. He'd set the mop down again and was leaning over the bar, the bucket list out once more. It was looking even more worse for wear than when we'd found it. Stained with red Slurpee, seawater, chocolate sauce from the giant sundae we'd dumped on an unsuspecting Noah, and covered in a bunch of different pens where we'd ticked things off or crossed them out after completing them.

Now Lee tapped the list. "You know, there's one thing on here we won't be able to do. Number twenty-two: Live together at Berkeley."

Guilt prickled across my skin, same as any time Berkeley came up in conversation.

I knew he wasn't trying to guilt-trip me now. Aside from our initial discussion about college, after I told him I'd be going to Harvard, Lee had been trying his best not to make me feel any worse than I already did about Berkeley. Even so, I still worried that whenever it came up, resentment was simmering just under the surface.

He just gave me a sad smile and said, "You think we should cross it off the list? It feels weird to leave something out."

"Well . . . what if we didn't have to? Maybe I could come up to Berkeley with you, help you, I don't know, get set up or move in or something. Go up and check the place out? It's not exactly what we had in mind, I know, but . . . we could make a weekend of it? Just us?"

Lee reached across to put his hand on mine. "It's a deal. Hey, I'll get some recommendations from Ashton for when we visit. See if there's any places we should check out."

"Ashton?"

"*Yeah*, Elle. Ashton? Came to our party? Yay high, blond

147

hair, great taste in comic books?" He laughed, talking about some things Ashton had told him about Berkeley already, including some comic-book shop Lee thought sounded like a lot of fun. I was barely listening, though.

Ashton lived on Jon Fletcher's street but went to a different school. Jon and a couple of the football guys had rented a place on the beach together for the summer after they'd seen us having such a great time at the Flynns' beach house. Olivia had begged her parents to do the same for her and a couple of the girls.

(And here I was putting ten-dollar bills in a piggy bank I'd labeled "college fund.")

So Ashton had been hanging around with the guys some days, and he and Lee had been talking. I knew that. I knew Ashton tagged Lee in funny posts on Instagram he thought he'd like.

But I kept managing to block it out of my mind. Ashton and Berkeley both.

I figured I didn't need the reminder of how I was letting my best friend down.

My second shift was just starting when Lee's phone rang. "Rach. She's outside. Guess that's my cue to go home."

"Save some dinner for me?"

"Not likely."

I knew he would.

"See ya tomorrow, May!" Lee called, tossing me his apron.

"No, you won't!" came her reply, even though I think

she knew that nothing she said would stop Lee coming by to hang out here, working for free. He hadn't said it exactly, but I got the feeling he was trying to make up for the time we'd lose now we wouldn't be at college together.

There was a handful of other people who worked at Dunes. A nerdy guy from the grade below me at school whose name I now knew was Melvin. A woman who'd been here about as long as May. An old guy who'd come out of retirement and mostly just made up drinks or helped prep food in the kitchen. A few college-aged kids I didn't really know but got on well enough with. They were all a little confused about why Lee was here so much, although none of them really said anything.

Right now, Melvin and one of the college girls were just arriving. They passed Lee at the door, saying hi to him and then to me.

And not far behind them came the start of the dinner rush. At this time of day, it was mostly families with little kids, just finishing up on the beach and needing to fill hungry bellies before they headed home.

I spotted May seating one all-too-familiar family over in Melvin's section and grabbed him. "Hey, you mind if I take that table?"

"Uh, sure." He looked where I was pointing and a knowing smile dawned on his face. "Isn't that the guy you broke up with Flynn for?"

I groaned. "I told you, that was just a stupid rumor."

"Oh yeah?"

"*Yes*, Melvin."

His smile stretched even wider. He pushed his round glasses up his nose. "So why's he staring at you?"

"What?" I turned to look over my shoulder, but Levi was studying his menu carefully. His cheeks were a little pink. I rolled my eyes at Melvin, who just kept grinning at me till I grabbed a water pitcher and marched over to the table.

I announced myself with a bright and unnecessary, "Hi! My name's Elle and I'll be your server today," then started to pour their water.

Becca, Levi's little sister, giggled. "We know who you *are*, Elle."

"Didn't expect to see you guys here."

"Couldn't waste an afternoon like this," his mom said cheerfully. "My husband couldn't get the time off work, so it's just us three today. Levi keeps talking about you working here, so we thought we'd give it a shot."

"Mom!" he hissed.

I bit my top lip, trying not to laugh as I saw Levi squirm out of the corner of my eye.

"Besides," she said, unfazed, "we haven't seen you around in a while."

She said it with a certain gravity, like she was trying to make a point. A point I got loud and clear. Throughout senior year, I'd spent a lot of time hanging out with Levi. He'd come over while I babysat Brad; I went to his place while he was looking after Becca. A lot of the time we just hung out together, for no other reason than that we were friends.

And yeah, maybe we hadn't been hanging out so much lately.

"Mom," he hissed again.

"Well, you know." My smile faltered and I shifted my weight to my other foot. "I've been busy with this job and . . . Noah's home now, so . . ."

"Ah, yeah. The boyfriend."

She shot a glance at Levi, which seemed to say something I really didn't get, and he let out a sharp, exasperated sigh. "Mom!"

Okay, well . . .

This was weird.

"Shall I give you guys a couple minutes to decide? Or, um . . . uh, would . . . would you like to order drinks?"

They ordered drinks. Levi was slouched right down in his seat by now, although I wasn't so sure what he had to look so embarrassed about.

"Are you gonna come hang out again soon, Elle?" Becca asked me, pouting, with puppy-dog eyes that were *way* more effective than Lee's.

"I, uh, maybe. I'll try! It's just a little crazy around here right now. But I'll come see you soon, okay?"

"Sorry," her mom said to me. "She just really liked having another girl around to hang out with. You've had quite the influence on her, you know. And on Levi."

"Right . . ."

Honestly, I wasn't sure what to make of that. And I wasn't totally sure it was a good thing, even if she made it sound like it was.

"And Harvard! Levi told us. Congratulations, sweetie, that's such an incredible achievement. Your dad must be so proud of you. It makes me wish Levi had applied to college. He graduated with such good grades."

I coughed. Talking to other people's parents had never really been my strong suit (not counting June and Matthew, of course), and it was uncomfortable to talk to Levi's mom about his decision not to apply for college during senior year. Frankly, I couldn't get out of this conversation quickly enough.

"He's just figuring things out," I said lamely, and snapped my notepad shut. "One veggie burger, one hot dog, one cheeseburger, and a side of onion rings coming right up."

• • •

I was taking a thirty-second breather at the bar when I felt someone standing beside me. They cleared their throat.

"I'm sorry, sir, I'll be right— Oh, Levi."

"Hey." He gave me a stiff half-smile, with only one side of his mouth, and raised his hand in an equally awkward wave. "I just, um, I . . ."

"You . . . ?"

He cleared his throat and tried again, running his hand through his hair. "I'm sorry about that earlier. If my mom made it awkward. It's just, you know, I mean, Becca's asked a couple of times if you're coming over, and I've been telling her you've got a job here and you're spending time with Noah and Lee. So . . . yeah. That's all."

"Right."

God, when did it get so awkward hanging around Levi? When had this happened? My palms felt clammy and I had a weird squirming sensation in my gut—the kind that made me wish someone would spill their drink or drop their food and yell for me to fix it.

Was this what happened when we didn't hang out face to face for a couple of weeks? (The Slurpee contest didn't count, not really.)

Was this what was going to happen to me and Lee, after time apart at college?

Or was this because Noah was back home and it had shifted the whole dynamic between us?

"Right," Levi said, nodding.

"I'm sorry I haven't been around much," I said. "Not . . . not just for Becca, but . . . I know we text, like, every day, and we talk on the phone, but we haven't hung out properly, and that's . . . that's on me."

Levi shrugged. His smile was soft even if his eyes were a little sad, and he laid a light hand on my arm. "It's okay. I know you're busy."

As if on cue, my phone buzzed in my pocket. I slipped it out to check it.

A text from Dad. *Don't forget to pick Brad up from soccer practice later!*

I groaned. "Shit. Shit."

"What's up?"

I kneaded my knuckles between my eyes, scowling at my phone. "I hounded May to give me a double shift today, but I'm supposed to pick Brad up from soccer. Shoot. How . . ." I sighed. "I'm gonna have to ask May to—"

"Well, we can pick him up," Levi offered. "What time does he finish?"

"Six-thirty."

"That's perfect; we'll be heading right by there. We can pick him up, take him back to your place."

"No, Levi, I can't ask you to do that."

"You didn't," he told me with a grin. "Seriously, Elle, it's no problem. I've got your dad's number; I can let him know. Spare key's under the flowerpot by the gate, right?"

"Yeah," I sighed, giving him a quick, grateful hug. "Thanks. You're a real lifesaver. He literally just needs a ride home. My dad had a late meeting and his office is on the other side of town, so . . . thanks, Levi."

A late meeting I had a sneaking suspicion was with Linda, but hey . . .

"Like I said, I know you're busy."

My shoulders sagged. At least the weirdness between us had evaporated—for now. As Levi turned to go back to his mom and sister, I grabbed his arm. "Hey, look, we're planning a day at the water park in a couple of days. Jon Fletcher's brother works there and he managed to pull some

154

strings for us. It's gonna be kind of crazy. Could do with an extra few recruits."

Levi's lips stretched into a smirk. "Does this have anything to do with the bucket list?"

"You know it."

"Text me the details. I'll be there."

I smiled, breathing a sigh of relief. Maybe it'd be in a group setting, but it'd be good to hang out with Levi again. Seeing him today made me realize just how much I'd missed him.

Levi went back to his table and I glanced over again—just in time to see him looking away, scowling at something his mom was saying and looking embarrassed.

Well, whatever that conversation was about, I was glad I wasn't a part of it.

Chapter Sixteen

When I got home, I found the beach house empty. Lee and Rachel were out on date night, I remembered, but there was no sign of Noah. The light was on in the kitchen and lounge, but the doors to the backyard were ajar, so I went outside to look for him.

It was only as I got farther down the path from the house to the sand that I heard his voice drifting toward me. He hung up the call just as I got near, looking up at the sound of my footsteps.

"Hey, gorgeous," he said, smiling.

My cheeks grew warm. "Gorgeous" was the last thing I was right now; sweat was making my hair feel greasy, I had various stains down my shirt, and my arm was still sticky where I'd spilled soda on it. But even so, I'd never get tired of hearing Noah compliment me like that and mean it.

I flopped down on the sand beside him, lying flat on my back, not caring about the sand that got in my hair and clothes. "Long day?"

"Long day. I saw Levi, though."

"Oh yeah?"

"His mom took him and Becca to the beach. They came by Dunes for dinner on their way home. I had to get him to pick up Brad from soccer because I forgot when I asked May for the double shift, so I'm expecting a call from my dad any minute now to tell me how disappointed he is in me."

Noah lay down beside me. I turned to face him, the sand scratching at the side of my cheek. He didn't have a shirt on and my eyes drifted over his broad shoulders, his toned abs. "So Levi picked him up?"

"Well, him and his mom and sister. I really owe him one."

"You could've called me. I could've picked Brad up."

"Well . . ."

That was a good point.

"Well, I didn't think about that," I told him. "And Levi was there. He offered."

Noah gave a quiet grunt. I couldn't tell if he was annoyed, but I didn't mention it. Levi had ended up being a source of contention when we'd broken up around Thanksgiving, especially after I'd gone to the Sadie Hawkins dance with him and Noah had seen us kiss.

It wasn't like Levi was the *only* problem we'd had, and I'd thought the air was all clear now, but even so, I decided not to push it.

"Who were you talking to anyway?"

I saw Noah bite the inside of his cheek for a second before he twisted to face me. "Amanda."

Ah, Amanda. Another source of contention in our

relationship last fall. Again, she wasn't the *only* source, but . . . Well, it hadn't helped that I'd found out Noah was keeping a secret from me that *she* knew all about. I'd thought he wanted to be with her (a theory backed up first by a photo online of her kissing his cheek and then by Noah bringing her home for Thanksgiving), but it turned out he'd just been struggling with his classes, and she was helping him out—something Noah had been too embarrassed to tell me.

Despite what I'd initially thought about Amanda, I liked her. She was British, with a permanently bubbly attitude as far as I could tell, which made her impossible to hate. The fact that she looked like a catalog model for "classic preppy college girl" had made me pretty jealous at first. Still did sometimes. I'd seen her when I visited Noah over spring break, and she'd been nothing but welcoming and friendly.

They had the kind of easy, platonic relationship that Lee and I had. It was still weird, though, for me to get my head around Noah having someone like that in his life.

"Oh yeah?" I asked, just like he had about Levi.

"Turns out she's gonna be in town for a while. She gets here day after tomorrow. Her folks are here. Some business deal her mom's working on. I told her she could crash here for a couple of days. Is that cool?"

"Sure, Noah. I guess we've got the space, with Lee's and my old room."

"You sure?"

I shrugged into the sand and offered him a reassuring smile. As jealous as I got of Amanda, I did at least feel confident that she wasn't a threat to Noah's and my relationship. "Why wouldn't I be? Did you know she was coming or was this her idea of a surprise?"

He smirked. "Her idea of a surprise."

"Hey, if she's around, you should invite her to the water park with us! Levi's gonna come, too. Lee and I figured we could make it a whole group thing; it'll be so much cooler that way. Lee was gonna ask Rachel, and Jon wanted to get involved, too, since his brother helped us organize the whole thing, so . . ."

"Oh, right. Cool. Uh, sure. I'll . . . give her a heads-up."

I realized then that we'd never actually *formally* asked Noah to get involved with it and laughed, swatting a hand lightly across his arm. "*Obviously* we want you to be part of it, too, you big doofus. Lee's got your costume planned and everything."

His eyebrows knitted together and one side of his mouth quirked. "No thanks, Elle. I'm sure you guys will have a blast, but . . . nah. Not my thing."

"Oh, come on! Please? The only reason we're even allowed to do it is because we're filming it and raising money for charity as some, like, PR promo for the water park. Please? It's for a good cause."

He laughed. "Why does this feel like that time you asked me to be a kisser at your kissing booth?"

"So?"

"I don't think so, Shelly."

I pouted, spinning onto my side and wriggling closer, so my face was nearer his. "What did you say last time?" I racked my brain, trying to remember the house party when I'd asked him to do the kissing booth for us, at the request of all the girls. "I *think* you said something like, would I go down on my knees and beg?"

Noah groaned, pulling his hands over his face and laughing. "Don't give me that look, Elle. You know I never meant it like that."

"Please?" I wheedled, my fingertip tracing patterns over his bare chest.

"I just don't think it's my thing." He sighed. "I'll come along to . . . support you or whatever, but there is no way I'm putting some stupid costume on."

I could see there'd be no convincing him tonight, so I gave up. Maybe Lee could give it a shot—heck, even Amanda might be able to convince him. Sometimes I forgot that where Lee and I could get carried away with the crazy, Noah was a lot more down-to-earth. Sighing, I settled for just resting my head on his shoulder, tucking into his side as he moved his arm around me and kissed me between the eyebrows.

"So what're your plans tomorrow?"

"Hmm . . ." I pulled up my mental calendar. "Breakfast shift, then I'm taking Brad to the dentist, running a couple of errands for my dad and back here all evening."

"No bucket-list stuff?"

"Nope." Then I added, "Lee's going to a movie with Ashton."

"Huh. And you're . . ." He trailed off, but I heard the words he didn't say: *You're okay with that?*

I shrugged, burrowing my face into his shoulder. "Yeah, I'm okay with it. Why wouldn't I be? I . . . I have to be," I mumbled. "Lee's allowed to have other friends. Same as me. He didn't get mad when I started hanging out with Levi."

"You don't *sound* so okay."

"Shut up. I'm *fine.*"

"Mmm-hmm."

"And if Lee ever asks, I'm fine with it."

"I think it's cute you're jealous."

Before I could stop myself, I said, "Did you think it was cute when I got jealous of Amanda?"

Noah stiffened. Then his arm tightened around me, his hand stroking up and down my spine and sending a shiver through me. He pressed a kiss to the top of my head. "No. But I will admit I think you're kind of sexy when you're shouting at me."

"Only kind of?"

"Very," he corrected himself in a murmur.

"Is that why you disagree with me so much?"

"Absolutely."

I softened, smiling, and pressed a kiss into his shoulder before shifting so I could kiss him properly.

The way Noah kissed me, the way he held me, it was with such total adoration, holding me so tenderly, with a grip like he couldn't ever bear to let me go. I could feel how much he loved me, and I knew that whatever had happened last year, I had nothing to be jealous of now.

I only hoped he could tell how much I loved him.

Chapter Seventeen

"Hello, hello, strangers! Anyone home?" a voice sang, ringing through the house. "Do you guys really leave your front door unlocked?"

There was no mistaking that peppy voice with the English accent. I heard someone moving around in the kitchen. Lee and Rachel's bedroom door opened. I launched myself out of Noah's and my bathroom, toothbrush still in my mouth.

Amanda was standing in the doorway. Her blond hair was cut short, hanging in chin-length waves that framed her face. She didn't seem to be wearing makeup, but her smooth skin had a dewy glow. She wore a cropped white T-shirt that hung off one shoulder and pink denim shorts. I could see a pink bikini top through her shirt and the ties of it around her neck.

Laughing, Noah dashed forward to draw her into a bear hug that lifted Amanda clean off her feet. She giggled, mussing his hair when he set her back down. "All right, muscles, no need to show off. Rachel! Elle! Hey!"

I drooled toothpaste all over the floor and down my

pajama top, which made Noah snort when he noticed. I shoved my toothbrush back into my mouth and gestured *one sec* with an incoherent mumble, dashing back to the bathroom to sort myself out. I patted the patch of toothpaste drool off my shirt before heading back out.

Amanda gave me a huge smile, pulling me into a hug. She smelled like vanilla. Like cookies.

For Pete's sake, was there *nothing* about this girl that wasn't perfect?

"It's so good to see you!" she was saying. "Where's Lee?"

"Sleeping in," Rachel said with an affectionate roll of her eyes. "He and Ashton ended up going out with the football team last night after their movie. I think he's gonna have a sore head today," she added in a whisper.

"Oh, oh right," Amanda whispered back with a serious nod, pressing her finger to her lips.

Noah caught my eye just long enough to wink at me, then drew a deep breath.

"Lee!" he bellowed, cupping his hands around his mouth. "Lee Flynn, get your ass out here!"

A few seconds later, there was a faint grumbling and scuffling coming from Lee and Rachel's room.

I laughed, while Rachel shot Noah a stern look and Amanda elbowed him and gave a sharp sigh.

Lee dragged himself out of his room, wearing just his boxers and rubbing his face. "What the hell, Noah? Are you kidding . . ." His eyes settled on Amanda, blowing wide.

His cheeks flushed, which only made me laugh harder. "Shit, Noah, you could've said we had a *guest.*"

"Don't worry yourself, big boy, it's nothing I haven't seen before," Amanda told him with a nonchalant wave of her hand. "Good to see so much of you, Lee."

He laughed. "Nice to see you again, too, Amanda. I didn't realize you were coming."

He said this with a cutting look at me and Noah, and all I could do was give him a guilty shrug. I hadn't even seen Lee yesterday, we'd both been so busy; Noah obviously hadn't thought to mention it to him either.

"Surprise!" She held up her purse, then a navy leather tote. "Oh, and I come bearing gifts."

She pulled out two little white squares, handing one each to me and Lee. A refrigerator magnet that read *I heart London.*

"I know technically you haven't been, but I thought you could add them to your magnet collection."

When Lee and I had taken our road trip on spring break, we'd made a point of picking up magnets in every state we'd passed through, as souvenirs of our epic trip. It was a really thoughtful gift, and we both grinned at Amanda and thanked her.

"I also brought shortbread because Noah told me he's never had it before, and you guys have not *lived* if you've not had proper Scottish shortbread." She pulled out a red tartan-patterned box from her bag and handed it to Rachel.

"Anything else in that purse?" Lee asked.

"Not unless you want my lipstick or a used tissue."

"Think I'll pass."

"Hey, you'd better get dressed anyway," Noah told Lee. "There's supposed to be a viewing today, remember?"

"No, there's not."

The three of us looked at Lee.

"Uh, yeah, Lee," Rachel said slowly. "Remember, your mom texted to remind us all a couple of days ago—"

"They canceled."

"What? Since when?"

"The . . . the realtor called to tell me."

Lee was an *awful* liar.

No one was buying it, but he clenched his jaw and glared around at each of us, daring someone to call him out. I didn't know what the hell Lee was up to, but he had to be up to something. Plus, this was like the fifth time something had been "canceled" in the last couple of weeks, which was pretty suspicious now that I thought about it.

Right now, though, I was happy to let it slide.

"Come on in," Noah said. "I'll give you the grand tour."

"Do you want some coffee, Amanda? Tea?" Rachel offered, the perfect hostess. "Cold drink?"

"Ooh, I wouldn't mind a cup of tea, if you don't mind?"

I wanted to laugh at how cliché she was, but I had a sneaking suspicion it'd just sound mean and bitchy coming out of my mouth, so I stayed quiet, smiling as Noah led her through the house, and took myself to the kitchen with Rachel.

"Is it still weird for you?" Rachel whispered.

I didn't have it in me to pretend right now. "A little. But honestly, mostly because it makes me feel so stupid for ever feeling jealous, you know? I trust Noah. And I know they're only friends. And she's great, right? So I just feel like such a bitch for ever believing otherwise."

Rachel pulled a thoughtful face, humming. "She was part of why you guys broke up, though, right?"

"Well, yeah, but it was more because he was keeping a secret, and he wouldn't tell me what. The distance was . . . It was hard. Plus the time difference. I know it's only three hours, but we both had our own schedules and our own social lives, and it all felt totally out of whack, so it wasn't like we were talking maybe as much as we should've been, and then when you throw in the new mystery female friend . . ."

I watched Rachel's face fall and a concerned look darken her features—and realized what she'd *really* been asking and what I'd just said.

"Not that you and Lee will be like that," I added hastily, and I hoped she could hear how much I meant it. "I mean, he's made that whole stupid schedule for when you guys can see each other. I'm sorry, I don't mean it's stupid. It's not. It's really sweet. I just mean . . ."

Oh God, this was why I'd mostly just stuck to hanging out with the guys for so long. I was the *worst* at this kind of stuff. I tried again, being as emphatic as I could. "Lee's devoted to you. He's made that whole schedule to figure out when you'll be able to see each other around the holidays and stuff. And you guys are smarter than me and Noah. You'll figure it out."

"But that's just it," she whispered desperately, eyes filling up, and oh crap, what had I said now? "You and Noah are like . . . You have all this *passion*. It's crazy how intense you two are. I can't stand to be in the same room when you two are *looking* at each other sometimes. And Lee and I aren't like that. So it just makes me worry, knowing how hard you two found it, and let's face it, if you hadn't had Lee, there's no way you would've seen Noah at Thanksgiving and ended up clearing the air and getting back together. But I don't have that."

I thought for a moment, trying to choose my words carefully.

Because honestly, as scared as I had been about the whole long-distance thing with Noah, I had never even *thought* to be concerned for Lee and Rachel's relationship.

"You're right. You're not like me and Noah. You guys are smooth and steady. You're probably way better at communicating than we are, and you don't bicker over things all the time like we do, so it's probably gonna be so much easier for you guys to air what you're actually feeling and if you're missing each other or finding it hard. And, no, you don't have a Lee to be a bridge between you guys, but you've got me. I know you probably feel like you got lumped with me because of Lee and that we're, like, a package deal, but I . . . I'd like to believe we're friends without him, Rach. I'd like to think of you as my friend."

Rachel took an uneven, stilted breath through her nose. She blinked rapidly, a couple of tears spilling from her eyes. She brushed them away quickly and gave me a watery smile before pulling me into a sudden hug.

"Thanks, Elle."

"S-sure. No problemo. Anytime." I patted her back awkwardly.

Rachel drew back, wiping her hands over her face again to finish making Amanda's tea. "For the record, you are my friend, too. With or without Lee. And you can bet your ass I'll be visiting you at Harvard next year and expecting you to visit me at Brown. You're not far enough away that we can't hang out for a weekend."

The suggestion caught me completely off guard. In all the time since I'd accepted my offer at Harvard, it hadn't actually occurred to me that I'd have another friend around. I'd told Lee he could visit both me and Rachel at once, but hadn't thought that *I* could just visit Rachel, to hang out.

I smiled at her. Maybe we never would've been friends if Lee hadn't asked her out at the carnival last year, but I'd never been so glad he did.

Chapter Eighteen

Noah and Amanda had headed out to the beach, according to the note on the kitchen counter; Rachel and Lee were nowhere to be found. I guessed I shouldn't be so surprised: one of the college girls at work had asked to take my second shift, if I could take one of hers in a few days. An afternoon off hadn't sounded so bad, so I didn't mind helping her out.

I looked at the note on the kitchen counter in loopy writing.

I wasn't jealous, because that would be stupid, as there was nothing to be jealous of.

I thought about joining them. The note didn't say they wanted to be left alone or anything—if anything, it implied the reader should come join them. But I thought about spring break and that, while I'd had fun hanging out with Noah and his friends, I'd wanted some time to Noah myself, just us. And I thought that if it were Lee or Levi, I'd want some time to hang out without a crowd.

I trusted Noah.

I grabbed a pen and left a note of my own: *Off work early. Heading back home to see Dad & Brad. See you guys for dinner!*

On my way home, I stopped off at the 7-Eleven.

Levi's face lit up when I got to the cash register with a couple of supplies. "Hey! What're you doing here?"

"I'm supposed to be watching Brad tonight, but I got off work early. I thought he could come hang with us at the beach house tonight. He's desperate to stay over."

Levi laughed, ringing up my items slowly. "Bet he'll love that."

"You'll have to come by, too. You haven't been yet."

He looked down for a minute. "Just been busy, you know. But I'll see you at the water park tomorrow afternoon?"

I beamed. "Dude, I'm so glad you're coming with us. Noah thinks it's kind of stupid."

"Well, maybe Noah's kind of stupid," Levi shot back with a grin.

I laughed. "Something only a Ravenclaw would say."

"Ah, so you admit it? I thought you were convinced I was a Hufflepuff."

Shit, he was right.

"Maybe, like, a sixty–forty split," I conceded. "Still mostly a 'puff.'"

"That's thirteen sixty-eight," he told me, bagging up my items. "And I for one can't wait for tomorrow. It's gonna be epic. You sure you don't need me to bring anything?"

I shook my head. "Nope, we've got everything under control. See you, Levi!"

Back home, I let myself in and immediately heard Brad's video game in the lounge. I stuck my head inside, grinning. "You beat my high score yet?"

Brad jumped, just about managing to pause his game before my shock arrival ruined it.

"Elle! I thought you weren't supposed to be here till later?"

"Change of plans. How would *you* like to come spend the night at the beach house?"

Brad gasped and threw himself across the sofa, kneeling on it to beam at me with wide eyes. "You mean it?"

"Absolutely."

"Wait . . ." Brad's eyes narrowed, his smile turning into a pout as he looked at me suspiciously. "Is this a trick?"

"Oh, come on. When do I ever trick you?"

"Hmm . . ." He thought on it for a minute but eventually decided that even if it *was* a trick somehow, it'd be worth it. "Okay! Awesome! I'll go grab my stuff!"

I'd picked up milk and peanut butter, knowing we were running low from last time I was home. But when I opened the refrigerator, I saw milk there already.

Huh. Weird. Maybe we'd had an extra bottle in the fridge and I'd not noticed.

I put it in there anyway and opened the cupboard to put the peanut butter away.

Even *weirder*, there was a brand-new jar there already, and it wasn't our usual brand. I stared at it for a second, trying to work out what the hell was going on. We always got the reduced-fat one with the blue lid—it was the one Mom always bought, but we'd switched to the low-fat option a year or two ago.

Why had Dad suddenly switched brands now? Besides, I'd thought he was expecting me to buy some.

I drifted out into the hallway.

"Hey, uh, Brad?" I yelled up the stairs.

"Yeah?" He popped out of his room and into view. "You haven't decided I can't come to the beach house, have you?"

"No," I reassured him. "Where'd the peanut butter come from?"

"What?"

I held up the jar to show him.

"Oh! Linda bought it."

He vanished back into his room and I stared blankly ahead for a second before going upstairs, following him. "What do you mean, *Linda bought it*?"

First the wine and the staying overnight and now this?

"Uh-huh. We went to get groceries yesterday after camp."

"She . . . picked you up from camp?"

"Uh-huh," Brad said again. "How many swim shorts do you think I need, Elle?"

"Just one pair," I told him absently.

Linda had picked him up from camp? She'd taken him grocery shopping? What the hell?

Why hadn't I met her? Brad had met her a couple of times now. That seemed like—

"Kind of a big deal, right? And if Brad needed picking up

173

from camp, why didn't Dad tell me? I could've done that," I complained on the phone.

"Weren't you working yesterday?"

"That's not the *point*, Levi!"

Finally, I paused for breath. I'd shut myself out on the porch to call Levi to catch up, while Brad was packing way too much stuff for just one night.

"Why don't you ask your dad if you can meet her?"

"I don't *want* to meet her," I snapped, hating how childish it sounded coming out of my mouth. It wasn't . . . Okay, fine, it was *exactly* like that, but so what? Gathering myself, I said, "I just don't get why she's looking after Brad and picking him up from camp and doing our grocery shopping when, like, a month ago she didn't exist."

"She—"

"Don't you *dare* point out she did exist. You know what I mean."

Levi laughed. "Okay. Well, what did Brad think of her?"

"Oh, he thinks she's great. Linda this, Linda that. Linda let him pick what he wanted for dinner. Linda let him pick the music in the car. Linda puts honey in his oatmeal. Linda, Linda, Linda." I sighed, squeezing my eyes shut. "I'm sorry, Levi. I didn't mean to call and steal your break and yell at you."

"I called you, remember?"

That was true—and made me feel just a *little* less bad. Although it did remind me I'd monopolized the entire conversation. "Oh yeah. What did you want to talk about?"

"Doesn't matter," he said.

I was going to ask if he was sure, because he *must* have called to talk about something, but I had to get back to Brad. I said as much, and we hung up.

Back inside, Brad had brought his backpack downstairs. It was stuffed full.

"Do you guys have video games or should I bring some?"

"We have video games, Brad. And I think we were planning on Chinese food for dinner. Unless Linda already got you Chinese yesterday."

"No. We had Mexican."

"I thought you hated Mexican food? It gives you gas."

"I liked the way Linda cooked it."

I was really, really glad Linda wasn't here right now. I had a feeling I'd snap at her and tell her where to stick her Mexican food and her wrong-brand peanut butter.

. . .

I was still sore about it later that evening. Lee and Rachel were still out, but neither Noah nor Amanda seemed to mind our surprise visitor. Right now, Noah and Brad were having an epic lightsaber battle in the pool with some sticks, making loud *whusch* noises. Brad was yelling about how this was the end of the Jedi, so Noah was arguing back about how he would defeat the evil Sith rulers.

It was sweet. And while Noah might not like getting involved with Lee's and my childish shenanigans, it was cute to watch him get involved with Brad's.

The leftovers from our Chinese takeout littered the table, and Amanda and I had picked up the video-game controllers Brad had abandoned to go play in the pool with Noah.

Now she threw hers aside with a huff. "Remind me never to play against you again. Maybe you should start a YouTube channel or something. You should get paid for this."

I managed a laugh, distracted for a second. "I'm not so sure about that, but thanks for the ego boost."

There was a melodramatically mournful shout from outside and a splash, followed by Brad's giddy laughter.

"Guess the malevolent Sith Lord won this round," I said.

"Your brother is adorable," Amanda gushed. "Kind of makes me wish I wasn't an only child."

"I guess he has his moments. Now that he's shut up about Linda."

Amanda gave me a sympathetic smile. "If it's any consolation, a bunch of my friends' parents are divorced, and my friends all seemed to hate the first person their parents dated after that. I know I'm dreading it!"

"Wait, w-what?" I stopped reaching for a dumpling to gawp at her. "Your parents are getting divorced?"

She shrugged, and even though she was doing a great job of looking indifferent, something felt off about it. Kind of like she was trying super hard to stay so laid-back, like this was the only way she knew how to talk about it. "Probably. Honestly, I think this is their last-ditch effort to make it work. Originally this trip was just supposed to be my mum; then it turned into this whole family thing. They've been seeing a couples counselor for a while, but I don't think it's really worked out. They think I don't know how much they're arguing, but . . ." She sighed, rolling her eyes, then added with a smirk, "Hey, do you think I'm too old to take advantage of the whole 'two birthdays, two Christmases' deal?"

Amanda caught the stricken look on my face, and her own rigid smile faded.

"I'm really sorry," I told her, not knowing what else I was supposed to say. "I had no idea."

"Noah didn't mention it?"

"N-no. Was he supposed to?"

She considered it. "I mean, I never said it was a secret, but I guess I also didn't tell him to tell you guys. I just sort of figured he would. That's why I asked him if I could stay here a couple of days. It's just exhausting to be around them all the time when they're like this."

I tried to fix the look on my face, not sure she wanted my sympathy or pity or whatever else she'd find there.

Although, honestly, how she could even sound so peppy about her parents' looming divorce, I'd never know.

"Well, hey," I told her, "you can stay here as long as you want."

Amanda squeezed my hand, and I was shocked to see her lips wobbling and her eyes fill with tears. Her voice was thick when she said, "Thanks, Elle. You're such a good friend."

At that moment, the door opened. Amanda sniffed

suddenly, blinking and taking a breath to steady herself. A trio of voices chattered, laughing, as people poured in. We both turned to see Lee and Rachel walking into the lounge in fluorescent outfits. Rachel's hair was teased and back-combed into something huge and springy, and Lee wore a bright pink headband. They were both in leg warmers.

Ashton was just behind them in his own bizarre and brightly colored eighties getup.

A creeping feeling of dread crawled up my spine as their laughter dimmed.

"Where have you guys been?" I asked. "Hey, Ashton. Didn't expect to see you here."

"Well, Shelly," Lee announced, "after Rachel and I spent the day at the mall doing some college shopping, we went to meet you for bucket-list item number twenty-three, as previously agreed, which, if you remember, we said we'd invite Ashton along after Noah turned down the invite. We waited for you after work like we'd planned, but May said you'd traded your second shift, and your phone went straight to voice mail when we called."

Bucket-list item number twenty-three . . .

The big hair, the leg warmers, the lurid clothes . . .

I gasped, clapping both hands over my face. "Oh my God. Eighties mini-golf night! No!"

"Yes," Lee crowed. "And it was spectacular."

"It really wasn't," Rachel said, ever the mediator, giving me an awkward smile. "You didn't miss out on much."

"You so totally did," Ashton said, not getting it. He gave Amanda a salute. "Hey there. I'm Ashton."

I bit my lip, a lump rising in my throat, interrupting Amanda as she started to say hello back. "Oh my God, I'm so sorry, Lee. I think I was on the phone to Levi when you called. I'm *so* sorry. Are you mad at me?"

He shook his head, but I got the feeling I wasn't *totally* forgiven. "So long as we're all set for the water park tomorrow, it's good."

"Yes! Yes, definitely. I'm driving Brad back for camp first thing, and then I'm all yours for the most epic item on the bucket list. I promise."

"Awesome." Lee smiled at me—not quite the smile I was used to, but enough that I knew he wasn't *really* mad at me. I made a snap decision to tell him all my complaints about Linda another time—tonight wasn't the time for it. "And, hey, Ashton's gonna come along, too. We need someone for car eight, right?"

Lee clapped Ashton's shoulder and they shared a laugh— some in-joke I didn't know.

And I *always* knew Lee's in-jokes.

"Right. That's . . . that's great! Glad to have you on board, Ashton."

The three of them grabbed some drinks and moved outside. Amanda got up, too. "You coming, Elle?"

I guessed I didn't have a lot of choice. Not if I didn't want my little brother and my best friend replacing me completely.

Chapter Nineteen

It wasn't quite a full-fledged Flynn party, but word had definitely gotten out about race day. Jon Fletcher had made it a Facebook event, and now it seemed like the whole school had turned up at the water park. I spotted guys from the football team lounging on the fake beach and cheerleaders grabbing rubber rings and running up a wooden staircase to a waterslide. A few people from the school's marching band floated down the lazy river. Dixon left the rapids looking half drowned, having lost his sunglasses.

It was a scalding-hot day. The sun shone bright and there wasn't a cloud in the rich blue sky. Perfect weather for a day at the water park.

Lee and I were meeting up with Jon at one o'clock, near a flip-flop and swimsuit vendor by the biggest waterslide in the park. His older brother was there—a less muscular, shorter, stockier version of Jon. He wore jeans and a white button-down and shook our hands as his little brother introduced us.

I felt like I should be wearing more than shorts and a bikini top.

Lee seemed to be thinking the same thing about his swim shorts.

The only reason we'd managed to pull this off was because we'd sold it as this big PR stunt for charity. Right now I felt like a total fraud. Like I should be wearing . . . maybe not a business suit, but at least I shouldn't have my hair in braided pigtails that hung over my shoulders, still dripping wet from the last ride we'd been on.

"So you two are the masterminds behind this whole thing, huh?" Jon's brother said.

"That's right," Lee said with a confidence only I knew he was faking. "We're really grateful for all your help on this, Mr. Fletcher."

Both Jon and his brother cracked up.

"Is this the bit where you say, 'Oh, please, Mr. Fletcher's my father'?" I joked.

"It is. I'm not *that* old. Will's fine."

"Well, thanks, Will," Lee corrected himself. "We're really grateful."

"The pleasure's all ours. We've been selling spectator tickets. Raised almost fifteen hundred bucks! You guys should be proud."

Lee and I exchanged a look. Fifteen hundred dollars? That was a lot of money raised—especially when we were just doing this for fun. But spectators? I knew some of our friends and people from school would be hanging around, but I didn't expect, like, an *audience*.

I could tell Lee was thinking the same thing, but he took it way better than I did.

While all I could think about was the thousand and one ways this could blow up in our faces, it only fueled Lee's excitement.

Will added hastily, "And you guys all signed those insurance forms, right? Water park's not liable for any injuries or accidents, blah, blah, blah . . ."

We nodded. I said, "I emailed them to you this morning."

"Awesome. Well, you guys are all set! Strictly no banana peels, though. Sorry, but we've gotta draw the line somewhere. We've got some GoPros and video equipment all ready, so see you in an hour?"

We nodded, saying our goodbyes, Jon lingering.

"Are you sure you're related?" Lee asked, squinting after Will.

"I know." Jon flexed his arms, making a show of kissing his biceps. "I got all the brains."

The three of us laughed.

"Are you gonna come with us now?" I asked him. "We wanna make sure everything's set up before we get changed."

Jon shook his head. "I'm gonna do one last round on this bad boy"—he jerked a thumb over his shoulder at the monstrous waterslide—"but I'll be there in time, don't worry. I wouldn't miss this for the world!"

We called goodbye after him and followed the wooden signposts pointing us in the direction of the go-kart track.

We lingered to watch the karts race past for a couple of minutes. They roared, tearing around the track, some skidding and knocking into the piles of tires lining the perimeter. A sign saying MUST BE 14 OR OLDER TO RIDE was nailed near the entrance. Bleachers rose up on one side of the track—mostly filled with parents; sour-faced, jealous younger brothers and sisters; and a nervous friend or two.

A kart careened into the tire wall near us, spinning in a full circle before hurtling back after the others.

"Whoa," I breathed.

"This," Lee said, "is going to be incredible."

It was scary, how easily we'd been able to organize this. What had seemed like the ultimate crazy fantasy as a couple of kids had been organized with a phone call, a couple of emails, an online order from a costume-rental store, and a trip to Target.

The contents of said trip to Target were now being unloaded from my backpack in a set of changing rooms near the track: we filled up the blue and red water balloons; a couple of the black ones we filled with whipped cream—although, honestly, I was sure more ended up on the floor (and in Lee's mouth) than in the balloons; three cans of silly string. Plus, Will had left us three giant red foam cubes from the children's soft-play area.

Lee and I stepped back to survey our arsenal.

A buzzer went off on the track, and we scooped up our

stuff and headed out to set up the karts before everyone else arrived, stashing random combinations of weapons into each one.

And then we headed back to get ready.

There were eight of us: Rachel and Amanda joined me in the women's changing area; Levi, Ashton, Jon, and Warren were back with Lee.

Amanda buckled her helmet and wrestled her costume over the top of it. She planted her hands on her hips, twisting and turning to pose for us.

"How do I look?"

Rachel and I cracked up as Amanda pouted, full-on voguing.

Only she *could pull off a gorilla costume,* I thought, trying not to roll my eyes.

Meanwhile, Rachel and I applied our fake mustaches carefully in the mirror.

"You a-ready?"

"I'm a-ready," I confirmed. We met the boys out near the main entrance to the changing rooms, and it was impossible to keep a straight face. But this was why we'd decided to meet up now: get the giggles out of the way before we went out there.

My stomach flip-flopped and my heart was racing. I felt kind of sick.

I wouldn't trade this moment for the world.

Lee stopped joking around with Ashton to curtsy to us in his cheap, crinkly pink dress, blond wig spilling out from under his yellow helmet with a crown sticker slapped on the front. "You guys ready?"

"As I'll ever be!" Rachel exclaimed.

He looked at me.

I launched myself at him, throwing my arms around his shoulders and hugging him tight. Our helmets knocked together and he cried, "Hey, hey, watch the dress!"

"Best summer ever," I whispered to him, and drew away.

Lee turned to the group, clapping his hands. "All right, folks, listen up. We've got one shot at this, and only one. I want to see foul play. I want to see underhanded, dirty tactics. I want to see you trying to run each other off the track and . . ."

I'd ended up standing next to Levi, who was wearing a yellow shirt and purple dungarees. A squiggly mustache was stuck badly above his top lip. He hooked his thumbs through the straps of his dungarees and grinned.

He leaned toward me, not daring to look away from Lee's serious pep talk, to whisper, "I can't believe you guys pulled this off."

"Don't jinx it," I whispered back. "We haven't raced yet."

Lee glanced our way with a reprimanding scowl, not faltering in his speech. Levi bumped my arm with his in lieu of a reply.

"Three laps, just like in the game. Winner takes all."

"I have a question," Amanda piped up, raising her hand as best she could in her costume. "What does that mean?"

"It means you win the fifth-grade state-spelling-bee trophy Elle has so kindly donated for the cause."

"I NEED that trophy," Jon Fletcher announced, bending forward and rubbing his hands like he was gearing up for a football game.

Lee wrapped up the speech with a shout of "Let's go kill this!"

We all cheered, and the door behind Lee opened.

Noah slipped in, saying, "Sorry, I just— Oh my *God*." He snorted, shaking his head. "I was expecting this, but . . . I still wasn't expecting this. You guys look sick."

"But me especially, right?" Amanda said, jumping forward. She crouched, hooking her arms inward and growling, stomping one foot, then the other, making Noah laugh.

"Good luck out there, Evans," Levi told me.

"Please," I scoffed. "I don't need luck."

"As if." Levi put his hands on his hips, head wobbling as he gave a dramatic, movie-villain-esque chuckle. "You're going down. I'll destroy you out there."

"Looking like that, you won't." Taking pity on him, I reached up to fix his fake mustache, pressing it into place properly.

He blushed. "Thanks."

A throat cleared behind me and I turned to see Noah looming behind us. I grinned up at him and gave a twirl. "Cute, huh?"

"I just wanted to come by and say good luck out there. There's a hell of a crowd."

"Didn't you know?" Levi joked, grabbing my shoulders to shake me gently. "Elle doesn't need luck."

I didn't miss the look Noah shot Levi, or the way a muscle jumped in his jaw.

Oh God, I so didn't want to deal with this right now.

I blew Noah a kiss, knowing I couldn't give him a proper kiss with this helmet on. "See you in the stands!"

I made my way back to the doors as everyone started to get in line to head outside. I took the first spot, just ahead of Rachel and Lee.

"All right, gang," I shouted over my shoulder. "Let's go!"

I wanted to push open the doors in one grand gesture, so they swept forward as they opened on either side of me. It wasn't as smooth as that, though. The doors were heavy, so I fumbled, Lee laughing behind me, and just held open the one door instead.

The whole thing was far from graceful. Amanda's and Jon's costumes both got stuck in the doorway and Jon's giant spiky turtle shell got caught on the door handle. It took three of us to free him.

But then we were back on track, walking out under the bleachers to a roar of cheering, with the music from the video game playing over the speakers.

The sound was deafening. I drowned in it, exhilarated, having to work hard to keep a serious face. Walking up to my go-kart, I stole a glance at the big screen, where our little slow-motion parade was being shown in HD.

It was surreal.

Right there on the screen, there I was, dressed up to look exactly like Mario, a white sticker with a red *M* stuck to my red helmet. Rachel was just behind me, wearing green where I wore red, the perfect Luigi. Lee gave a skip and a twirl as Princess Peach, and Ashton jumped into the air, pounding it with a fist to yell "Woohoo!" in a scarily accurate imitation of Yoshi.

Amanda came next, beating her big gorilla chest as Donkey Kong. Levi strode after her, a leaner, less squat version of Wario, Jon ambling behind him as Bowser.

I did a double take as I got to my kart.

Where the hell was Warren?

I looked back at our group and the empty kart, and by the time I was turning back to the screen I saw for myself: Toad was running out of the bleachers, giant head wobbling. But it wasn't Warren in the costume.

Noah?

I glanced back at Lee, who looked just as confused as I felt. He shrugged.

Maybe he'd had a change of heart after all and realized just what he was missing out on. I hoped Warren wouldn't be too mad about missing out.

(And I hoped Noah wouldn't flip over in his kart and break something. He hadn't signed a form, and the last thing I needed was the water park suing us.)

"Racers!" Tyrone, our old school council president and commentator for the day, yelled over a microphone. "Take your marks!"

We all got into our karts, some with a little more difficulty than others. There was a crackle in my ear as the microphones and earpieces in our helmets came online.

Lee's voice crackled through, drowning out the cheering crowd. "Princess to Plunger One, Princess to Plunger One, *chhh*, we are a go for race day. I repeat, we are a go for race day!"

"This is Donkey Kong to Princess, DK to PP, you don't need to make the *chhh* noise."

"Plunger Two to Donkey Kong, let it be noted that my boyfriend will make the *chhh* noise if he wants to."

Rachel's comment was met with a series of *chhh*s from the rest of us, mimicking radio static and dissolving into giggles. I collected myself, flexing my fingers around my steering wheel.

A buzz sounded across the track. A red light lit up, hanging over us.

"Plunger One to Toad, what's with the change of heart?"

"What, I can't support my girlfriend?"

"This is Bowser. Plunger One, Toad, take your relationship drama off the track. This is a race, not *Pride and Prejudice*."

Before either I or Noah could bite back, or anybody else could make a jibe over the radio, the buzzer sounded again, and an amber light showed up. I caught my breath, inhaling sharply, suddenly hyper-focused.

Lee and Elle's Epic Summer Bucket List
19. Do a real-life *Mario Kart* race

Tick, complete.

One more buzz.

Green light.

I floored it. Our karts swung to life, engines growling furiously. I was vaguely aware of Jon Fletcher cursing down the headsets, his kart stalled at the first post—but I was already yanking on the wheel, twisting around the first bend in the course.

Lee's kart drew up beside me. I saw him raise a red balloon. "Enjoying first position, Shelly?"

"Princess Peach, you don't have to yell when we have headsets, *chhh*, over," Ashton/Yoshi told him with a laugh.

As Lee raised his balloon, a blue one soared forward, smacking into the back of his helmet and smearing green slime everywhere. He howled, dropping his own balloon and drenching himself in water as it burst on his lap.

He fell back and Rachel/Luigi took his place.

I narrowed my eyes, trying to focus on the track while fumbling in my foot well for a can of silly string I could hear rattling around.

There was grunting over the radio. Cussing, muttering.

I took the corner too quickly, skidding around. By the time I righted myself, I was in fifth position. Jon Fletcher was still lagging behind in last place, his giant Bowser suit weighing him down. Ashton/Yoshi had fallen back, and Amanda/Donkey Kong was just edging out in front of me. I gripped my can of silly string.

But then a black water balloon burst against Amanda's helmet, whipped cream exploding out, splattering across her face and the car, making her shriek. "Who did that? Who did that? Fear the wrath of Donkey Kong!"

"Woohoo!" Ashton/Yoshi yelled, punching the air again as he shot past both me and a whipped-cream-covered Amanda/Donkey Kong. Rachel/Luigi had fallen back, too, she and Lee/Princess Peach vying for third and fourth as we started our second lap.

And out in front—

I winced as Noah's kart smashed into Levi's.

Levi jerked sideways, smashing right back into Noah.

Somewhere in the background, Tyrone was narrating the whole thing, talking about Wario and Toad going head-to-head in a vicious fight for first place.

Vicious was right, I thought.

I eased off the accelerator as I took a corner. Lee hit a tire, spinning out, and I managed to grab a balloon to launch at Ashton at the same moment that Rachel hurled a slightly squashed-looking red foam box back at him. I'd have missed if not for her: he swerved to avoid the box, right into the path of my water balloon. I shot out ahead of him, starting my third and final lap. Lee was now lagging somewhere in the back. Jon wasn't far behind me.

"No fair!" Ashton cried. "The Plungers teamed up! If we're teaming up, I want Donkey Kong and Wario on my team."

"No teaming up!" Jon was yelling. "Plunger Two, you got any more boxes to take out Plunger One?"

I laughed, hands clenched around the wheel. "Back off, Bowser."

Amid the giggles and shouts on the headsets, I heard "Back off, Wario."

"Eat my dust, Shroom."

There was a *bang!* a little way ahead. Levi's and Noah's karts crashed together again, Noah's almost pressed into the tire wall. As they swerved across the track, Rachel yelped, jerking her kart out of the way before she crashed into them. I shot past her.

"Cool it, Toad," Levi snapped.

"Hey, doofus, what're you playing at?" Amanda shouted.

I could hear the smirk in Noah's voice as he barked, "Winning!"

A water balloon flew past me. It smashed on a tire and slime spattered over Noah. He yelped and I swerved sideways before Ashton could overtake me, and—

A cheer rose through the stands as Tyrone shouted, "And we have a winner! Wario wins the match! Followed by Toad . . . Mario . . . Yoshi . . . Bowser . . . Princess Peach . . . Luigi . . . Donkey Kong!"

We all slowed our karts to a stop. Amanda had stopped where she'd run into a tire wall, her kart facing backward. Jon, Lee, and Rachel hadn't quite made it to the finish line either. Ashton's kart stopped just next to mine and he gave me a wide-eyed, manic grin—reminding me uncomfortably of Lee for a split second.

"That was awesome!"

But I didn't have time to high-five Ashton right now because while Levi climbed up from his kart, draped in silly string, arms raised in victory as Tyrone came forward to present him with my old spelling-bee trophy, Noah was tearing himself out of his kart, ripping off his helmet.

He looked pissed.

And it didn't take a genius to work out all that anger was directed at Levi.

Chapter Twenty

Trophy in hand, Levi beamed around at us, surveying his opponents. He tugged off his helmet, his hair matted and frizzing underneath. He tucked the helmet under his arm and stepped toward Noah.

Uneasiness prickled at me and I clenched my jaw.

This was a bad idea. This was a *very* bad idea.

Noah was still scowling, hands balled into fists at his side. His hair was damp, stuck to his forehead. Slime was streaked across his cheek and shirt.

I pulled my helmet off, setting it on the seat of my kart. Ashton had done the same and stepped toward me, his eyebrows raised. "Damn, I know Lee said he had a temper, but your boyfriend's a real sore loser, huh?"

Levi stopped just in front of Noah.

He stuck out his hand.

"Good race."

Come on, Noah.

I didn't know what was going on here, but I didn't like it

one bit. Apprehension continued to nag at me, and I willed Noah to just shake Levi's goddamn hand and walk away. It wasn't that hard.

But I guessed it was, because Noah just glared at him before storming away.

Levi blinked, lowering his hand. Rachel and Jon rushed toward him to congratulate him and Ashton joined in.

I was tempted to go after them. I *did* want to congratulate Levi. I wanted to grab his arm and lift it in the air and cheer for his win and pull some of the silly string off him. I wanted Noah to stew, to give him the cold shoulder and make him come crawling back to Levi to apologize.

But watching Noah walk away, I was just angry.

My feet were already carrying me after him.

"What the hell was that all about?" Lee asked as I got near him.

Amanda was lingering, too, lips pinched as her gaze trailed after Noah. "You want me to talk to him?" she offered.

I shook my head, gritting my teeth. "I'll be back in a sec."

Noah was halfway under the bleachers when I yelled his name. He stopped for a moment before carrying on. I ran after him, catching the back of his shirt.

"What the hell was that?" I asked.

Noah glared past me for a second before taking a sharp breath and unclenching his jaw. "I got slimed. I almost had him."

I knew that wasn't what the problem was, but for a second, I played along anyway.

"Come on." I tried to sound a little more upbeat and not too pissed at him. "Don't be mad just because you lost."

Noah smirked briefly, mirthlessly, dragging his eyes back to mine. "I thought the Wario costume was supposed to be mine. That's what Lee said."

"It was," I said slowly, not sure what that had to do with anything. "And then you didn't want to get involved, so we gave it to Levi. So . . . what, you stole Warren's Toad outfit because you decided you didn't want to miss out? I don't get why you'd take that out on Levi. He's—"

"I'm just trying to figure out if you're always gonna go running to him," Noah burst out, breathing hard. His brow furrowed and there was a vulnerability in his eyes I wasn't used to. He didn't look angry so much as . . . scared.

My mouth dropped open and I stared at him for a few seconds, trying to work out if he'd *actually* said that.

And . . . yeah. He had.

So he could wipe that sorry-ass expression off his face, I thought, because I was not buying it.

"Oh my God," I scoffed, stepping back. "That's rich, Noah, that really is. It's not my fault you thought this whole thing was stupid and you didn't want to be part of it. I told you days ago that he was gonna be part of this! Why're you getting so mad about it now? I thought you and Levi were good."

"And I thought you said there was nothing between you," he shot back, frown deepening.

"What . . . what are you *talking* about?" I cried, my hands flapping. I racked my brain, trying to think where the hell he'd gotten that idea, and then realized . . . "Wait, is this because I was fixing his mustache? I put Rachel's mustache on for her, so, what, are you going to accuse me of trying it on with her next?"

"It's not you, Elle! It's . . . it's *him*! I saw the way he was looking at you. If you think he's over you, you're being naive."

"Oh my God. Okay. I'm . . . I'm so not doing this again, Noah. I thought we were past all this crap! Are you seriously going to stand here and do the whole 'uber-protective boyfriend' shtick because you think you saw Levi . . . looking at me? He's one of my best friends; he's going to look at me."

"He's a best friend you kissed. Who has a crush on you."

"*Had.*"

"Has," he argued. "I know what I saw, Elle."

"I'm . . ." I drew a deep breath, closing my eyes as I took a minute to compose myself. Maybe it was only fair for Noah to be jealous—wouldn't I be if he'd kissed Amanda?

(Wasn't I sometimes still jealous of Amanda, even though their relationship was purely platonic?)

But this wasn't Amanda we were talking about: it was Levi. We'd kissed *once*, and it had been months ago. I took another breath, pushing my temper back down.

"All you had to do was shake his hand and be the bigger person, Noah. Would that have been so hard?"

I watched his Adam's apple bob and heard him gulp. He glanced down at the ground between us.

He might still be angry, but I could feel the regret pouring off him in waves.

"I'm not gonna fight about this here," I told him. "Not today, Noah. I'll . . . I'm gonna go congratulate Levi on his win. I'm gonna go see my friends. I'll see you back home."

I didn't walk too quickly. I wondered if he would follow me.

I kept walking, slowing almost to a stop as I got back to the track.

I heard Noah's heavy footsteps—but they were going in the other direction.

Fine. If that was how he was going to be, well, *fine.*

After I'd congratulated Levi, given him a hug, and mussed his matted hair, telling him he'd better take good care of my old trophy, Lee pulled me aside.

"Everything okay?"

I wasn't so sure, but I beamed at him and grabbed his shoulders. "Okay? Lee, we just pulled off *race day*. Why wouldn't everything be okay? We did it, Lee! We pulled it off!"

He gave in, grinning back at me before wrapping me into a hug and shaking me. "Hell yeah, we did! And you deserve full credit for this one, Shelly. The water park was your idea.

I don't know how we would've managed all this without that."

"Hey, you two. Mario and Peach."

We both turned to see Will approaching, beaming. He clapped us on the shoulders. "That was incredible, you guys! Totally epic. The footage we got was amazing. It's already got a few thousand hits on Facebook Live!"

"Whoa!"

"And I'll email you guys the video, as promised."

"Thanks, Will."

He sighed, looking around the track. A couple of staff had appeared to clean up the whipped cream and slime and collect the red blocks that had been thrown. One guy was pulling the karts back inside. The crowd was gradually filtering away, for regular business to resume on the go-kart track.

"I am so fucking glad nobody got hurt." Will sighed, smiling as he walked off.

Lee laughed. When he looked back at me, he wrapped his arm around my shoulders. "Hey. I've got an idea. I promise it'll cheer you up. It's not a bucket-list thing, but I think you're going to love it. How about we get out of here? Rachel and Amanda can meet us back at the beach house later. And . . ." He sighed, glancing toward the changing rooms. "And Noah, if he's not off somewhere drinking himself into oblivion and trying to forget what a ginormous douchebag he is."

I hated the idea that Lee might be right, that that might be exactly what Noah was doing.

But no, screw him. Let him wallow. Let him get over this whole stupid thing. Let him realize what a jackass he was being.

So I nodded. "That sounds great, Lee. Whatever it is, count me in."

Chapter Twenty-One

"Where—"

Lee shushed me, and my confusion only grew as he led me down the boardwalk. The sun was still shining, but a couple of clouds had gathered now, so it wasn't quite as sticky and sweltering as it had been a few hours ago at the water park. The breeze coming in off the sea was a welcome relief.

The smell of the boardwalk took me right back to my childhood. The smell of cheap hot dogs, cotton candy, and salt water. I breathed in deep. A Ferris wheel turned slowly up ahead. Bike bells rang out, children racing each other. A couple of kids on their skateboards swerved around the pedestrians, pulling stunts.

"So Noah seemed pretty upset," Lee said lightly, with a breezy, conversational manner, like he was commenting on the weather. I cut him a look, but he kept up the pretense.

"It was stupid," I muttered. "He's being *stupid*."

"Three guesses what it was about," Lee said, snorting a

little. I frowned at him until he sighed, his resolve breaking. "Well, obviously he was mad about Levi."

It *was* obvious, I supposed: the way they'd been going at each other on the track, Noah refusing to shake his hand . . .

But then Lee said quietly, "I kinda don't blame him. Don't be too mad at him, Shelly."

"Excuse me?" I choked, stopping to gawp at him.

Lee sighed. His mouth twisted up on one side and he shrugged helplessly. "I'm just saying. You know, I get where he's coming from. I know he said he was cool with Levi, and he's really been trying hard, Elle. I know he has. And it's not like he doesn't trust you. But I just . . . get where he's coming from."

"You don't even know what he was mad about," I scoffed. I did my best not to glare too much at my best friend right now. Wasn't he always meant to take my side?

"I'd probably be pissed if Rachel was always hanging out with her ex."

"Okay, *first*," I snapped, ticking off one finger, "he's not my ex. Second, if Noah really *did* trust me, he wouldn't have gotten so mad. And—"

"Point taken," Lee said gently, holding his hands up to me. "But I mean . . . I know *you* don't have feelings for Levi anymore—"

"I'm not even really sure I ever did," I pointed out.

"—but I see the way he is around you. And all I'm saying is, if he did still have a crush on you, it wouldn't surprise me. You know you'd feel *exactly* the same if Noah had kissed Amanda or if she had a crush on him."

"That's totally different. She's staying with us. Levi just took part in race day. Same as Rachel and Ashton and Jon Fletcher and Warren was going to . . . That doesn't mean anything. He saw Levi at graduation! He's been on FaceTime when I've been hanging out with him. They've been totally fine around each other. I don't know why he's suddenly lost it."

Lee thought about it. "I guess he's never really *been* there when you two have been hanging out. Graduation was a different thing."

"He asked if I was always gonna go running back to Levi."

He blinked at me. I gave Lee a second for that to sink in. "All right, well, that was out of line. But it's gonna be hard for him, Elle. He thought you broke up with him for Levi for *weeks* before you two figured things out. I'm not saying he was right to be such a little bitch earlier, but don't be too hard on him."

I pursed my lips before my shoulders drooped and my expression relaxed. Hard as I wanted to cling to this frustration at Noah's behavior and at what he'd said, Lee put forward a pretty good argument.

I didn't think he'd have been so convincing if he hadn't been so earnest. It was a rare occasion for him to take Noah's side on something like this. Next to me, Lee was the first person to call Noah out on his bullshit.

"Besides," Lee added, seeing my resolve fracture, "I don't think I can handle having to be in the beach house if you two are going to be at each other's throats and then have crazy makeup sex. That is *not* something any of us need to hear, Shelly."

"Fine," I said. "But only for you. And he has to apologize."

"Don't look at me! I can't promise he will."

"Hmm."

Lee slipped his cell phone out of his pocket—three guesses who he was texting and what it was about. Lee hadn't exactly been the most enthusiastic supporter of my relationship with Noah when he first found out about us, but he loved both of us; times like this, I was glad of it.

"Okay!" He clapped his hands together, looped his arm through mine, and started walking again. "Putting all your relationship drama behind us . . . can we just appreciate again how freaking awesome today was? Did you see that crowd? I bet the video looks incredible."

"I can't believe you got so far behind."

"I was so close to catching up on that last lap, but then Amanda took a corner too fast and spun straight into me and Rachel went into the back of me. It was a three-car pileup that cost me precious seconds." He gave a mournful sigh and shake of his head, but when he looked back up at me, he was beaming. "And, hell, if I'd known it'd raise so much money, I would've made a bigger deal out of it. We should've done it *ages* ago."

"For charity, Lee?" I shot him a sly smile.

He laughed. "Always, Shelly, always. And—" He broke off, snorting and laughing suddenly and taking me by surprise. His eyes began to water. "Can we also appreciate how goddamn stupid Noah looked in the Toad costume?"

I allowed myself a smile and snickered as I remembered. Warren was shorter than Noah, a different build. The white trousers had hung a couple of inches above Noah's ankles and the blue waistcoat with yellow trim had looked a little snug on him. I hadn't even really been able to appreciate the sight of his bare chest, I'd been too angry at him when we'd finally been face to face. And the giant mushroom hat that had been secured to his helmet . . .

Lee was laughing so hard he was wheezing, and I leaned heavily on him, a stitch pulling tight at my side as I tried to sober up.

"How in the hell did he manage to look so mad dressed like that?" I asked breathlessly. "How? Nobody should be able to dress up like Toad and look so pissed."

"Imagine how much better it would've been if he'd kept the helmet on to be mad."

Picturing it, I started laughing all over again.

We'd just about managed to stop laughing and breathe again when Lee pulled me to a stop. Quickly, he covered my eyes.

"All right, Elle. Do you know where you are?"

"Uh, the boardwalk?"

"*Elle.*"

I huffed, but indulged him, turning my focus from the hands covering my face to the electronic pinging sound somewhere in front of me. A clattering noise like . . . like foosball. Something that sounded like the go-karts, along with a tinny voice that said, "Player One wins!" The plastic-y bang and slamming of air hockey.

I gasped, pulling Lee's hands away and snapping my eyes open to stare in awe at the arcade in front of me. I turned to Lee to find his eyes glittering. He seemed to be shaking. So excited he could barely contain himself. Lights from the games flashed across the arcade and kids ran back and forth. A couple of preteens were trying to win something from the claw machine and a few parents hung around.

"Lee . . . this is the arcade."

"Elle," he said. "This is *the* arcade."

Both of us holding our breath, we stepped across the threshold and into the arcade. It was like stepping back in time. Our moms used to bring us here when we were really small. Lee and I had come out to the arcade by ourselves during the summers when we were in middle school—and even played hooky one day to come here. (We got caught and were grounded for two weeks each, but it had felt so totally worth it at the time.)

I couldn't remember the last time we'd come out here. I guessed, at some point, we'd just grown out of it.

But I could remember our favorite game: the *Dance Dance Mania* machine was sitting proudly in the center of the arcade. Its silver steel was flecked with rust and was a little misty-looking, but the blue and pink flashing arrows were bright as ever.

Wordlessly, Lee and I approached it.

I ran a hand over the handlebar at the back of the game. I could see Lee beaming at me, proud to share this.

"We came out here for the eighties mini golf," he explained, "and walked right past this place. I'd forgotten all about it till then."

"Oh my God" was all I could say. Because—oh my God. It was still here. How many hours had we devoted to *DDM* when we were kids? I wasn't always especially coordinated, but this game had been one of my few strong suits in that area. We used to rule this game.

Lee fished in his shorts pocket for a bunch of quarters. He held them out to me, cradling them like diamonds. They even seemed to sparkle in the glare of all the flashing lights.

"Ready, Player Two?"

"Oh, you are *so* on."

The two of us leaped up onto the machine, taking up our old spots. Lee fed the quarters in and the demo video on the screen switched to a list of songs. Lee paused on "All Summer Long" by Kid Rock.

"That's it," I told him. "That's the one."

He selected it and then gave me the biggest, most impish grin imaginable as he selected *Difficulty level: Expert.*

"You don't think we're a little rusty for expert, Lee?"

"*Bwok-bwok-bwok-bwok-bwok,*" he clucked, fanning his arms at his sides, elbows out. "Is that a chicken I hear?"

I narrowed my eyes, turning back to the screen. "Mind you don't trip over those two left feet, Lee. I've got a game to win."

The screen switched to the game.

THREE.

Chicken? I'd show him chicken. I'd crush this.

TWO.

There was no chance in hell of me winning. I bet Lee would suck, too. We were in an arcade surrounded by little kids half our age and we were about to make utter fools of ourselves, trying to play at expert level on *DDM*.

ONE.

I sucked in a breath, my hands clenching into fists. The blend of anticipation and pure, childish delight that was fizzing through me was intoxicating.

GO!

Arrows flew across the screen and my legs lurched into action. I could hear Lee thrashing about beside me, our feet stomping frantically as we did our damnedest to keep up with the game. I didn't dare spare him a look. I was completely focused on the screen and I knew he would be, too.

It was a different version of the song from the one I was used to. It was more electronic and furiously fast.

And it was over too soon.

My chest heaved as I tried to catch my breath. I definitely had a stitch now. I collapsed back against the metal bar, and Lee flopped right down on the floor of the machine, hand on his stomach and panting.

The screen racked up our score: *54%*, it declared. *NOT BAD!*

"Not bad?" I wheezed. For Pete's sake, when did I get so out of shape that I couldn't keep up with a kids' dancing game? I'd spent months on the track team! And Lee was a *footballer*. "Not bad?"

"Shelly," Lee gasped, hand clutching my ankle. "I don't think we were good."

"We used to hold every spot on the leadership board of this game. Come on, get your ass up. We've got two more songs before those quarters run out. Not bad! Ha! We're. Gonna. Kill this."

"It's gonna kill me first," Lee muttered, but he hauled himself up, shaking it off. "I don't remember it being this much exercise, Shelly."

"I guess this explains why we used to eat, like, three hot dogs a day."

Twelve dollars and nine songs saw us both drenched in sweat, but finally, *finally*, back on the leaderboard.

Even the game screen was proud of us: *92%! WOW!*

A celebration video rolled across the screen, and I let myself sit down at last.

"That song . . ." Lee puffed. He shook his head, bending over his knees while he caught his breath. He tried again: "That song is going to be stuck in my head for weeks."

"Hey, it can join your one other brain cell, keep it company for the summer."

Lee groaned, swiping blindly at me. "Don't make me

laugh. I don't have the energy to laugh right now. Oh man. How did we do this all day long as kids?"

"Get it together, old man." I picked my phone up from where I'd left it on the floor next to Lee's wallet and cap and my sunglasses and took a picture of our score and spot on the leaderboard.

It had taken the second round of songs for us to get back in the groove. The muscle memory for *DDM* must have been in there somewhere because Lee and I had found our rhythm again. We even pulled a couple of tricks as we got more and more into the game. Nothing as great as we used to do, of course, but nothing too shabby either.

Ninety-two percent expert.

I'd take that.

"I know you kids," a voice said. We both turned to see an old guy standing nearby wearing a red cap and a red polo shirt with the arcade's name in swirly writing on the pocket. "Don't I know you?"

We both looked at him for a minute before Lee said, "Wait . . . Harvey? Oh man! We almost didn't recognize you! It's us—Elle and Lee. We used to be here all the time."

He squinted back at us. "Didn't you get your arm stuck in the claw machine?"

Lee blushed, but he was grinning. I climbed to my feet as he proudly confirmed, "Yup! That was me!"

"Back for one last round on this thing, huh?" Harvey fondly patted the side of *Dance Dance Mania*.

"Oh, I don't know about that." Lee laughed, saying exactly what I was thinking. "We'll probably be back here all summer, taking over that leaderboard again."

Harvey's wrinkled face pulled into an apologetic smile. "Well, good luck with that. This old gal's going out to pasture in a couple of weeks. Retirement date's set for sixth of July."

The words punched the air out of my lungs in a way that none of the dancing had.

"What?" I demanded. "But . . . but why? This machine's been here for years! We've practically been dancing on this thing since we could walk!" *With the exception of the last few years.* "You can't get rid of it!"

He sighed heavily, full of sympathy. "There's not much I can do about it. This thing's starting to fall apart. Costs more to repair than it makes." He tapped at the edge of the screen, where there was a fuzzy black spot in the corner that I hadn't noticed until now. Then I saw the duct tape slapped across the metal panels on the sides of the machine. The lights in one of Lee's arrows were out completely and two of mine were flickering. Lee seemed to be noticing all of this, too; he wiggled the metal handlebar behind us. It was a little loose and it creaked. I bet with any amount of force, you could've pulled it right off.

But still!

The *DDM* machine had been the staple of the arcade for us for so many summers. The last forty minutes or so with

Lee had been pure joy and had wiped my mind of the stress of the future, of college, of the fight with Noah and his attitude toward Levi.

Lee's face had fallen, too, but there was so much more than simple disappointment in it.

"Sorry, kids," Harvey told us with a shrug.

I did my best to give him a polite smile and sound upbeat. "That's okay. Guess we'll just have to come back to take over that leaderboard before you get rid of it!"

As Harvey walked off, Lee muttered under his breath and kicked at the machine. The screen fizzled out and back on and off again, then started showing the demo video again. Lee stepped off completely, huffing, and hunched over the handlebar.

I knew that look all too well. I'd seen it plenty of times this summer. His eyes shone wet and he clenched his jaw tight. His lip wobbled just a little.

"I don't believe this," he bit out. "First the beach house. Then you and Harvard. And now this? Is nothing sacred?"

Melodrama was one of Lee's strong suits, but I didn't think he was being melodramatic right now. Not in the slightest.

I put a hand on his back, leaning next to him. "Tell me about it."

It didn't matter that we'd forgotten all about the arcade and *Dance Dance Mania*. What mattered was that we'd shown up here to relive a golden hour of our childhood, just to find it was falling to pieces and being scrapped.

Which, honestly, felt like a way-too-accurate metaphor for everything else that was going on. It *hurt*. It wasn't about the machine. There would be other *DDM* machines, other arcades.

It was about us.

It was about the future.

It was about this being a summer of lasts.

Lee sniffled next to me, and I wished there was something I could do. A huge part of the melancholy hanging over us all summer, however distantly, was because of me, because of my decision to not go to Berkeley. I wished I could stop him hurting like this.

I wished—

It hit me like lightning. I stifled a gasp to tell Lee, "Stay here. I'll be back in a sec," before running off to find Harvey, who was exchanging a kid's tokens for a baseball mitt.

Barely a minute later, I was back with Lee, who hadn't budged from his despairing stance at *Dance Dance Mania*. He eyed me curiously as I grabbed his wallet off the floor and riffled through receipts and dollar bills and—

I held up a condom. "Seriously? You're so classy."

"Put that away!" he hissed. "There are kids around!"

I shoved it back into his wallet, only for him to murmur, "It never hurts to be prepared, Shelly. I bet Noah keeps one in *his* wallet."

"I will neither confirm nor deny this."

I could totally, absolutely confirm this.

I pulled out the sheet of paper I was looking for. We'd

been carrying the bucket list about all summer, folding and refolding it a hundred and one times. It hadn't been in the most pristine condition when we'd found it; by the end of this summer, I got the feeling it'd be falling apart.

"What're you doing?" he asked, straightening up. I took a seat under the handlebar. Lee sat with me, hitting his head and muttering, "Ouch."

Lee and Elle's Epic Summer Bucket List

27. ~~Take a hot air balloon ride—NO PARENTS ALLOWED!~~
28. ~~Turn Noah into a human ice-cream sundae~~
29. Go to Berkeley together for college!
30. One last dance on our DDM machine at the arcade

"New item," I told him. "One final dance on this old gal—July fifth."

"Hmm," he murmured approvingly. And then, "You sure you got the time for it?"

I glanced at number twenty-three, the mini-golf night I'd missed yesterday. Lee had crossed it through lightly in pencil. Half done. Kind of done. Not done enough.

"Absolutely," I told him, reaching up to chuck a finger under his chin. "Now get that mopey look off your face, okay? I know I've been crazy busy the last couple of weeks— working, looking after Brad, spending time with Noah as well as doing all the bucket-list stuff, but this is important to me, too, Lee. And I *promise you*, I'll be here for one last dance, no matter what. I wouldn't miss it for the world."

Lee gave me a soft smile, his head tipping onto my shoulder. "You're such a mushy loser sometimes, Elle, but I love you."

"I love you, too, buddy."

Chapter Twenty-Two

It was dark out by the time Lee and I got back to the beach house. We had the next couple of days all planned out. Race day may have been the biggest thing on the list (and the biggest coup to pull off), but it was by no means the end of it. We'd managed to plan our weekend at Berkeley, too.

Indoors, the lights were on in the rumpus room and laughter filtered out from that direction.

"Who's that?" Amanda sang down the hallway.

"Tweedledum and Tweedledumber," Rachel replied, followed by a giddy laugh.

"I resent that!" Lee and I called back in unison, which only made her laugh more.

In the rumpus room we found them watching their way through a bunch of old home movies. A mostly empty box of chocolates sat between them and—

"Where did you guys even get wine from?" I asked. Jealousy tinged my voice to see them hanging out, having a girly night in together. I knew I'd have been welcome if I'd been around, but even so.

"I went to see my parents," Amanda said. "Picked up some more clothes and stole some wine from them. They're not gonna miss it. Just like they're not gonna miss their only daughter when they're too busy fighting. Ha-ha!"

I exchanged a glance with Lee, not really sure how to react.

Amanda topped their glasses off. "To self-involved parents and their stashes of wine!"

Rachel laughed again, swatting at Amanda's knee like she'd said something truly hilarious. "Where've you guys been?" she asked us.

"Was it a bucket-list thing?" Amanda wanted to know.

Lee and I exchanged a look and nodded. I didn't think either of us was about to explain how our old favorite arcade game was being retired soon, and what a big deal that was. Although in fairness, they'd probably take us more seriously while they were tipsy than any other time.

"We saved you guys some dinner," Amanda told us. "Mac and cheese."

"We grabbed some burgers on the way home," Lee said. He glanced at me. "But I'm gonna heat up some mac and cheese. You want some?"

I smiled. "Nah, I'm good. So, uh, did Noah join you guys for dinner?"

Both the girls shook their heads. Amanda said, "Haven't seen him. I tried calling him, but he sent me to voice mail, like a tool."

Rachel scoffed. "Toad the tool."

They both dissolved into giggles again.

"Aww, but he doesn't look like a tool here." Amanda gestured at the home movie. It was Fourth of July, judging by the fireworks and the flags. On the screen, Noah was holding a toddler Brad on his shoulders. She wriggled around to peer over the back of the sofa at me. "Was it about Levi?"

I caught my breath and let out a sharp laugh. "Oh my God, seriously?"

"It was probably about Levi," Rachel agreed seriously, sipping her wine.

"You too? This is crazy. Noah's got *no reason* to be jealous of Levi."

They both pulled a face and then tried to go back to *not* pulling a face, but it was too late by then. Rachel was helpful enough to point out, "But you did kiss him."

"He did kind of have a look," Amanda added with a sympathetic expression.

"What *look*? What are you talking about?"

"You know, that . . ." Amanda's head wobbled and her eyes drifting side to side as she looked up at the ceiling, her lips pursed lightly and her eyelashes fluttering. There was something dreamy and wistful about it.

I snorted. "Okay, I don't know what you're talking about, but *that* is not a look I've ever seen on Levi's face."

"Looks pretty accurate to me," Rachel mumbled into her wine.

"Okay!" I grinned at them both, knowing my eyes told a different story—one that said, *Screw you both, I don't have time for this.* "Well, you guys are drunk and clearly don't know what you're talking about, and I've got a missing boyfriend to track down and talk some sense into."

"No, stay! Watch home movies with us! Um . . ." Rachel looked at the bottle of wine, which wasn't far from being empty. "I *guess* you can have what's left of the wine."

"But no chocolates," Amanda decided.

"I'm good, thanks. I'd really better go find Noah."

"Good luck," they both called to me. I stopped by my room to grab a jacket, then passed Lee on his way back from the kitchen, already digging into a heaping plate of macaroni and cheese.

"I'm gonna go look for Noah."

"You sure you don't wanna stay and hang out? He'll probably come crawling home soon."

I shook my head, fidgeting with the jacket I was holding. "Nah, I . . . I'd rather just clear the air, you know?"

"Any idea where he is?"

I shook my head. "I figured I'd go check down on the beach, then—"

As I said it, we both turned at the noise of Noah's motorcycle engine growling outside. The sound cut a moment later.

"Mystery solved," Lee muttered. He shoved some more pasta into his mouth, set the fork down on the plate to pat my shoulder, and then carried on to the rumpus room. I braced myself as I went in the opposite direction, opening the front door to find Noah stopped halfway up the porch, fiddling with his keys and scowling at the floor, his lips moving silently—like he was giving himself a pep talk.

He glanced up, looking surprised to see me. "Oh."

"Expecting someone else?"

"I . . . figured you'd still be mad at me."

I shrugged. Maybe I still was, just a bit. Enough that I wasn't going to forgive him *too* quickly.

Noah sighed heavily. His hair fell into his eyes, such a bright blue that they were striking even through the dark. He was wearing the T-shirt I'd seen him in earlier and his usual leather jacket. "Can we go for a walk?"

I nodded, pulling on my jacket and closing the door behind me. Noah offered his hand, and for a minute I considered not taking it and walking ahead of him, just to make a point, but . . .

My hand slipped into his, fitting so well. Our fingers slotted together like this was exactly where they belonged. I got a waft of that citrus scent I would forever associate with Noah. It was comforting, even if we were technically still having an argument.

This far out, it was a private stretch of beach, for residents only. We both took our shoes and socks off, leaving them behind as we walked down to the shore, the sea washing over our ankles.

"It's so quiet. I've never seen it this quiet."

I felt Noah shrug beside me. "Like my mom said, the land's valuable. People have been selling up, I guess."

We kept walking in silence. There were a thousand

things I could say to him, and wanted to say, but I knew Noah had something on his mind, something he wanted to say. He was unnervingly quiet and I could see the tension in his shoulders. His breathing was a little too measured: slow and even, in for three, out for three, in for three . . .

Besides. This whole stupid fight was his fault. I wasn't going to give him the satisfaction of forgiving him before he apologized.

Eventually, Noah came to a stop, stepping in front of me and turning to face me. "I'm sorry. I know it looked like I was being a dick earlier, and . . . and I know I probably was," he added in a huff, "but I really didn't mean to ruin race day for you. I'm sorry."

"I'm not mad you ruined race day," I told him.

"Yeah, I know." His mouth twitched humorlessly. "I'm sorry about that, too, though. It wasn't *just* my fault, you know. He was getting pretty rough on the track, too. Which . . . yeah," he added, seeing me raise my eyebrows, "isn't an excuse. I'm just saying, it's not all my fault. But you were right. I should've been the bigger person and . . . and . . . and just shaken his hand."

"And you think maybe you should've not made a bitchy comment about me always going running to Levi?"

Noah took my other hand in his, looking down at our hands and nodding. "Yeah."

"I know you thought I broke up with you to be with Levi last fall, but that's not what this is about. It's not like he's my backup plan for you. He's my *friend*. And that's all there is."

"For you."

"Oh, Jesus, Noah." I started to draw back, but Noah held me fast, one of his hands letting go of mine to cup my face instead. I pushed it away. "Okay, fine. Look. Just . . . for argument's sake, okay, let's just *say* that you were right, and Levi does have a crush on me still. *Just say.* I don't feel that way about him. And Levi *knows* that. He knows I'm in love with you. And he's not the kind of guy who's going to make a move on me as long as we're together. I'm not saying you have to like him, but . . . I'm not going to stop being friends with him."

"I'm not asking you to do that."

"You say you trust me, Noah. We had whole fights about trusting each other last year and I *can't* do that again. So right now, I . . . I need you to trust Levi."

He scowled. "I hardly know the guy, Elle."

"Then be civil to him," I tried. I reminded myself that if I were in his shoes, I'd probably be finding it hard to trust a relative stranger, too. It was easy for me to say he could trust Levi, but another thing for Noah to know that for himself.

"I'll try," he promised me. "And I'm sorry."

"Yeah, you'd better be. You big lug." I pushed gently at his chest and he caught my hand, using it to pull me into his arms. His lips ghosted over my temple, down my cheek, along my jaw, and down to the crook of my neck. He pressed a kiss there and held me tight to him. I wrapped my arms around him in return, fingers reaching up to play with the hair at the nape of his neck. Noah sighed into me.

I loved him so much it hurt sometimes. I'd found it really tough, being away from him this last year. Living together so far this summer hadn't exactly been a picnic twenty-four seven, but it wasn't as hard as being apart. I knew how wonderful it would be to be at Harvard with him next year.

But sometimes, like today, being in a relationship was tough.

It all felt worth it, though, to be in his arms like this.

"I love you," I murmured into his shoulder. "But you make it real hard sometimes, Noah."

"Don't ever let me forget it, huh?"

"Cross my heart. Where did you end up all day anyway?"

"You know that place I took you on your birthday last year? The hill, where we went to see the fireworks? I just needed some space."

Ah. That made sense. I should've thought of it earlier.

"I'm glad you came home," I told him.

He pressed another kiss to my neck and I held him tighter. The waves broke quietly around our feet and the rest of the world was silent but for our breathing. Maybe we weren't perfect, but for now, it was all I needed.

Chapter Twenty-Three

I worked the breakfast shift the next day, and the lunch one. I'd have done the dinner shift, too, but I had to pick Brad up from camp. It was an exhausting day: I'd dropped an entire ice-cream sundae, some woman screamed at me for getting her Diet Coke instead of regular, even though I was *sure* she'd ordered diet. And right now, I was a mere twenty-five minutes away from finishing my shift when a crowd of rowdy college-aged guys poured into the diner. Most of them had damp hair and sand stuck to them. I spotted a truck outside with a couple of surfboards in the bed.

"You want me to take them?" Melvin asked, seeing me roll my eyes. I had to hand it to him—he had a *lot* of guts to even offer. With his round glasses and head of springy curls and soft face and braces, they'd eat him alive. And despite the nervous glance he cast their way, he puffed out his chest, ready to jump in on my behalf.

I shook my head. "It's okay, I've got this."

Marching over to the table, a fresh jug of water clutched in my hands, I plastered on a smile. "Hi. My name's Elle and I'll be your server this afternoon. Can I start you guys off with some water?"

They barely paid me any attention, too wrapped up in a heated debate about who'd had the best day out on the waves. One guy grunted and waved absently at me, not even looking over. "Sure, sweetheart."

Wow, what a charmer.

I poured their water and cleared my throat. "So, the soup of the day is leek and potato. Our specials are lobster rolls with avocado, which I'd highly recommend, and a chickpea-and-halloumi burger with—"

"How about dessert?" one of the guys asked, turning to me with a cocky grin.

"Uh . . . sure. The dessert special today is a hot fudge sundae with cherries or banana sorbet."

"What about you?" the first guy asked. "Are you on the menu, sweetheart?"

I gave him a flat smile. "Sadly, we're all out of single waitresses, and it looks like you're all out of pickup lines."

A couple of the guys laughed at their buddy, but he was persistent. "Aw, come on. How about you give me your number, baby?"

"How about I get my manager to throw you guys out?" I offered, batting my eyelashes.

"Quit it, dude," the guy in the corner muttered, shoving his friend's arm. "I'm starving."

"I'll give you a minute to check out the menus and then be back to take your order."

"I know what I'm checking out," one of them said as I turned around, and a hand pinched my butt.

I whirled around, upending the water pitcher.

"Ohh, I'm so sorry, *sweetheart*," I told him in a sickly sweet voice. Grabby guy was drenched, and his friends were trying and failing to stifle their laughter as he gasped, sputtering and wiping his face.

"Bitch," he snapped at me.

"Guilty as charged!" I told him in a gleeful tone. "Now please leave, before I ask our chef to come out here and make you leave. He's a real pro with a meat tenderizer."

Grumbling, the group clambered out of the booth. The guy who'd asked if I was on the menu mumbled an unenthusiastic sorry at me, and another one shoved the grabby guy, telling him, "You're such an asshole. That lobster roll sounded so good."

I gave them a bright smile, following them to the door and waving. "Don't come back soon!"

Turning around, I spotted May gathering up an order from the kitchen. She arched a penciled eyebrow at me and I winced.

"Sorry. I'll clean it up now."

"You handled those douche-bros like a pro," she told me instead. "And go on, get out of here. Haven't you got a little brother to pick up? Melvin—paper towels in section five, please!"

I ducked into the back to grab my backpack. I didn't bother to change out of my uniform, deciding I could do that once I was back at home. And it was just as well May let me clock out a couple of minutes early and I didn't waste time changing my clothes, since I drove straight into traffic. The freeway was down to one lane and I crawled along, grumbling under my breath, watching the time slip past on the clock on the dash.

By the time I got to the field where Brad's baseball camp was taking place, there were only a few stragglers hanging around. The parking lot was mostly empty. Two moms were standing outside their cars smoking while their kids played catch. I jumped out of the car, searching through the kids still hanging around, but saw no sign of Brad.

Fear curling like a fist around my heart, I ran to the squat brick building off the field. There was a mess hall being cleaned up, where a couple of the coaches sat talking over some papers without even sparing me a glance, but no Brad.

Shit. Shit, shit, shit.

Okay, Elle. No need to panic. This is fine.

My legs shook as I returned to my car, fumbling with my cell phone to dial Dad. It rang twice before I was sent to voice mail and I hung up.

A text buzzed through only seconds later.

In a meeting. What's up?

Shit. If Dad hadn't picked him up . . .

No, I didn't need to panic yet. I ignored my dad's text and jammed the keys into the ignition. I stalled the car twice before managing to pull out of the parking lot. Maybe Brad had just gotten a ride home with a buddy. Maybe one of the parents picking their kids up from camp had seen him waiting around and taken him back home.

My fear only grew the closer I got to the house, though, because Brad never disappeared like this. And sure, maybe he was old enough to look after himself by now, but he was still just a kid. He was my little brother. He was my responsibility. I was supposed to take care of him. And if he'd gone missing . . .

I parked the car haphazardly, throwing myself out of it and at our front door. It gave way, not even locked, and my blood froze before—

"Oh, thank God!" I panted, snatching Brad up into a hug from his seat at the kitchen counter, where he was shoveling hot nachos into his mouth. He smelled sweaty and like grass and I buried my nose in his hair. "Thank God! I couldn't find you anywhere. Did one of the moms give you a ride home? You know you're supposed to wait for me, or call me if something like that happens. Do you have any idea how scared I was?"

"I'm right here," he said, shrugging me off with a huff and looking at me with total confusion. "What are you doing here?"

"What am I— I was supposed to pick you up! What do you mean, what am I doing here?"

"Oh!"

I spun around to see a total stranger standing in the doorway. The woman wore a black sleeveless blouse and blue pencil skirt and sparkly blue stud earrings. Her shoulder-length dark hair bounced into curls at the ends, not a flyaway in sight. She looked like she'd come straight out of an office somewhere.

It didn't take a genius to figure out who this stranger was.

"Elle!" she exclaimed, a broad smile stretching over her face. "We weren't expecting you!"

I scoffed. Was she serious?

"You weren't expecting me?" I repeated. "Oh, I'm so sorry for coming here to my house. And who the hell are you?"

I knew exactly who she was, but the whole "we weren't expecting you" thing was so goddamn rich I didn't even try to hide my indignation.

She gave a light laugh. "Of course, silly me. I've just heard so much about you, I feel like I already know you! I'm Linda. I'm your dad's—"

"Yeah, I know."

I kind of didn't want her to finish that sentence.

"What I don't know," I went on, "is what you're doing here."

"She picked me up from camp," Brad said, like it was obvious—which, now that he was pointing it out, I guessed it was. But the why wasn't so obvious.

I scowled at him. "No. I was meant to pick you up from camp."

"You've just been so busy lately," Linda said kindly, and oh my God, if she didn't stop pottering around the kitchen like that, I was going to scream. "Your dad keeps talking about how much you've got on your plate right now, so I offered to help out and pick up Brad from camp a couple of days. Didn't he tell you?"

I thought about the string of messages Dad had sent me yesterday that I'd been too preoccupied to look at and said nothing.

"Speaking of having a lot on your plate, can I fix you one?"

"What?"

"Nachos," she explained, gesturing at Brad's plate. "Do you want some?"

"No, Linda. I don't want nachos."

She shrugged and carried on cleaning up, running water at the sink.

"I can do the dishes," I told her.

"It's no trouble. Besides, I made the mess! I'm so sorry for the confusion about pickup today for Brad. We really didn't mean to worry you."

We. No, there was no "we." The only "we" was me, Brad, and our dad. Not one that included this . . . this . . . his . . . whatever the hell she was.

"I've been managing just fine without your help, Linda."

"Well, I . . . I know that, Elle." She turned from rinsing dishes to give me an awkward-looking smile.

Good, I thought bitterly. She should be uncomfortable. This was my house, not hers. She was the intruder here, not me. "Your dad's always saying how much you take on and what a good job you're doing of it all, but since I could be around to help out . . . We thought it'd give you more time to hang out with your friends. Work through that bucket list

I've heard so much about! Brad was showing me the race-day videos—how amazing! You and Lee must have such wild imaginations to come up with something like that. And all that money you raised for charity!"

What do you know about the bucket list? Don't talk about me and my best friend like you know anything about us. I don't need you to help out. You're not doing me any favors.

But I bit my tongue, swallowing every mean retort back down.

Brad looked at me with awe in his eyes. "I wish I could've been there to see it, Elle. Levi and Noah really went for it! And when Lee got slimed!" He burst into laughter.

I softened a little. "Wish you could've been there to see it, too, buddy."

(Dad and I had quickly made the decision that Brad absolutely should not have been there—I'd be too busy to look after him all day at the water park, and he'd only want to get involved; that the go-karts were strictly fourteen-plus had given us an easy excuse to talk him down before he asked.)

"Can I come back to the beach house this weekend, Elle?"

"Maybe. I'll talk to the guys. But I promise you can come back soon. And hey! It's almost Fourth of July! You'll be there for that! We're throwing a huge party, since it's the last year we've got the beach house. Dad even said you could bring a couple of friends along. Huh? That's gonna be cool, right? Being at a grown-up party with college kids?"

Brad rolled his eyes. "You're not in college yet, Elle."

But he did look totally thrilled at the idea.

I glanced at Linda, wondering if Dad had invited her along, too. I guessed I couldn't say anything about that. I just had to hope I wouldn't run into her on the night.

She caught me looking and, instead of mentioning Fourth of July, just said, "I'm really sorry this is how we ended up meeting, Elle, but it is so good to finally meet you. Maybe, if you've got a free evening, the four of us could go out to dinner somewhere? Get to know each other better?"

"Like you said," I told her, "I'm busy."

• • • •

As I parked at the beach house, after driving around for an hour trying to clear my head, my phone buzzed.

Don't forget! Lee's text told me. *#9 tonight! Meet you at the mall.*

Bucket-list item number nine: be part of a flash mob.

Lee had found one being organized for tonight online. If you signed up, you got sent an email with a video of the choreography, which had been pretty straightforward to learn. And with all the effort we'd put into organizing race day and scheduling other activities around my hectic schedule, it had been easier to take part in an existing one than to organize an entire flash mob ourselves.

I sighed. I hadn't changed out of my work uniform and was still carting my outfit for the flash mob around in my backpack—and I'd been so caught up in Brad missing and the Linda drama that I actually had forgotten all about the flash mob. I grabbed my backpack now, heading inside. Quick change, then back to the city and the mall.

Inside, the lights were low and something orange flickered from the direction of the kitchen.

Following the flickering, I found several tea lights and saw more on the table outside. A bowl of salad waited outdoors, too. And then Noah stood up from the oven, pulling out a casserole.

"Hey! You're here." He beamed at me, dimple showing, eyes sparkling.

"What's . . ." I stared around at the candles, the food. "What's all this?"

"I wanted to make it up to you, for yesterday. And you've been so busy, I thought you could use a night in."

"You did all this yourself?"

"Of course," he declared, puffing out his chest, then smirking and saying, "No. Amanda totally helped me prep the casserole."

"Where is she?"

Mixed as my feelings could be about Amanda, I would feel terrible if she had to shut herself up in Lee's and my old room all evening so Noah and I could have a romantic dinner.

"She headed back to the hotel to have dinner with her parents. They said they had some stuff to talk to her about. I think she's staying there tonight." He set down the dish and shook off the oven mitts before coming over, putting his hands on my hips and bending to kiss me.

"Noah, this . . ." Despite myself, tears sprang to my eyes and I had to gulp to keep my voice steady. "This looks amazing. It's so sweet, but . . ."

I pulled back, feeling my shoulders hunch and my head bow. My hands fidgeted in front of me.

I could feel Noah's eyes roaming over me, taking in my guilty expression, the frown on my face, the sigh I was barely managing to hold back. Even though I was staring determinedly at the floor and trying to block out the delicious aroma of the casserole and the romantic glow of the candles, out of the corner of my eye I saw his excited smile fade away.

"Elle? What's up?"

What's up?

That was such a loaded question. Between an exhausting double shift, complete with some grabby jackass, the panic over Brad not being at camp, and the whole ordeal with Linda, now Noah had made a romantic meal for us to spend the evening together and I had to say . . .

"I'm sorry," I told him, my dejected sigh finally escaping now as I fell back another step. "Noah, I'm sorry, because this is all so amazing and honestly it's exactly what I need tonight, but I can't. I have somewhere I need to be."

I saw it dawn on him, and he let out a sharp, frustrated noise. "Please tell me this isn't another bucket-list thing."

"I'm sorry!" I cried. I felt genuinely awful, especially given how much trouble he'd gone to. "I promised Lee, and I already missed one thing this week. I'm trying really hard not to make a habit of that."

I was already backing away through the door.

"You're seriously gonna leave?" he asked, gawping incredulously.

"It's not like I have a choice! I promised Lee. It's not like this is something we can just rearrange. I'm gonna be with you all next year. I need to make that up to him this summer. I'm sorry, Noah, but I have to go."

He followed me through to our bedroom. I pulled the flash-mob clothes out of my bag and started to get changed. Noah scoffed again.

"So just because you picked Harvard over Berkeley, I don't get to spend any time with you this summer?"

"That's not what I said. Don't blow it out of proportion."

"You keep saying this summer is all about you and Lee, all about the bucket list. I didn't think I was reaching for the stars by hoping for an evening in with my girlfriend."

He'd picked up my shirt, and I snatched it back from him. "You're not! But not tonight, Noah. That's all."

"Then when? Tomorrow?"

Tomorrow, Lee, the guys, and I all had plans to go to the movies.

He sensed me faltering.

"The next day?"

"I'm on the late shift."

"How about August eighteenth? Two years from now? How does that work for you, Elle?"

I'd put the T-shirt on backward. Huffing, I wriggled my arms back out of it, working it around to put it on properly. "Noah, come on. Don't be like this. I'm sorry I ruined your surprise dinner and already had plans that I can't bail on now. Okay? But right now, I've gotta go."

"Fine," he snapped. "Have fun with Lee."

I hated that I'd upset him. I hated that I couldn't stay, because I really, honestly did want to—but I also knew I couldn't let Lee down. Not again. I hated that I had to leave in the middle of a fight and I hated that we were fighting again.

So I told him, "I love you."

Noah gave a noncommittal mutter as he left the room, but then said, "Yeah. You too."

Which was about as good as I was going to get tonight, so I'd take it.

Maybe I'd crash in my old bed tonight and we could clear the air tomorrow.

I passed Rachel on my way out the door. She didn't look overly happy either. There had to be something in the air tonight.

"Bucket list?" she said to me in a way that told me she already knew.

"Uh-huh. Catch you later!"

She huffed, muttering, "Have fun, I guess."

Maybe I wasn't the only one whose relationship was taking second place to the bucket list.

As I shut the door behind me, I heard Rachel asking Noah, "What's all this?" and him muttering, "It's nothing," and blowing out the candles.

* * *

"You've got such a stick up your ass tonight, Shelly," Lee told me. "Come on! Flash mob! This is supposed to be fun!"

"Sorry. I promise I'm having fun. And I'll be smiling when it starts."

We'd taken up a perch on a bench by a fountain in the mall near the food court. The flash mob was eight minutes from starting. So far, we'd been playing a game of "Are they shopping or are they with the flash mob?"—a game that I, apparently, wasn't engaged enough with.

Lee scooted closer to me. "What's up?"

I was so close to telling him. It had been such a horrible shitshow of a day that I was three seconds from bursting into tears, and I knew I would if I told him.

Aside from when I'd started dating Noah, I didn't make a habit of keeping secrets from Lee or lying to him. (The application to Harvard didn't count, I kept telling myself, since I never thought I'd get in.)

It would be so easy to just tell him.

But I couldn't do that. I knew exactly how it would sound: that I didn't want to be here, that I didn't want to be doing the bucket list, that I wanted to pick Noah over him yet again, that our friendship was a burden and getting in the way of my relationship.

I knew exactly how it'd sound, so I kept my mouth shut.

"It's just been A DAY, you know?" I settled on saying.

He gave a breath of laughter. "Tell me about it. I totally forgot to tell Rachel about this, so she thought we were going to have dinner with her folks. My bad, totally. But she was cool with it. She gets this summer's important to us."

That makes one of them.

I decided not to mention how disgruntled Rachel had looked when she'd gotten home to the beach house earlier this evening.

Lee started talking again about race day (how many hits the video had now, how epic it had been), what was next up on the bucket list, if we'd have time to head to the arcade again in the next couple of days. I indulged him, doing my best to put the fight with Noah out of my mind.

It wasn't about picking one Flynn brother over the other. It never had been.

But when it came down to it, Lee was like a part of me. Without him, I'd feel like I was missing a limb. I'd be missing part of my soul. I already knew what it was like to be apart from Noah and that had been enough of a struggle. I was dreading leaving Lee.

So while it wasn't about picking Lee or Noah over the other . . . maybe it was, just a little. And this summer it had to be Lee.

Chapter Twenty-Four

If I'd thought things had been rough two days ago, it was only getting worse. Noah and I had barely spoken. He'd been out yesterday to show Amanda around the city a little—an impromptu decision, with an obvious reason behind his sudden zest for local tourism—and I'd pretended to be asleep when he came to bed last night.

It was probably totally childish, but I didn't really have it in me to care. I just hadn't been able to face another discussion that'd probably turn into a heated debate, if not a full-on argument.

After an early start to go tick off another bucket-list item with Lee (number twelve: rappelling), I was back at work, doing the lunch and dinner shifts.

My dad had been trying to get a hold of me for the last couple of days, too.

I'd sent him a short text to say I was busy, I had things to do, and if he needed someone to help out with Brad, maybe Linda could do it. Precious Linda. Stupid Linda. Making-herself-at-home-in-my-kitchen Linda.

Lee knew something was up. He knew me too well.

Weirdly, the only person I felt like talking to about Linda was Amanda. She hadn't been judgmental when I'd told her about Linda originally and it somehow seemed less scary to tell her than to talk to Lee or Noah about it. (Not that Noah and I were exactly *talking* right now anyway . . .)

So without wanting to hurt Lee's feelings by explaining that the tension between me and Noah was because of him and the bucket list, and without going into the whole Linda thing, I just kept shrugging it off and saying, "It's no big deal. I'm just kind of tired from everything that's going on. Work's crazy, you know?"

The last part wasn't even a lie.

Work *was* crazy, today especially. There had been some surfing competition on the beach and we were swamped. There wasn't even a lull between lunch and dinner the way there usually was.

The douchebags from earlier in the week had shown up, but May was quick to tell them, politely and in no uncertain terms, that they would have to take their business elsewhere. They started to object until one of them spotted me and I gave an enthusiastic wave, holding up a tray of brightly colored virgin cocktails I was taking to table thirty, at which point they gave in and left.

That was about the best part of the day.

I dropped an entire order before I even made it out of the kitchen. I mixed up at least three other orders. I forgot to pick up the check at table twenty-four for so long the dad eventually marched up to me, credit card in hand, and demanded to speak to my manager if he was going to be kept waiting like this. The kids at table thirty-three left it a total *mess*—spilled drinks, ketchup all over the table, half a burger smooshed into the seat, and fries floating in half a milkshake.

My pants had ripped at some point. I didn't even know *when*, but I did know the right leg was currently torn halfway up my shin, the fabric flapping around even though I'd tucked the ends into my sock. When I took a bathroom break, I realized there was pen on my face. I didn't even bother trying to rub it off.

I had just finished taking the order from a large family group of twelve and given them what I hoped was a smile, when, as I stepped away, I careered forward. My arms flung out, pulling a plate off one table and half strangling some poor girl at another as I tried to catch myself.

Struggling to stand back up, I found the laces of my shoes tied together. Some snot-nosed kid who couldn't have been more than four or five at the table I'd just been waiting on was giggling hysterically.

His mother looked mortified, taking turns apologizing profusely to me and scolding her son.

"It's fine," I told her, leaning forward to fix my shoelaces. Damn, the kid tied a good knot. Finally fixing them, I trudged back to the bar, clipping the order up for the chef.

A hand landed lightly on my shoulder. "You doing okay there, Elle?"

I looked at May. She had such a concerned look on her face I almost cried. Not trusting my voice, I nodded.

She didn't look totally convinced, though. "Why don't you take a break? Kaylie just got here. She can look after your tables for a little bit."

"B-but—"

"Hey. No arguing with the boss. Take a break. That's an order, okay?"

I sniffled, giving her the world's most pathetic smile and trudging outside. I just needed some fresh air, that was all. A couple of minutes to get some fresh air, and I'd be fine. I was just tired. I was just run off my feet.

I was just . . .

Falling apart.

"Elle?"

I jumped at the sound of my name, a familiar voice—and then jumped again when a car door opened and clipped me on the hip. "Oof!"

"Shit, sorry. I didn't realize you were that close." Levi pulled himself out of his car and cracked a smile. "We've gotta stop bumping into each other like this."

The first time we'd met, he'd opened a car door into me. I tried to smile at the joke, I really did, but all I managed was a twitch of the muscles somewhere in my cheek. His face fell.

"What's up? Wow, you look like a hot mess. Not hot, like, *hot*. But you're . . . Well, that's . . . Never mind. You doing okay, Elle?"

I couldn't talk to Lee without hurting his feelings. I *wasn't* talking to Noah right now. I couldn't talk to my dad about Linda without sounding like a brat, and I couldn't talk to Rachel or Amanda without the very good chance they would go back to Lee or Noah and tell them everything, and then it'd be a big deal because they'd *know* what I wasn't talking to them about—and that there was even something going on that I wasn't talking to them about.

But Levi . . .

Levi was looking at me so sadly, his forehead creased and his mouth twisted downward, his eyes so warm and friendly. He looked like he just wanted to help.

"Elle?" he asked again.

And I burst into tears.

• • •

I told Levi everything. I even told him about the fight I'd had with Noah on race day and how Noah thought Levi still had a crush on me and everything else that had been said. I told him about Linda: that if I wasn't so busy working, maybe she wouldn't need to be around so much, but if I didn't have this job, I couldn't really do the bucket list. And speaking of the bucket list, I told him about missing eighties mini golf and then having to bail on Noah like that . . .

"He thinks just because he cooked and lit a couple of candles, everything's fine again?"

I shook my head. "No, it's not like that. He'd already apologized. He was just trying to be nice and wanted to spend some time with me. And then I bailed on *him* to do the flash mob, which I *did* want to do, but . . . I feel like I keep getting stuck between them, and the last time this happened, I almost lost Lee and Noah went off on some stupid bender because he thought he'd, like, ruined everything or whatever."

"No offense, Elle, but your boyfriend sounds like a real piece of work sometimes."

I grunted. *Yeah, but he's my piece of work.*

"It's not like I'm so perfect myself." I snorted. "If he wasn't like this, he wouldn't be Noah, and I wouldn't love him the way I do."

"Hmm."

We were sitting on a pile of rocks between the parking lot and the beach. I hugged my knees up to my chin. Levi stretched out beside me, his hands planted just behind his hips.

"It's just," I tried, "between all that, and Linda, and things being so crazy here, I feel like I can't breathe some days. You know? Don't get me wrong, I love doing the bucket-list stuff. It was my idea! And I'm having a blast doing it all. And I'm happy to help look after Brad, and I wanted to work here—and I like it. Aside from the occasional"—I sighed, long and loud through my nose, gesturing at myself and the state of disarray I was in—"day like today and the odd ass-pincher. But it's just getting to be a lot."

"You don't have to try to do everything," he said gently.

"I do, though. I need money for college and so I can keep

up with all the bucket-list stuff, which Lee doesn't get because he's *always* had money and it's never even been a question for him. If he needs a hundred bucks, he just asks his mom and dad. And, like, I know if *I* went and asked them, they'd give me that money, too, but that's not the point."

"I know."

"And, like, with Linda, you know, I'm happy for my dad. It's not like I *want* him to be miserable or whatever. And if Linda makes him happy, then that's great. But I don't need her barging into my life and taking over when I had things under control. And at the start of summer, Noah was talking about how, if I went to college in Boston, we could live together. Well, we are right now and look how that's turning out! We aren't even *speaking* to each other! What does that say about us?"

I sighed, fresh tears springing to my eyes just when I thought I was all cried out. I rubbed my face into my knees.

"Everything's falling apart," I said, the words muffled by my legs. "And everything's changing. And I hate it."

Levi wrapped his arm around my shoulders, pulling me into him, and I let him. I sniveled into my knees and let him hold me and rub his hand up and down my arm soothingly.

"What're you even doing here anyway?" I asked when I'd finally gotten the tears back under control. I found a napkin somewhere in my apron pocket and wiped my nose with it before looking up at Levi.

He blushed a little and shrugged, his arm still around me. "I just came by to see you."

"Why?"

"You're always showing up where I work," he pointed out with a brief laugh. Then, more seriously, he said, "We haven't really talked since the water park. I wanted to check in, see if you were okay. Noah was obviously pissed at me—guess now I know why—and I probably shouldn't have taken the bait and gone at him like that on the track. I wanted to apologize for that, too."

"Thanks," I said. I guessed he didn't *really* have so much to apologize for, but I appreciated it anyway. Besides, it wasn't as though he'd been entirely innocent. "You really just came by to check on me? Not for the lobster rolls?"

"You know I came for the lobster rolls," he deadpanned. I'd brought him one not long after I'd started working here, stopping by his 7-Eleven on my way to pick up Brad, and he'd kept texting me about how much he'd loved it and needed another one. He'd had one the day he'd come with his mom and sister, even though it hadn't been on the specials menu that day.

"Plus," he added, "I got the feeling Noah wouldn't be too happy if I showed up at the beach house."

I scoffed. "Noah can suck it."

"Ouch, strong words for someone in love, Elle."

"Sorry." I sighed, rubbing my face. "I do love him. I do. I just meant he can suck it because we're friends, and it's not like he can stop you showing up to the beach house. Amanda's been staying with us and if I'm cool with that, then—"

"Yeah," Levi murmured, then said, like everyone else, "but he didn't kiss Amanda."

I glanced at Levi. His cheeks were flushed pink and he hastily withdrew his arm from around me, looking away.

I could feel the awkwardness radiating from him and hated it. I never should have kissed him on Thanksgiving. It really hadn't been fair of me.

But like I said, I wasn't perfect.

Hoping to at least lighten the mood a little, I nudged him in the side. "Hey, listen. Thanks for coming to check up on me and putting up with me while I just off-loaded all my stupid stuff onto you like that. You know you can tell me your stupid stuff anytime you need."

"Yeah, I know." He smiled at me. There was something withdrawn about it, which I assumed was due to the lingering awkwardness of him mentioning our kiss. We were close, but I didn't know him as well as I did Lee: he wasn't always as easy to read.

"Speaking of coming by the beach house," I went on, "you're definitely coming by for Fourth of July, right?"

Levi sighed. "I . . ."

"Oh, please? Please, please, please? The whole gang is coming! Everyone's going to be there and it won't be the same without you! Please, Levi?"

He made a show of sighing and rolling his eyes, and then broke into a smile. "Of course I'll be there. Anything for you, Elle."

Chapter Twenty-Five

That night, after I helped clean and close up the restaurant, I sat back on the rocks for a while, where just a few hours ago I'd taken a long-ass break from work to have an admittedly very one-sided heart-to-heart with Levi.

I checked my phone, having ignored it until now.

A few messages from Lee, but none of them too important or pressing.

A couple from my dad. How about dinner next week with Linda? Did I mind that she would be joining us for Fourth of July? He really thought I'd like her if I got to know her but he understood I had a lot going on right now and he understood this might be weird for me. . . .

Two from Levi. Some baking joke in meme form, followed by: *Glad we got to chat earlier! Hope your day got better x*

Nothing from Noah, but I was surprised to see one from Amanda. In all caps.

WILL YOU AND YOUR DUMBASS BOYFRIEND PLEASE SORT YOUR SHIT OUT. I CAN'T KEEP LOOK-ING AT HIS STUPID POUTY FACE. ALSO I'LL BE BACK

AT THE HOUSE TOMORROW AND WILL BRING MORE WINE—SHALL WE KICK THE BOYS OUT AND HAVE A PROPER GIRLS' NIGHT?

Then: *Sorry for all the caps, his stupid face and all the whining just make me kind of nuts. Like, why is it so hard for him to just TALK TO YOU?????? Also, you SHOULD TALK TO HIM TOO. Love ya! xxxx*

I laughed a little. There was a definite irony to be found in the fact that while Amanda had been such a big part of me breaking up with Noah last year, she was the one trying to help pull our relationship back together now and looking out for us. She really was a sweetheart.

And . . . I really did need to talk to Noah and clear the air.

I was just turning my car on when a headlight swept around the corner of the road and the familiar noise of Noah's motorcycle drew near. I blinked, startled, killing the engine and jumping out of my car as he parked his bike and climbed off, tossing the helmet aside.

"Noah—"

I barely got his name out before he crossed the distance between us in a few strides, wrapped his arms around me, and pulled me into a searing kiss that set my entire body on fire. All the tension and the irritation that had been hanging around me for the last couple of days went up in the flames, too, scattering like embers on the breeze, and I forgot everything that had been bothering me as his mouth moved over mine.

When we finally stopped for breath, I uncurled my fingers where they'd fisted in his jacket.

"Hi," I whispered.

He chuckled. The sound reverberated through his chest against my palms. "Hi."

"Is this the part where you apologize and I apologize and we try not to do this again?"

He smirked, his mouth still against my skin. "It is. Should I have music? Roses?"

"You're telling me you didn't bring a boom box, John Cusack?"

"Who's John Cusack?"

I laughed, nudging my lips back against his. Eventually he drew back, holding my face in one hand, the other brushing stray hairs back where they'd fallen out of my ponytail.

"I know the bucket list is important," Noah told me. "I know this summer is important for you and Lee. I know it's a big deal, you not going to Berkeley. I promise you, I know. It's just . . . I miss you?"

"Are you asking me or telling me?" I couldn't resist saying. He was too easy to tease sometimes—and teasing Noah was too familiar a habit to let go of, even during a more serious conversation like this one.

He groaned, leaning down and pressing his forehead to mine, his eyes shut. "I get it, I do, but it's hard seeing you make so much time for Lee when *I* want to spend time with you. I *know* it sounds stupid, because I see you every day and we sleep in the same bed together, and it's not like we're never around each other, but it just feels like it's been a while since it was just us two, you know? Without a whole crowd hanging around us, or without you needing to run around looking after your brother or doing stuff with Lee or working. And I'm not trying to say you shouldn't do those things . . . but I miss you."

"I miss you, too," I told him. I knew exactly what he meant.

"And it's hard for me to watch you running yourself into the ground, trying to make everyone happy."

"I'm not . . ."

Okay, maybe I was. A little. Just a very little.

I smiled, nudging my hand against his chest again.

"I can't wait for next year." He sighed. "I know we'll both be busy with classes and stuff, and you'll have new friends to hang out with, and maybe work, but . . . it won't be so crazy."

"Yeah. No flash mobs or race days."

"And like I said, we could . . . we could maybe see about living together. I know it hasn't been, like, the easiest thing, but I don't think we've done *that* bad, right?"

"Even though I stole your side of the bed?"

Noah laughed. "Yeah."

"Yeah. I don't think we've done too bad."

"I've missed you," he breathed again, kissing my nose and drawing a giggle out of me. "I hate fighting with you like that."

"Me too."

"But I will fight *for* you," he told me.

I was touched, and the intensity of his gaze along with the sincerity behind his quiet words made my heart skip a beat—but I still snorted with laughter and buried my head in his chest. "And you think *I'm* the cheesy romantic."

"I thought you liked me being all romantic and shit."

"I like you," I told him, plain and simple. "So . . . how about we head back home and I show you just *how* much?"

"Now that," he said, kissing me once more, "sounds like something I can't pass up."

. . .

The next day, I wasn't working until the dinner shift. Noah had promised Amanda he'd meet her for breakfast, but he lingered in bed a little longer than he should've to cuddle and make out with me. I'd fallen back to sleep after he left, the stress of the past few days catching up to me all of a sudden. Judging by the glaring sunlight that poured into the room even though the blinds were shut, it had to be almost lunchtime by the time I finally woke up again and dragged myself out of bed.

I didn't even bother to wash my face or clean my teeth before stumbling out to the lounge. Lee was lying on the couch, playing a game.

"Look who decided to join the land of the living," he said. "Nice hair."

I patted it, feeling how tangled and messy it was, lifting a good couple of inches away from my scalp. Wow, I must've been a *great* sight for Noah to wake up to this morning.

Ignoring Lee's comment, I fixed myself a coffee and looked around. It felt as though I'd hardly been here the last few days—I wasn't sure when the beach house had turned into such a junkyard. Pizza boxes were stacked up by the window. Empty mugs and cups were dotted around. Clothes I could only assume were dirty littered the floor.

It surprised me. Rachel was pretty uptight about us keeping things clean. Had she not been around much the last few days, too? Had she decided to give up?

Or, more likely, had Lee managed to turn this place into such a mess just this morning alone?

"You wanna maybe tidy up in here?" I asked him.

"Okay, *Mom.* I'm kinda busy right now."

"I'm serious, Lee. I thought your parents said they have buyers coming this afternoon? And that guy's meant to be coming to measure for new flooring . . ."

"He can measure around some mess."

"Lee!"

"Fine," he grumbled, pausing the game and tossing aside the controller. He surveyed the room for a second before starting to gather up trash. "And the buyers canceled just this morning. For the record."

"What? But that's . . . that's, like, the *eighth* time people have canceled viewing this place."

"Guess they keep changing their minds."

"Lee, are you . . . Have you . . ."

"Careful, Shelly. You know if you finish that question, you're gonna get an honest answer."

I sighed, throwing up my hands and going back to pouring my coffee. "You know what, you're right. I'd rather stick to plausible deniability, thanks."

"Good choice." He threw me a smile. "So what time do you want to leave tomorrow?"

"What?"

"Tomorrow," he said again, pausing to look at me. The enthusiasm froze on his face, his features stiffening. The hopeful lilt in his voice faltered only slightly as he chuckled and said, "You know. *Tomorrow*. Our trip to Berkeley?"

Oh, *fuck*.

"Elle?"

I was the biggest asshole in the world. I couldn't *believe* I'd forgotten all about the trip this weekend. We'd had it planned for ages now, and here I'd been thinking I had a Saturday clear of bucket-list plans. I hadn't even questioned it. I'd just sort of assumed Lee had plans with Rachel or something.

Wrong.

He had plans with *me*. Big plans. Huge plans.

The absolute most *monumental* plans of the entire summer.

"Seriously?" he cried, reading me way too easily.

"I'm sorry! I don't know how I forgot about it. I really don't, Lee. And I've made plans with Noah. . . . We have reservations at some fancy restaurant your mom recommended, and we were gonna head out to that chocolate shop he took me to last year for my birthday."

"Of course you have plans with Noah," he said dryly.

He dropped his pile in the garbage and unearthed a laundry basket from under a bunch of throw pillows and started gathering up the clothes instead, snatching them up one at a time.

I gulped, seeing Lee's face all scrunched up. He was angry, sure, but it was worse than that—he was plain old upset. I really couldn't cope if he started to cry.

I'd thought forgetting about eighties mini golf had been shitty of me, but this . . . this *really* took the biscuit.

"Noah," he snapped, "who you're gonna see, like, literally *all* the time next year. Noah, who you can hang out with any other day aside from tomorrow. It's just really . . . It's real fucking rich, you know, Elle? You gave me shit for applying to Brown because of Rachel and then you went and did the *exact same thing*, only worse, because you kept your Harvard application secret from me."

"Lee—"

"I honestly thought we were done with all that after I found out about you dating Noah behind my back. But, nope, you did it again. And you're doing it again now."

Here it is, I thought. The anger that had been simmering away since I'd told him about Harvard, that he'd been working so hard to crush down and ignore in favor of an epic, fun summer.

"I'm sorry," I told him again. "Lee, I am, but I've . . . It's not like that. I'm not *sneaking around* or anything. I just made a mistake this weekend . . . and with mini golf. I messed up, okay? But we talked about college. You said—"

"I know what I said!" Lee erupted, tossing the laundry basket down now. It spilled onto its side. "I'm super proud of you, Elle, but I'm allowed to be pissed off, too, okay? *Excuse me* for being upset that our plans for college have gone to shit so you can live it up in Boston with your boyfriend."

He sighed, pinching the bridge of his nose. My hands were trembling now, but all I could do was wait, let him say his piece.

"I know you're trying to make up for it with the bucket list, Shelly, and I appreciate that, but . . . it's not . . . I hate that it feels like a last-ditch effort to rescue our friendship, okay?"

"Whoa, hold on. Since when did our friendship need *rescuing*?"

"Since you went on this manic one-woman mission to give us the best last summer ever before we start college!"

"Because I thought that'd make you happy and make up for me not being at Berkeley!"

"You know what would make up for you not coming to Berkeley? You going there with me this weekend."

"I already made plans with Noah. I genuinely can't believe I forgot tomorrow was Berkeley, but it was an honest mistake. Noah and I *really* need some quality time this weekend, you know? It's just been a bit tense with everything going on. You get that, right? What about Sunday? We can go Sunday instead."

I was working, but I could try to swap my shift with

someone. And I had a bunch of stuff to do, but that could wait. We'd talked about going to the arcade again and I was supposed to look after Brad so Dad could go to dinner with Linda, but I could make it work. Noah could totally look after Brad for a little while till we got back from Berkeley; Brad would love that, I knew.

But Lee informed me, "I have plans on Sunday."

"Oh. Oh, r-right."

"Can't you change your plans with Noah?"

"I . . ."

He took my silence for what it was: that I was *choosing* not to do that.

"We can't do Berkeley another weekend, Lee? What's the rush? We've got all summer."

"The plan," he said through his teeth, "was to go to Berkeley tomorrow. And that's what I'm gonna do. You do whatever you want, Elle."

"Lee . . ."

He kept tidying, saying nothing, not even looking at me. I knew better than to push him or keep apologizing.

When had my life turned into this circus act of spinning plates? And why was it that every time I got a handle on Lee's plate, I lost control of Noah's? When did it become so hard to manage being Lee's best friend and Noah's girlfriend?

When did that even become a thing I had to *manage*?

I could tell Noah I couldn't hang out with him tomorrow

anymore. I could tell him I was going to Berkeley with Lee. I *could*, but I needed this weekend with Noah, too. This wasn't just something I was doing for him.

I could suggest Rachel and Noah come along and we make a group thing of it—but that would ruin the whole point. This was the compromise for me bailing on our plans to go to Berkeley together, and all I'd done was . . .

Bail on these plans to go to Berkeley together, too.

Way to go, Elle.

"We can find another day to go," I said, hating the silence. "Lee?"

"Sure. Maybe."

Which meant: *No.*

"Lee, I'm sorry."

"Yeah, I know."

The silence stretched on, and this time I let it. As I made myself some breakfast and drank my coffee, Lee cleaned up the beach house. I watched him move around, but it was like someone had put a pane of frosted glass between us. Like I was watching him on a screen that hadn't finished buffering properly.

I could practically see the void that yawned between us.

But if I closed this one, I'd just open a new one between me and Noah.

I hated feeling like I had to choose.

It was a draining, horrible few minutes while Lee put in a load of laundry. He came back into the kitchen, and I said quietly, "I didn't mean to make you feel like I was trying to rescue our friendship, or make this whole bucket-list thing feel forced. I just wanted to do something to make you happy. Make some awesome memories, and help say goodbye, I guess. To the beach house. To being kids. But not to each other, Lee."

He sighed, giving me a half-hearted smile. "It's okay. I know you've got a lot going on. And I wasn't mad about the mini golf. It was a genuine mistake, it's all good. And I'm not mad about Harvard. It's . . . it's fucking *Harvard*. Of course you're gonna go. That was about more than Noah. I really am proud of you. But, you know, I really thought that this . . . I thought you'd come through for me on this one."

He broke my heart.

He really, really did.

"I don't like fighting with you, Shelly, and I'm not gonna. I love you. Always will. You do what you've gotta do. But I'm going to Berkeley tomorrow, with or without you."

I didn't say anything. I didn't have anything *to* say to make this better. Not when we both knew I'd already made my decision.

●   ●   ●

Later that night, when I was tossing and turning and unable to sleep, Noah wrapped his arm around me, tugging me into his body and spooning me.

"What's up with you tonight?" he murmured, tucking his head over my shoulder.

"Sorry. I didn't mean to wake you up."

"Are— Elle, are you crying?"

"No." I sniffled, turning my face into the pillow, using it to mop up a stray tear.

"You're a real bad liar, Elle. Talk to me. What's up?"

"It's . . . Lee's going to Berkeley tomorrow. Like we talked about."

"Number twenty-two," Noah said. "I remember. You guys were gonna go up for the"—his body went rigid as he realized—"weekend. Shit. *Shit*, Elle, why didn't you say something yesterday?"

"I forgot. Till this morning."

"I'll cancel our reservations," he said. "It's fine."

I knew it was. I knew he wouldn't be mad, not over this one and not after we'd talked things over yesterday.

But I shook my head. "It doesn't matter now. I already let him down just forgetting about it. It won't be the same. He'll think I'm only going so he'll stop being mad at me."

"Elle." Noah sighed. "Not everything has to be perfect. We can rearrange. You should go to Berkeley."

Not everything has to be perfect.

"But this does have to be perfect, Noah." I sniffled again, frustrated with myself for crying, and wriggled around so I was facing him. "That was the whole point of this summer and the bucket list. It's like . . . it's like with the road trip Lee and I took over spring break. Sure, we didn't *have* to stop off in New York on our way to Boston, but it would've ruined the whole plan and the trip. This is just like that. We were meant to do it all just the way we planned. If I go now—"

"If you go," Noah reasoned, nuzzling his nose against mine, "you'll get to tick off bucket-list item number twenty-two. You'll get your trip to Berkeley with Lee like you guys planned, and you'll have a great time. Isn't that the most important thing? If you're not going because of me, don't even worry about that, okay? I know this is a huge deal for you two. We can hang out some other time. Hey, we've got all next year, like you said, haven't we?"

I groaned, burrowing into the space between his face and the pillows. "Stop being right. You'd better not have that smug look on your face."

"I'm sure I don't know what you're talking about, Shelly."

"You *sound* smug."

"When have I ever been smug?"

I pushed a fist into his chest weakly, not pulling my face out of the pillow yet. Noah kissed the little bit of the side of my face he could reach.

"What time is he leaving?"

"He said something about leaving at seven." I felt him stretch over me, heard the quiet sounds of his thumb tapping at my phone.

"There. Alarm set for six-thirty. Now, you think you can stop tossing and turning and get to sleep? Some of us don't have to work tomorrow."

I told Noah I loved him and fell asleep easily in his arms after that.

At six-thirty the next morning, I jumped out of bed as soon as the alarm went off, instead of snoozing it for a while to buy myself another two minutes under the covers the way I always did. I all but skipped across the hallway to tell Lee I'd be coming with him, but—

His and Rachel's bed was empty. It was made, the covers pulled up neatly.

I ran to the kitchen, but there was no sign of them.

I flung myself out the front door.

His car was gone.

Chapter Twenty-Six

Lee, it turned out, had gone to Berkeley for the day with Rachel. Ashton and his girlfriend met them up there. They had a great day, if Lee's Instagram story was anything to go by. They did everything Lee and I had talked about.

The worst part was, I wasn't even jealous. I didn't resent Lee that day in Berkeley. And I didn't feel like I was missing out. I knew I should've felt like that. Hadn't I been set on going there for college practically my whole life?

So why did I suddenly feel like Lee was the only reason I wanted to be there?

Noah did his best to cheer me up. I was so mad at myself for feeling so shitty about letting Lee down and missing the trip to Berkeley, it kept me distracted all day. Noah didn't seem to mind, though, which I really appreciated. We spent most of the day together on the beach, and he'd made reservations for us at some fancy restaurant, so we got all dressed up to go and eat five exorbitantly priced and too-small-to-be-really-filling courses.

Eating at some fancy restaurant with Noah made me

feel so grown up. I could picture us doing stuff like this at Harvard. I could picture us in some apartment together, cooking. I could picture us walking hand-in-hand around the city like we did over spring break, getting coffees and studying.

I wasn't so distracted by the end of dinner. I was even less distracted by the time we got back to the empty beach house. Having the day to just the two of us had made us both giddy. We didn't even make it to the bedroom before ripping each other's clothes off.

"We should probably go to bed," I told Noah afterward, lying across him on the couch with my legs tucked between his, my fingers lightly drawing circles on his chest. "Before anybody gets home."

"They're not coming home," he told me. "Lee said yesterday he was planning to stay over at Rachel's tonight. They've got plans tomorrow. Which means," he added, nipping at my earlobe with his teeth, "you're going nowhere."

We fell asleep on the sagging old couch, a faded throw tossed over us.

I woke up with a crick in my neck and Noah's elbow sticking into my stomach and to the sound of the front door slamming shut. A sigh tinkled through the room as someone started pottering around in the kitchen.

"I know, I know, I said I was spending a few days with my parents, but it's driving me *crazy*. I can't stand it. Every other minute it's 'I'm keeping the wedding china' and 'Good, I never liked that crap anyway; I want the air miles' and 'You wouldn't have those air miles if not for me' and 'Amanda, tell your mother I'm keeping the air miles' and 'Amanda, tell your father he can have the air miles when he stops sleeping with that tart from the wine club' and 'Amanda, tell your mother I'm not sleeping with her and she's not a tart.' I swear to God, I'm going to kill them both, and then *I'll* get the air miles and the wedding china and all the other bullshit they're arguing over in my inheritance. See how they like it *then*."

I froze against Noah, who was stirring at all the noise, as Amanda slammed down a mug and the box of tea June kept on the kitchen counter.

"Uh," I said, for lack of anything better to say.

"Oh, don't worry, sweetie." She waved a hand at me. "I've walked in on my roommate having sex with a whole bunch of people. Not all at once, obviously. She always forgets to put a sock on the door or whatever. Plus, I've seen *that* moron running butt naked across a football field after losing a bet. This is *nothing*."

"Uh," I said again.

"Wha's going on?" Noah mumbled, wriggling his arm. "My arm's dead." He tried the other one, shifting the elbow out of my stomach to rub his hand over his face and look over at the kitchen. "Oh, thank God. I thought it was my mom."

"Nope, just me." Amanda grinned and waggled her fingers before her scowl reappeared and she went back to slamming things around in the kitchen. "Normally I wouldn't barge in, but, hey, if you give me a key and my parents are driving me up the wall with this whole divorce thing, I'm going to barge in. You guys want coffee? I'll make you coffee."

"I thought this was, like . . . a last-ditch family holiday?" I said, recalling my previous conversation with her about her parents.

"It was *supposed* to be, but neither of them seem to be able to remember that. Pair of tossers."

"Hey, Amanda, you think you could pass us that blanket?"

She kept ranting, launching into this whole thing about how her mom was mad at her dad for a supposed affair, but how *she'd* been having an affair, too, and they were both as bad as each other—but she did take pity on us and passed me the blanket I'd pointed to, turning her back to give us a little privacy while Noah and I wrapped the blankets around ourselves and gathered up our clothes from across the room.

I got the impression that Amanda wasn't looking for sympathy so much as someone to vent to. I liked her—but not enough to hang around with her wearing only a blanket. I figured Noah could take the lead on this one.

"I'm gonna go take a shower," I said. "I have to be at work in a few hours anyway."

"You want pancakes, Elle? I'm gonna make pancakes. Ooh! A waffle iron. I'm gonna make waffles."

"You do you," I told her. "I'll eat anything."

"I'll have both," Noah told her.

She whacked his knuckles lightly with the wooden spoon

she'd just grabbed. "You'll get what I make, pretty boy. So, anyway, then they start arguing about who gets custody of the wine club. The sodding wine club! Not me, their *daughter*, the wine club! And Mum only wants that so Dad will have to go somewhere else with the tart. Although she's not really a tart. She's my old Brownie leader. She's quite lovely, really. And . . ."

Amanda's rant faded out of earshot once I was in the bathroom. I felt bad for her, I really did. I decided my own rant about Linda that I'd been dying to talk to her about could wait. I'd told Noah about it all yesterday, and he'd been sympathetic enough to tide me over for a while.

Back in the kitchen, they'd moved on from Amanda's parents' looming divorce to talking about the house.

". . . I know there's kind of no point in cleaning things up if they're only going to tear it down," Noah was saying, "but not everyone who's interested is a developer. Some of them just want to buy the beach house as it is. Or, you know, they say they do, but they keep canceling."

"How do you know there are developers interested?" I asked him, pulling my wet hair into a bun. "Did your mom say something?"

"Lee told me."

"How does *he* know?"

Noah gave me a flat look and said, "Elle, you know I don't ask him questions I don't want to hear the answers to."

"Plausible deniability. I'm with you there."

"He changed the number," Amanda told us, clearly only

half listening as she made me up a plate of waffles, smothering them in chopped fruit. "On the sign outside. It's his phone number."

"What part of 'plausible deniability' don't you get?" Noah barked at her, but there was a playfulness to his scorn. He sighed, rubbing a knuckle between his eyes. "I should've guessed he'd pull a stunt like that."

"You're telling me you guys missed that? He's your best friend! And *your* brother! How did you not know that?"

Noah and I both pulled a face. "Uh, because his number hasn't changed in about seven years?" I said. "There is no chance in hell I'd be able to tell you Lee's cell number. I barely remember mine sometimes."

Amanda shook her head at both of us. "What, and you guys thought the painter just canceled last week out of nowhere, and the guy coming to check the roof 'forgot' his ladder, and that every buyer wanting to view this place mysteriously changed their mind? And none of that was, like, at all suspicious? You guys are such *morons*."

"Plausible deniability," I repeated.

But hearing her lay it all out like that, I couldn't say I was surprised. Lee had been against selling the beach house since the very start. This was *exactly* the kind of thing he would pull to stop it all going ahead.

(Plus, it wasn't like I'd been around that much to really pay it a lot of attention.)

"You think we should talk to him?" Noah asked me.

"I'm not doing it," Amanda said. She slid my breakfast in front of me. "I like the kid, but he's not my problem."

"That's really gonna put me back in his good books." I snorted, moping over my plate of waffles. "Yesterday I missed the trip to Berkeley, and now you want me to tell him to stop getting in the way of your parents selling the beach house? Nope. I like the kid, but he's not my problem," I said. "This one's all yours."

"Oh, great. *Now* you decide you're not part of the family. What happened to 'this beach house is just as much mine as it is yours'?"

I waved my fork at him dismissively. "This one's all yours, Noah."

He grumbled but eventually muttered, "Fine. Jeez. I guess we've just gotta hope our mom doesn't find out. . . ."

Chapter Twenty-Seven

On the morning of Fourth of July, a weird tension hung around the beach house. I hadn't really seen Lee since he'd gone off to Berkeley without me—he'd gotten back on the Sunday while I was at work, and we'd somehow managed to stay out of each other's way later that night.

Amanda was back staying with us. She was making pancakes when Noah and I got up.

"My mother's working," she told us. "And my dad is out playing golf with some guys he met. It's not like Independence Day is a big deal for us, so we don't have any plans. We *did*, back when this was still a last-ditch happy-family holiday, but . . ." Amanda blew a raspberry to make her point.

"You're welcome to celebrate it with us," I offered, like she wasn't already counting on doing just that.

"I'm going to spend every holiday with you guys if you're not careful," she joked. "If my parents keep fighting, I'll be begging for a spot at your Christmas dinner, too. Oh look!" she said. "I have strawberries and blueberries and cream. Red, white, and blue! Themed breakfast!"

"She's more into this holiday than we are," I stage-whispered to Noah from behind a hand, giving her a melo-dramatically wary look. "Do you think we should, like, go throw all her tea in the sea to remind her what today's all about?"

"I vote we throw *her* in the sea," Noah replied in the same way, hiding his mouth behind his hand.

"Hey, don't forget who's making you guys breakfast."

She finished arranging a dollop of whipped cream on one of the plates before gesturing for us to sit, then putting heaped, colorful plates in front of us and chopping more fruit.

"Thanks," Noah said. "You really don't have to."

"Oh, please." Amanda waved the knife dismissively in our direction. "You know I'm an early bird, mister. And a little cooking is the least I can do for you guys, for letting me stay. You have *no* idea."

"None at all," I deadpanned. "It's not like we heard the rant for, like, three hours solid yesterday."

Noah cut me a look but relaxed when Amanda laughed.

"What's so funny? Oh, man, *something* smells good." Lee hopped into the kitchen, clicking his ankles together and then hunching forward, eyes shut and head leading, as he weaved through the kitchen, sniffing noisily, mimicking a cartoon character who'd just detected a pie on a windowsill.

"Mmm," he said, straightening up and leaning around Amanda. "You're back again? I thought we finally got rid of you."

"Lee," Noah huffed.

"Guess you didn't try hard enough," Amanda told him, waving her spatula before going back to easing the pancake away from the edges of the pan.

"Pancakes?"

"Happy Fourth of July!"

Lee turned around to look at us. He arched an eyebrow, catching my eye and whispering loudly, "She knows what this holiday is all about, right?"

I felt a rush of relief at how normal he was acting.

"I'm not convinced, so we're doing a whole reenactment for her later. I get to be Jefferson," I told Lee. "You can be John Adams."

"Aw, man. Can't I be Franklin? I'll get the old kite out of the den and everything. I will even throw in the Twinkie I found under my seat in the car yesterday."

"Hmm. You drive a hard bargain, Lee Flynn."

"You know, Noah," Amanda announced, "when you told me they were a pair of freaks, I was like, 'Nah, he's just exaggerating, he doesn't mean it,' but, oh man, did you *mean it*." She finished planting another pancake on a plate, then delicately decorated the stack with blueberries, chopped strawberries, and a flourish of whipped cream before handing Lee the plate. "Voilà."

"Hey! Red, white, and blue! Nice!"

"I'm glad someone appreciates it."

"We appreciate it," I told her, my mouth full of pancake, gesturing my fork between me and Noah.

"Is Rachel up?"

"She's taking a shower," Lee told Amanda, who set about making even more pancake mixture.

With Lee sitting next to me eating his breakfast, the crackle of tension I'd been expecting appeared between us. The cracks that had been there a couple of days ago when I forgot about the trip to Berkeley were back. His elbow knocked mine while we ate, but he felt a million miles away in that moment.

It was only afterward, when the two of us were doing the dishes, that he said, "Noah told me, you know. That you guys changed your plans."

"I thought you weren't leaving till seven," I mumbled. "You were gone when I got up."

"We were ready early, and . . . I didn't know we were supposed to be waiting for you." He nudged me, catching my eye again—looking at me properly for only the second time that morning. "I'm sorry, Shelly. I really am."

I shook my head, focusing on the plate I was drying off. If I looked at Lee too long, I was kind of worried I'd start crying. "You're right. You didn't know. How could you have known? I should've, like, I don't know. Texted you. Or something."

"Maybe we can go another weekend. Just us two. Don't get me wrong, it was a great day with Rachel, and Ashton gave us the grand tour, and his girlfriend's great, too, but it wasn't the same without you there. We should go. I can recreate Ashton's tour and everything."

He made my heart melt.

"That sounds perfect. Thank you, Lee," I whispered, resting my head on his shoulder.

Maybe, at least for today, I could keep both Noah's and Lee's plates spinning steadily.

• • •

June and Matthew showed up midmorning. June, Rachel, Noah, and Amanda headed straight back out to buy some extra supplies for the day, while Lee, Matthew, and I got to work tidying the place up and getting things ready for the party.

Lee's parents had brought a big white folding table. We set it up outside, rearranging the rest of the furniture to fit it in. I laid out stacks of paper plates, plastic cutlery, and napkins, while Lee hung a string of flags around the porch to decorate. Matthew got started making a vat of potato salad—his mom's recipe and a Fourth of July tradition for us.

When the others got back, Amanda was decked out in a big glittery blue cowboy hat with a red ribbon tied around it and a sprig of white stars sticking out of the top, and she had a huge plastic flag that was probably intended to be a tablecloth tied around her neck like a cape.

"This is my first time celebrating this holiday," she

argued. "I'm going all out. Chances are, I won't be back next summer."

"Oh, sweetie, you're welcome to spend holidays with us anytime," June told her warmly. "Elle, what time are your dad and brother getting here? He's got the ribs and the fireworks. And Linda's bringing pie."

"I . . . I thought you were making pie."

Although, now that she'd said it, I hadn't seen any and I guessed we had enough to get by without making pies as well.

"Well, I was planning on it, but Linda offered, so . . . It's nice! Don't you think?" June smiled at me. "She seems really great, Elle."

"You've— Wait, you met her?"

"We all went to dinner last week. Your dad didn't tell you?"

"I guess he forgot."

I gritted my teeth and went back to prepping salad. Fine, great, *Linda* was bringing pie. Whoopee. Good for her. They wouldn't be as great as June's, but . . . fine.

Much as I wanted to stay out of her way, I knew I'd run into her at some point. At least it couldn't be as awful as last time, right? Or anywhere near as awkward and weird as the first time I'd met Amanda?

But I couldn't be the only one who thought it was all moving a little fast, right? A month ago, I'd had no idea about her, and now she was bringing over pies to spend the holiday with us.

No, Elle, come on. Not today.

I did my best to shake it off. Today was supposed to be something special. Not just because all of us were getting together to party and eat way too much food, not just because all our friends were coming over, but because it was the last Fourth of July at the beach house. It was special. It mattered.

So I'd swallow whatever feelings I had toward Linda (none of which, I hated to admit, were particularly favorable) and enjoy the day. Hell, I'd even enjoy her damn pies.

Besides, I'd only just gotten a grip on things with Lee and Noah. I didn't think I could handle any kind of emotional turmoil over anyone else right now.

We took a break long enough to get changed. While Amanda was almost aggressively red, white, and blue with her extra accessories, Rachel kept it simple in a pair of denim shorts and a cute T-shirt. My outfit was a happy medium between the two: while my shorts were bright red, the loose cami I threw on over my bikini was pale blue, and I finished the look with a pair of dangly silver star earrings. And while Noah, like Rachel, wasn't particularly dressed up, Lee had a pair of American-flag swim shorts on, paired with a white T-shirt with a gray star pattern. We did love a theme, after all.

Dixon, Olly, and Warren arrived midafternoon. A couple of Rachel's friends were only minutes behind—including Lisa, Cam's girlfriend. Olivia and Faith showed up with Jon Fletcher and a couple of the football guys. Ashton and his girlfriend arrived next. I threw myself into playing hostess, chattering away to everybody as they showed up.

June ushered everyone outside, and we quickly decided to head down to the beach to hang out and start tossing around a football—but only after pilfering a bunch of snacks from the kitchen while June and Matthew weren't looking.

"Plus"—Warren produced a bottle of vodka with a flourish and a grin—"I got this for later."

"Or now," Olivia suggested, bouncing over to him to pluck the bottle out of his hands. She unscrewed the cap, took a sip, and then sputtered, almost spitting it all back up onto the sand and sending the rest of us into fits of laughter. Half the group suddenly found themselves in a competition to see who could take a sip of straight vodka without reacting.

Jon Fletcher was pretty good, but Amanda won by a mile, taking three large gulps without so much as blinking, to everyone's astonishment and a round of applause.

As the afternoon wore on, more people started to arrive, filtering down to the beach to join us. They brought more drinks, some snacks. Someone brought a Bluetooth speaker and set it on someone else's towel. People sunbathed, swam, played ball . . . Jon Fletcher made the mistake of lying down to take a nap and was currently being buried in sand up to his chin.

Our first night at the beach house, the housewarming party Noah and Lee had organized had made the place feel cramped and crazy. Today might have started out as something for a more intimate crowd, but it definitely hadn't turned out that way. It wasn't just our close friends—somehow, word had gotten out. This was a whole thing.

When I pointed out as much to Lee, he just shrugged and said, "Hey, gotta do this one justice, Shelly."

"Guess you've got a point."

I headed back up to the beach house to check on things. The five of us had been taking it in shifts to go see when the barbecue was starting up and food was ready, and right now it was my turn.

My dad was just starting to fire up the barbecue, and Matthew was laying out platters of meat next to him. They were deep in discussion about something. A cry came from the pool, followed by a splash—Brad and two of his friends were playing there. One of them had a water gun and squirted me with it as I approached.

"Oh no! I've . . . been . . . attacked!" I gasped, staggering and clutching at my wet leg. "Tell my brother . . . he . . . gets all my . . . *agh.*"

I collapsed to the ground.

"I heard gets all her money," Brad announced. "Right, Dad?"

"Hmm, I heard gets all her chores."

I climbed back up, stopping to ruffle Brad's hair and dunk him abruptly under the water on my way to say hi to my dad. I gave him a hug.

"Happy Fourth, bud."

"You too, Dad."

"You guys having a good time down there?" Dad asked.

"Sure sounds like it," Matthew added with a smile.

"Are we too loud?"

"Nah, it's good. It's not like we've got many neighbors left around here right now to worry about, huh?"

"I guess so. Yeah, it's . . . it's great. I'm just starting to think we don't have enough food for everyone. I swear, I thought this wasn't gonna be such a big thing."

"Don't even worry about it," Dad reassured me. "A lot of your friends brought food. We're gonna be eating hot dogs and potato salad and pie for weeks. Hey, bud, uh . . . L-Linda's in the kitchen with June. It'd be good if you maybe went to say hi."

I wanted to tell him I wasn't a little kid, that he didn't need to *tell* me to go say hi to her, but he looked so god-damn nervous I didn't have the heart to bite back with a sarcastic remark. I wasn't used to seeing my dad nervous. But right now, his eyebrows furrowed behind his prescription sunglasses, his forehead lined with deep creases, and he snapped the barbecue tongs closed repeatedly, agitatedly.

So I chirped, "Sure! Of course. And, um, a couple of people brought some drinks? Not much, just a little. Maybe keep Brad and his buddies off the beach for a little while?"

My dad sighed. "Why am I not surprised?"

"So long as nobody pukes in the pool, it's all good," Matthew told me. "Anyone pukes in the pool, or anywhere else for that matter, you kids are cleaning it up."

"Roger that." I saluted them both and left them to the barbecuing.

Inside, June and Linda were chatting and laughing over something, moving about the kitchen together organizing bowls and platters, many of which I didn't recognize, and I could only assume—

"Oh, Elle! Thank your friends again from us. They've all brought so much food. Although"—June held up a tub of potato salad, sniffing and squinting at it—"if Matthew asks, their potato salad isn't as good as his."

I mimed zipping my lips shut.

Linda was wearing a gray linen sundress with a brown woven belt tied around her waist and matching flat brown sandals. She gave me a smile that was borderline wary and said a hopeful, "Hi, Elle. It's great to see you again."

I remembered how nervous my dad had been to tell me about Linda, and how nervous he'd looked again outside. She'd apparently heard so much about me; I imagined that she hadn't been overly honest about our first meeting, since my dad hadn't said too much about it to me and what a disaster it had been. Maybe I owed her one for that. Brad liked her. June and Matthew seemed to like her. Dad *obviously* liked her a lot.

Okay, take two. Let's try this again.

Drawing a deep breath, I decided in that instant to give her a second chance at a first impression.

I mean, she sure looked like a nice person.

"You too," I told her, giving her the broadest, sincerest

smile I could manage. "And June said you brought pie! That's really nice of you."

I didn't miss the relief on her face over the fact I didn't snipe at her.

"Oh, it's nothing. My pleasure."

"Did you, um . . ." I glanced at June, who gave me an encouraging little nod. "Did you not, uh . . . want to spend the day with your family?"

"My parents have their own plans for this evening," she told me with a laugh, not explaining any further, and I decided that as willing as I was to give her a second chance, I didn't care *that* much to ask. "I saw them this morning. And my ex and I aren't exactly on 'spend the holiday together' terms."

"Oh. Uh, right. Well . . ."

June gave me another look, and I didn't have to be a genius to figure out what it meant.

"Well," I tried again, "we're happy to have you here."

There was a knock at the door, and a familiar voice yelled, "Hey, anybody home? Sorry we're late!"

Grateful for the distraction, I excused myself, running out to greet Cam.

"Sorry," he sighed. "I had some car trouble." He grinned at me, giving me a quick hug before stepping aside to reveal Levi, laden down with Tupperware.

"What he means," Levi said, "is he got lost."

Cam rolled his eyes. "Dude. Come on."

Levi laughed, then held the Tupperware up. "I come

bearing baked goods. Brownies and snickerdoodles and cake pops."

"*We,*" Cam corrected him. "We come bearing baked goods. I helped."

"You put the cake pops in a container."

"That counts as helping in my book," I decided, and told Cam gravely, "Thank you for the cake pops, Cameron. We're very grateful for them. So, uh, everyone's down on the beach. Food's not gonna be long. Tell everyone I'll come grab them when it's ready?"

"Gotcha." Cam bounded off, calling, "Hey, Mrs. Flynn!" as he went.

I closed the door behind Levi, then led him to the kitchen, aware he hadn't been here before like Cam had. I announced him and all his baked goods, and snuck a cake pop before June could tell me not to.

"I thought you were coming up to check on the food."

I turned around to spy Noah hanging in the doorway from outside. But he wasn't looking at me.

"I am. I sent Cam ahead. I'll come grab everyone when it's ready. Hey, you want a cake pop?"

Noah was staring past me at Levi, and no sprinkle-covered cake pop could distract him right now. I found myself holding my breath.

"Levi," he said.

"Hey, man."

Noah nodded. Levi was nodding beside me. Noah cleared his throat and left again, stopping to help out at the barbecue, where our dads were currently debating over something to do with the ribs. (But seriously—it was grilling some meat. Could it really be that much of an art form?)

Levi let out a long breath and bent to whisper in my ear, "Think he's still mad at me?"

"I think you're off the hook," I told him. I shoved the cake pop I'd just offered Noah into my mouth before grabbing Levi's hand to tell him, "Come on, I'll give you the grand tour."

Chapter Twenty-Eight

There was a time when Lee and I were attached at the hip pretty permanently. But right now I was nibbling at my second hot dog, hanging out near the guys as they joked around and talked about plans for next year at college, and Lee hadn't stopped talking to Ashton for maybe an hour now.

They were practically attached at the hip.

Dixon said, "Right, Elle?"

I had no idea what he'd just said.

"Right," I said.

What was Ashton saying that had Lee's face all lit up like, well, like the Fourth of July? What the hell could they even be talking about? What was so funny that Ashton was almost doubled over, half choking on his burger?

I chomped on my hot dog angrily, trying not to glare in their direction.

Wasn't it good that Lee had such a good friend for when he went to Berkeley?

Wasn't it *good* that he was replacing me so easily?

I shook myself. I knew I was being ridiculous and it

wasn't like Lee was actually replacing me, but this was weird. Seeing him hang out with someone else like he did with me.

I kept watching, mumbling, "Oh sure," and "That sounds great," whenever the guys reeled me back into their conversation. Lee and Ashton gestured wildly as they talked about something; then Lee took out his phone and the two of them pored over it for a while.

"Hey."

I jumped at the hand on my arm, smiling when I saw it was Noah.

"You're gonna burn a hole in that poor guy's head if you keep staring like that." Noah nodded in Ashton and Lee's direction with a gentle, somewhat amused smile. "Jealous is a cute look on you. When it's not directed at me, obviously."

"Mmm-hmm," I mumbled, blinking a few times and dragging my eyes away from them. "Ugh, am I that obvious?"

"Hideously obvious," Cam said suddenly just behind me. "Warren told you that you had mustard in your hair and you said, 'Sounds good.'"

I ducked my head, trying not to be *as* obvious about looking for the mustard apparently in my hair. Noah's hand was still on my arm and he tugged me aside.

"I promised Lee I'd help set up the volleyball net, but I just wanted to check you're okay. Are you?"

"Just dandy."

"And not at all jealous that Lee's made a new friend?"

I sighed, rolling my eyes. "I'm fine. Just . . . It's weird. It'll take some getting used to, that's all. Ashton seems great. He does," I enthused, not sure whether I was trying to convince Noah or myself. "I'm glad they're getting on so well."

"Let's hope they're not too much of a team, huh?"

"What?"

"They put together the volleyball teams," Noah said, folding his arms and jerking his head in their direction. "They're on the same team, so let's hope they're not too great together."

"They . . ." I swallowed the lump that had suddenly appeared in my throat. "Ashton and Lee made the teams up?"

"Yeah. *And*"—he dropped his arms and laced one of his hands through mine, smirking—"I happen to know that you're on my team. So don't worry, we'll win. Show them who's boss."

My mouth was still dry, the lump still in my throat. Lee and I were supposed to put the volleyball teams together. And we were *supposed* to be on the same team. I was awful at the game (at most sports, generally), but Lee and I were always on the same team for things. We'd obviously planned to put together the best team for ourselves, just so Noah would be on the losing team. We'd discussed all of this.

So why had the plan changed?

Noah didn't seem to notice how bothered I was over the volleyball thing and excused himself to go set up the net—at which point I noticed Lee and Ashton had gone, too.

I stood for a couple of minutes, looking around at

everybody. The sun was still high and blazing bright, the sky a clear, brilliant blue, smattered with a few cotton-soft clouds. Music played from the speaker system Noah had set up earlier, muted by the busy, enthusiastic chatter that spilled from the house and across the patio. There were smiling faces and laughter everywhere as people splashed about in the pool or sat on the edge with their feet dangling in while they ate or sipped drinks.

Everybody looked like they were having a great time.

I caught Amanda's eye as she talked to June and Rachel and hastily put on a smile. It wasn't like I was having a *bad* time. The volleyball thing had just thrown me, was all.

It wasn't much longer before Lee was back up by the beach house, cupping his hands around his mouth to holler, "Ladies and gentlemen, boys and girls, we are proud to announce the first and final annual Flynn volleyball game. Players—to your positions!"

Most everybody poured down onto the beach. Levi fell into step beside me, grinning.

"Annual volleyball game, huh?"

"First and final," I said. We'd usually play a couple of games, and the boys would always end up tossing a ball around, whether it was a football, baseball, volleyball, whatever. I'd usually sit it out. But not this year. Not when Lee wanted it to be such an event.

(And not when "host a kickass volleyball game" was on the bucket list.)

"So, uh, Noah and I had an interesting chat earlier," Levi said.

I let out a sharp laugh. "Since when do you and Noah *chat*?"

I never got to hear the answer, though, because Rachel dragged him away and everyone was getting in place for the volleyball game.

Dixon and Olly were on my team, as were Lisa and Amanda. On the other side of the net, playing with Lee and Ashton, were Rachel, Tyrone, Levi, and Jon Fletcher.

"Hope you're ready for this," Lee called, tossing the ball lightly from hand to hand and wriggling his toes in the sand. "You guys are toast."

"Please," Noah scoffed. "You're going down."

I glanced around at our team. Lisa and Dixon were enthusiastic, but not . . . Well, I wouldn't have put them in the "talented" category when it came to sports, but they were better than me. I wasn't so sure about Amanda. And while Olly wasn't too bad, I didn't think we stood much of a chance against the others.

I tried to catch Lee's eye before the match started, but he was too busy muttering some game plan to Levi and Ashton and giving Noah the stink eye over his shoulder. He didn't even seem to notice me there.

Part of the idea behind the volleyball game being on the bucket list was that we were supposed to beat Noah. (How else would it be so kickass?) But maybe this was turning into Lee's list—especially after the trip to Berkeley and me missing out on eighties mini golf. . . .

As far as putting Noah on the losing team went, it was looking up within the first minute or so, when Levi spiked the ball hard into the sand near Dixon's and Noah's feet, sending up a spray of sand and a chorus of cheers from the crowd. Levi whooped, arms in the air as he ran a victory lap on their side of the net, high-fiving everyone on his team.

I heard Noah muttering under his breath. He shook his head, one hand ruffling his hair as he lined up and waited for the next serve.

This time the game went on a little while longer before anyone scored: Lisa got in a couple of decent hits, the ball saved by Amanda and Noah and sent soaring back over the net; Dixon and I fumbled, hitting the ball back and forth between us, to everyone's amusement, before he managed to knock it in Amanda's direction. She proved herself a much better player than most of us; Olly even almost scored, but the ball was saved at the last minute by Levi, who dived forward to knock it back up into the air and Jon Fletcher sent it our way.

As the ball sailed toward me, I leaped into the air, arm swinging to hit it, and my fingertips barely grazed the ball. Amanda was standing just behind me, though, and grunted as she hit the ball in a tall, graceful arc over the net.

It was looking like we might score, until Lee hopped up on Ashton's back to hit the ball right to the corner by

Lisa—and despite her best efforts, she missed it completely. Lee gave a delighted cry and jumped back down, high-fiving Ashton with both hands.

That should be me.

Not that I'd have been much help just then, but . . .

Noah managed to score a point. The next time, I hit the ball right into the middle of the net. Tyrone almost scored with some fancy trick shot, until the ball hit Dixon on the head and bounced right back over, so unexpectedly that none of them noticed until it was too late.

I was starting to enjoy myself, much to my surprise. Even with Lee and Ashton looking so buddy-buddy over there. I was still recovering from the stitch in my side after laughing so hard at Dixon getting hit by the ball, grinning and giggling, when the game restarted. Amanda caught my eye briefly and mimicked the startled look on Dixon's face, making me snort all over again.

I had barely stopped laughing when I heard Lee yelling, "Yes, Levi! Nice one!"

They'd scored again. Levi did another victory lap, jumping into the air and punching his fists up.

Noah scoffed, picking up the ball. He muttered something—the only word of which I got was *arrogant.*

I caught his arm.

"Is he always this bad?" Noah said.

"He's just having fun."

"Yeah, and he was just having fun on the go-kart track, too?" Noah shook his head. "This isn't a game, Elle."

"What are you—"

"Hey, lovebirds!" Ashton called over.

"Yeah, throw us the ball so we can serve already!" Jon shouted.

I stepped back, wondering what the hell Noah had meant by it not being a game. And wondering what the hell was with the glare he was giving Levi, and . . .

And why the hell was Levi glaring right back at him?

I stared between them in utter confusion. What had I missed? What had happened?

This was like race day all over again.

Levi had said something about a chat with Noah. Had Noah said something to him? Something . . .

I was still trying to figure out what the weird tension between them was all about when I realized that Tyrone had served and Noah had already scored, winning us the first set.

As the game continued, it was dominated by Noah and Levi, both of them darting around trying to get another hit in to score the next point. Amanda actually jumped onto Noah's back at one point to intercept an increasingly vicious volley between him and Levi, redirecting the ball to Rachel. I was pretty sure I wasn't the only one to breathe a sigh of relief—and I *definitely* wasn't the only one confused about what the deal was with Levi and Noah, judging by the looks everyone kept shooting them.

Lee's team won the second set, but as the third and final one drew to a close, we were neck and neck. Amanda stepped up to serve for the game. Jon smacked the ball back over the net and it came my way. Olly intervened, knocking it toward Noah, who jumped up to spike it hard, and Levi charged forward to block it—

The ball made a sickening *smack!* as it collided with Levi's face.

I let out a shriek, hands flying to cover my own face, and I wasn't the only one.

But Levi was still standing, and my team was celebrating. Lee flung himself backward into the sand with a melodramatic howl of despair over losing the game. A few people from the crowd looked concerned, but mostly people were just celebrating the end of the game and our win.

It had definitely *looked* like an accident—but Noah didn't seem overly sorry about it.

I shot him a look while he was celebrating the win with our team, then ducked under the net to check on Levi. His nose was bloody but seemed to have already stopped bleeding. He wiped the back of his hand across his face, apparently oblivious to me as he glowered at Noah.

"Nice shot, asshole," he called.

Noah turned, smirking—gloating—and stepped forward. "Now who's the sore loser?"

"I'm just here for a good time."

The laugh Noah gave in response was blunt and mirthless. His mouth twisted, tongue sticking out over his teeth as he shook his head. "A good time? Is that what you're calling it?"

"I'm not the one out to hurt somebody. Just like on race day. You know, everyone told me what kind of guy you are, but I guess I really had to see it for myself."

Everybody had fallen quiet to listen to their argument—not that it was exactly difficult, with both of them raising their voices. Levi barged forward, ducking under the net to face off with Noah. He was shorter, skinnier, but that didn't seem to bother him right now.

I did try to reach for his arm and hold him back, but he was too quick.

I'd never seen Levi so riled up like this. I definitely hadn't ever seen him look so pissed off—it stunned me into silence. I felt Lee drifting closer, his arm brushing against mine.

"Oh shit," he whispered.

"What?"

But he only shook his head with a look that said, *I knew this would happen sooner or later.*

Amanda was standing with her arms crossed, looking warily between the two of them. She caught my eye and gave a small shrug, the look on her face not too dissimilar to Lee's.

What the hell had I missed?

"Watch your mouth, kid," Noah was growling.

"Ha. There he is. The infamous *Flynn*, the school badass."

"And what about you? You think this act is fooling anybody? This whole 'innocent friend' thing you've got going on—it isn't fooling anybody. Everyone knows why you're here, why you're still hanging around."

He was invited, I almost said.

And why shouldn't he be here? He was our friend—of course he was here.

What was Noah *talking* about, with the "innocent friend" thing?

"And I'm sure you're gonna tell me why," Levi snapped.

"Because you're still pining after Elle!"

The words felt like a punch in the gut. My mouth fell open and I stared at them both.

It seemed to hit Levi pretty hard, too: he fell back half a step. "Shut up."

"It's so obvious," Noah carried on ruthlessly. He took a step closer to Levi, his hands balling into fists. "Everyone can see it! You're spending all this time acting like her friend, acting like that's *enough* for you, but we can all see it."

"Shut up!"

"She doesn't want you," Noah barked at him, their faces only inches away, both of them scowling and glaring. Levi was shaking. "She didn't want you then and she doesn't want you now. And the sooner you get that through your thick head, the better for everyone."

Noah punctuated it with a final smirk.

Levi's fist went swinging.

I gasped as he punched Noah in the jaw—pretty hard, actually. Way harder than I would've expected from Levi.

(Although considering it was *Levi,* any kind of punch was unexpected.)

My eyes flew to Noah and I braced myself, waiting for

the familiar sight of his shoulders squaring, his feet planting firmly against the ground, his hands curling into fists at
his sides. . . .

His jaw clenched, the muscle there jumping.

Amanda hesitated, not sure if she should intervene or
not. Rachel was tugging on Lee's other arm, saying, "Do
something!"

Noah's eyes slid across to mine.

I'd seen Noah get into fights before. Any second now,
he'd launch himself forward, tackle Levi to the ground, lay
into him. . . .

Only . . .

When he turned back to Levi, his hands were limp at his
sides and his jaw unclenched.

"You're not worth it."

He turned sharply on his heel, marching past the crowd
of onlookers and back up toward the beach house in long
strides.

I stared after him. Lee made a strangled, startled sort of
noise beside me. Our friends whispered, looking between
Noah's retreating back and Levi, who stood trembling and
breathing hard, fingers still bunched into fists.

Levi turned around, catching my eye.

"Elle—"

But I was already moving, already running after Noah.
Amanda started to follow but I gave her a quick look and
she hung back. Even with all that time I'd spent on the track
team, I still had a hard time catching up to Noah and his

long legs. I kicked through the soft sand and up to the beach house. There was no sign of him, but I heard the front door and chased after him.

Noah had snatched up his T-shirt from a seat on the patio where he'd left it earlier, and right now he was climbing onto his motorcycle. He seemed determined to ignore me.

"Noah!"

He gritted his teeth but kept on not looking at me. I caught his arm, pulling myself around in front of him.

"Noah, what . . ."

I trailed off, not even sure what to say. What had he been doing? What had he been talking about when he'd said all that stuff to Levi?

What made him walk away from a fight for maybe the first time ever?

"I . . . I thought we talked about this. I thought whatever you think about Levi, this . . . this stuff about him having a crush on me . . . Noah—"

"That's what you wanted me to do, right? Be the bigger person."

He was right.

So why did it feel so wrong?

Chapter Twenty-Nine

I *did* want Noah to be the bigger person. On race day, that was all I'd wanted him to do. I'd been so mad at him, so annoyed he couldn't just see sense, that he was still so caught up over this whole thing with Levi, that he still held on to the ridiculous idea that Levi had a crush on me.

They'd had a talk earlier.

Was it about me?

This isn't a game, Elle.

And Amanda, Lee . . . none of them had seemed too surprised to see things really start to kick off.

I faltered, stepping back just a little, my hand slackening around Noah's arm.

I did want him to be the bigger person.

But maybe not like this.

Noah turned on the engine and I took another step back. I didn't even know what to say to him right now, and I was still trying to process what had just happened. Noah obviously needed a little space, so that was exactly what I'd give him.

He gave me a fleeting smile before pulling the bike around, easing it between all the cars that clogged up the driveway.

I let him go.

Besides, there was someone else I needed to deal with right now.

As I stepped through the double doors leading outside, I was met by Levi, who stopped in his tracks just at the other end of the patio.

For a second, we both just stood there.

Levi's face crumpled. There was sand in his brown hair and smeared up his leg and on his T-shirt. There was some dried blood under his nose. His hair stuck up on end and he dragged his hand through it, lurching forward toward me.

"Elle, I'm so sorry."

I stormed toward him, jabbing a finger at his chest once I was close enough. "I cannot *believe* you just did that."

"He was pushing me."

"You punched him! You . . . you started it!"

"He hit me in the face with the volleyball! You saw! He . . . he was playing rough. Like on race day."

"I saw," I argued. "And it was an accident. You tried to block. Everyone saw. I know he was . . . The stuff he was saying was . . . But you didn't have to hit him." I sighed, pressing my hands to my face. "What . . . Levi, what did Noah say to you earlier? You said you guys had a talk."

Levi shook his head. "Nothing. It's nothing."

"Come on. This is me." Softening, I searched his face. "Levi, tell me. What's going on? What's all this about?"

"It's not an act," he told me instead, so earnest that I could see his eyes shining with tears. "I'm not just pretending to be your friend, Elle. And it *is* enough. This wasn't . . . this isn't . . . I don't just hang out with you because I like you. I mean, I . . . I do *like* you, obviously, but I mean I don't just hang out with you because I *like* you, like you. You're one of my best friends."

He gulped, breathing hard, chest heaving. His eyes roamed over my face, looking desperate.

And then I got it.

Despite everything I'd said to Noah, everything I'd believed about my relationship with Levi, he *did* still have a crush on me.

I'd really thought he'd gotten over that. That it was just some fleeting, silly thing, exacerbated by the time we'd kissed.

That kiss had felt like a huge mistake at the time.

It had made me realize that whatever I'd been feeling toward Levi last year paled in comparison to my feelings for Noah. It had made me realize I didn't like Levi that way, not really.

I'd always just kind of assumed it was the same for him.

I was *such* an idiot.

Maybe that time we'd kissed had just made Levi's feelings for me stronger.

"I'm not just pretending to be your friend," he said again. "It's not an act, whatever Noah thinks."

"Levi—"

But he was still barreling on: "I'm sorry. I didn't mean to get in between you guys or anything. I *know* I shouldn't have hit him. Maybe . . . maybe I should've said something to you before, or . . ."

Oh God, I was such a terrible friend. All this time and I'd had no idea. I should've *known*. I should've noticed. I wasn't exactly sure what I would've done differently, but I should've done something. Whatever else, Levi was my friend.

"I . . . I can't do this right now, Elle. Thanks for the invite. I'm sorry I screwed up. Tell Noah I'm sorry. But right now I think I should go."

"Levi," I said again.

He continued to look at me with that same desperation, the same soft, pleading look, and then suddenly his hands were on my arms and he tugged me toward him, pressing his lips to mine just once, just for a second, just briefly.

I gave a squeak of surprise, but he had already stepped back and let go by then.

"You're right," I mumbled. "You should go."

"I'm sorry," he said, and then he was staggering indoors and through the beach house, running out.

I touched a finger to my lips, listening to the front door slam.

And I let him go, too.

It felt like I'd been standing there for hours when footsteps clattered up onto the patio.

Lee's eyes flitted around before settling on me. "What happened? Was that Levi? Where's Noah?"

I froze.

"Was that the door?" Rachel said, going to look. "I thought I heard Noah's bike. . . . Where's Levi?"

"They've gone," I managed to say. "They've both gone."

Lee sighed. "Maybe just as well. First time I've ever seen Noah walk away from a fight. What the hell was that all about?"

I was shaking my head, but then Amanda piped up, sparing me having to come up with any kind of answer. (Because how exactly was I supposed to explain what had just happened? I wasn't even so sure myself.)

"Well, I can't say I'm surprised," she told us all. "Not after that talk they had earlier."

I huffed, exclaiming, "Oh my God, what talk? What the hell did they even say? What was so damn special about this *chat*?"

Amanda blinked at me. "Well, Noah confronted him. Told him to stop mooning over you. It's a little bit sad, really. The way he looks at you. I feel bad for the guy."

I suddenly remembered last spring, before Noah and I got together, when I found out he'd been "warning" guys to stay away from me in some stupid and misguided attempt to look out for me.

Frowning at Amanda, I folded my arms and demanded, "Did he tell Levi to stay away from me? Keep his distance or something?"

She shook her head, looking startled. "No! He just said it was about time Levi got over you and that it wasn't fair to either of you to carry on the way he was. Then, of course, they had that big bust-up down on the beach *anyway*. I did tell him, I said, if you're going to talk to the boy, at *least* try to be a grown-up about it." She sighed and rolled her eyes; there was something almost indulgent about it, though. "That idiot, honestly. There's no talking to him sometimes. He's so bloody headstrong."

"That's one word for it," Lee muttered.

They were all looking at me.

Waiting for me to protest, I guessed, like the last time this subject came up.

"I . . ."

They kept looking at me and waiting.

I flushed. "Okay, so . . . so maybe you guys have a point. About Levi having . . . having a crush on me."

"Oh!" Rachel sighed, throwing her hands in the air. "Now she sees it! Did it really take Noah getting punched in the face for you to realize that?"

It *maybe* took Levi kissing me again to realize that, but . . .

"Don't look at me like that," I muttered. "He's still my friend. It's not *my* fault I never noticed."

Lee slung his arm around my shoulders roughly, pulling me forward and ruffling my hair. "You're an idiot sometimes, Shelly." He let me up. "So what did he say? Levi? And Noah, for that matter."

"Noah didn't exactly say much," I explained. "Levi . . ."

Oh man. That was a whole other can of worms. One I wasn't quite ready to deal with just yet.

Chapter Thirty

Noah hadn't come back, but none of us were too worried about him. The mood down on the beach took a while to pick back up after the intensity of the volleyball game, but soon enough it seemed that everyone was enjoying themselves again.

"Everything okay?" Lee asked me as our friends cracked open some beers and Amanda explained the rules of some drinking game to everybody.

"Sure," I told him, and plastered on a smile to prove it. There was no way I was going to let Noah—or Levi—spoil the rest of my final Fourth of July at the beach house.

As the evening drew on, Matthew and my dad set up the fireworks. June brought out desserts, with Amanda and Rachel and Linda helping. I'd decided to stay out of the way at that point. Too many hands and all that.

"Shouldn't we wait for Noah?" Brad had asked me and Lee. "He can't miss the fireworks."

"How about we video them for him?" Lee suggested.

I'd tried calling Noah, left him a message to say he should come home.

He ended up texting his mom, saying he was just out clearing his head.

I had an idea of exactly where he was but decided to leave him be. He'd come home when he was ready. And today was about all of us, about our final Fourth of July at the beach house, not about me chasing after Noah.

That evening, after all our friends had gone and Brad's buddies had been collected by their parents and after we'd cleaned the place up a little, we piled into the rumpus room at the back of the house with drinks and plates of leftovers to snack on.

Dad was setting up Monopoly. The board was old, used so many times it frayed at the edges and felt soft to the touch. A lot of the cards and game money were faded, crinkled, and bent, some of them stained from our games as careless, messy children.

There weren't enough pieces to go around for us to all play by ourselves, since we'd lost two of the tokens years ago. Rachel and Lee teamed up. Brad would be playing with Dad. June and Matthew were a team. Amanda, Linda, and I would play by ourselves.

"We get the race car!" Brad cried, grabbing for it.

"Not so fast," Linda told him with a laugh. "We have to roll to pick the pieces."

I pulled a face at Lee. We *never* rolled to pick pieces.

We all had our own pieces. We just rolled to see who went first.

But, hey, fine.

Whatever.

I rolled a one when it was my turn. I didn't really care, until Linda rolled a six—the highest of everyone—and said with a great big smile, "Looks like the honor is all mine! And I think I'll pick"—her fingers danced over the pieces— "the doggy!"

My hand flung out before I could stop it, snatching up the dog.

"Sorry," I blurted, realizing what I'd just done. "It's just that I'm always the Scottie dog."

"Oh, no, Elle." Linda laughed, holding her palm out to me patiently. "Those are the rules. I get first choice."

June gave me a sympathetic look from her spot next to Linda, but all I could do was scowl. I'd been so willing to give her another chance today, but this was where I drew the line.

My voice was biting when I retorted, "I don't care. *I'm* the Scottie dog."

I knew I was being a brat. But I couldn't stop. I couldn't wipe the scowl off my face or compose myself or stop the irritation that boiled away in my veins the more I stared at her.

I knew I was being a brat, and I knew someone was going to try to talk me down, but I *really*, really didn't expect it to be Dad.

"Elle, come on," my dad said, sounding unusually stern. "Why don't you just give Linda the piece?"

I scoffed, glaring at *him* now in utter disbelief.

He was really going to take her side? On this?

I saw June wince, but she didn't step in to defend me either. In fact, when she caught me looking her way, she gave me a small nod, with an expression that said, *Go on, Elle, listen to your dad.*

Well, fine.

If that was how they were going to be.

"It's just kind of tradition," Lee tried on my behalf. "Elle's always the Scottie dog."

"No," I snapped, pushing myself up from the floor and throwing the little metal piece savagely at the table. It hit the Chance cards, sending them scattering. Rachel was quick to tidy them up. "It's fine. Take the dog. I didn't want to play anyway."

"Oh, no, no, it's okay! Hold on, Elle," Linda said, picking up the tiny dog and holding it out after me even though I was already at the door. "If being the dog is tradition, you should absolutely be it. Here."

"I don't need your *charity*," I spat, wheeling around. "You know, you can't just barge into our lives like this, spend the holiday with us, play board games with everyone, and act like you've been here all along. Because you don't belong here. And it's pathetic how hard you're trying."

"Elle!" both my dad and June shouted. I heard one of them jump up.

Matthew said, "Don't mind her, Linda. Teenagers, eh?"

I made sure to slam every door on my way outside. I heard heaving footsteps tromping after me but didn't turn around, not until my dad shouted, "Rochelle! You stop right there, young lady!"

I did, crossing my arms and turning back around just before I got down the path to the beach. It was already dark out, and the outside lights on the turquoise pool water cast eerie patterns across the patio, the house, even my dad's face.

Which was a pretty furious face.

I stood my ground, arms crossed tight and brow furrowed.

"What was that all about?" he demanded.

"What are you *talking* about? You know exactly what that was about!" I objected and jabbed a finger back at the house. "You know I'm always the Scottie dog, Dad. It was Mom's token. Every time we played. *Every time.* And you were just going to let her have it? What, should I give her the watch Mom left me for my seventeenth birthday, too? Should we get all Mom's clothes out of storage in the attic for her, let her use Mom's favorite mug with the pink stars on it?"

He sighed, taking his glasses off to clean them on his shirt, pausing to rub his eyes before putting them back on. "Elle. It was just a Monopoly piece."

"It was *Mom's* Monopoly piece. This is our last summer here. The Flynns are selling the place and . . . and we're off to college, and when are we even going to have a family game night like this again? She shouldn't even still *be* here. It's a *family* game night. All the guests went home ages ago."

"Now stop it. That's not fair and you know it."

"Fair?" I scoffed, my eyes bugging. "You want to talk about fair? What's not *fair* is the way she's just . . . just . . . just suddenly around all the time, trying to force herself into our lives! You got her to pick up Brad from camp, she's been to the house cooking dinner with you guys, she's been hanging out with Matthew and June. She was *in our house*, acting like she belonged there, acting all . . . *chummy* with me, and I can't stand it. I know you like her, and I'm sorry, but I don't. And I think it's selfish of you to force her into our lives like this."

I watched my dad's face turn pale, the way he blinked in total shock as he digested it all.

And I kept my arms folded and gritted my teeth, because I didn't regret a word of it.

He *was* forcing her into our lives. It wasn't as though I didn't want my dad to be happy, but it was too much, too fast. Linda wasn't part of our family and I hated that she was acting like she was.

I hated that she'd been getting on so well with June and Matthew all day. I hated that she'd been talking to Rachel and Amanda in the kitchen earlier, and they had been chatting so happily back, with friendly smiles on their faces. I hated the way she'd "snuck" Brad an extra brownie, like it was their little secret, like he was five years old and she could win him over with some baked goods—and I *hated*

309

that Brad was already so won over by her, calling for her to join in, and had she tried our favorite potato salad, and had she seen all the photos in the hallway, and she was still picking him up from camp in a couple of days and taking him for pizza, right?

I hated that everybody else seemed to have welcomed her in so easily when she *didn't belong*.

By now, Dad had recovered enough to stand up a little straighter, his cheeks turning ruddy. "Selfish? Are you serious, Elle? You and Brad have been my number-one priority your whole lives, *especially* since your mom died. But you're both old enough now, and after I got to know Linda, I realized maybe it was time I stopped putting part of my life on hold. Jeez, Elle, I know I haven't always been around a lot, but that's because I took a job I didn't want in order to earn more money to help you go to a better school, to give you and your brother a better life."

He was breathing raggedly, so heavily I could hear it from even a few feet away, and the lines on his face seemed to deepen while I stood there slack-jawed.

"And don't *talk* to me about selfish," he went on. "I asked her to help out with Brad so much to give you more free time this summer! So you could spend it gallivanting around with Lee, doing all those bucket-list things and spending time with Noah and your friends. Do you have any idea what a big step that was for Linda—for me to ask her to suddenly be part of my kids' lives like that? Looking after Brad, looking out for you?"

"I . . ."

I'd had no idea. I'd just always assumed he hadn't *met* anybody he liked, that he'd found it hard to move on from my mom; I didn't think for a second he'd actively decided to put any kind of dating life "on hold" for us.

And I knew he found his job exhausting. I knew he worked long hours sometimes and occasionally had to spend a night away or do something for work on a weekend, but he never *said*. Whenever we'd ask him about work, he'd just smile and say, "Oh, you know. Same old, same old, bud!"

It's not as though I didn't know he was, you know, *human*, with his own thoughts and feelings, but he never let on. About any of it.

"I'm not trying to force her into your life, Elle," he told me, his voice serious and weary. "I was hoping to take things slow. Give you guys a chance to get used to it, I guess. That's why I took a while to tell you. But with you being so busy this summer, it just . . . happened. And Brad really seems to like her. And Linda likes him, too. She treats him really well. And she's desperate to get to know you better. I'm not . . . For God's sake, Elle, it's not like I'm *trying* to replace your mother. Nobody could do that. But don't stand there and call *me* selfish, and don't take it out on her. If you're going to act like a child, Elle, I'll treat you like a child. But I would like to think that you're old enough now that we can have this conversation like adults."

"You never said" was all I could manage. "The . . . the job and"—*ew*—"dating."

"Of course I didn't! You were just a kid, Elle! You're *my* kid. Those weren't your burdens to bear. It was bad enough I needed to rely on you to help out with Brad so much and with chores around the house."

"But . . ." I gulped, not sure where the lump in my throat had come from or when the tears in my eyes had appeared.

My dad stepped forward and lifted my chin, sighing and giving me a sad, small smile. "You had to grow up so quick after your mom died. I just thought . . . this summer, why not let you be a kid a little while longer? I didn't realize Linda being around like this was so upsetting for you. And I'm sorry about that. I should've known, bud."

At least he was back to calling me *bud*, I thought. He couldn't be too mad at me anymore for yelling at his new girlfriend.

I sniffled, feeling a couple of tears drop down my face. I ducked my head, trying to wipe them away quickly. "I guess I should've said. And I guess I was kind of being a brat."

"Just a little," he agreed, pulling a face and making me give a snotty, wobbly laugh before he tugged me into a warm hug, letting me cry a little into his shirt.

And just for a little while, everything seemed okay.

Chapter Thirty-One

Noah didn't come home to the beach house that night. I was back at work on the morning shift so didn't get to stick around to see if he'd show up.

I was hoping, though, that by the time I got home things would be back to normal.

Some guy was at the beach house painting the doors. I gave him a polite smile and scooted past to find Amanda in the kitchen, packing some stuff into a box. The place was quiet, which felt unusual—especially after the chaos of yesterday.

"Let me guess," she said, squinting thoughtfully at me, head cocked to one side. "You're looking for . . . Lee?"

"Anyone, really."

"Master Flynn the younger has thrown a tantrum and left to cool off," she told me with a helpless shrug. "June sent someone to paint—"

"I kind of noticed. She did mention something about it."

"—and Lee flipped out when the guy went to paint over some door frame with all your heights marked into it. Which was very cute, to be fair, so I can see why he got so mad. Rachel went with him, but she's going to see her parents this afternoon. And, uh, Lee said . . . Hold on, I jotted it down."

She set aside the brown packing paper she was holding to rummage around the worktops, eventually coming up with a pink Post-it note.

"He said to remind you about the arcade later. Your phone was off."

"It died midshift." Which reminded me—I started searching the lounge for a charger. With five of us here, you'd think it'd be easy to lay your hands on an iPhone charger pretty much anywhere, but they always seemed to disappear on us.

I didn't need the reminder, though. I'd remembered that we'd made plans to go to the arcade today. How could I forget? Our beloved childhood *DDM* machine was being retired tomorrow, and today was our final chance.

"What're you doing anyway?" I asked her.

"Oh! There's a ton of plates here. There must be fifty-odd. I was a little too scared to count, to be honest. June said yesterday about needing to empty the place out soon, and I figured we wouldn't need so many after the big party yesterday. Thought I'd be helpful. Earn my keep, you know!"

I wondered what Lee would say about half the kitchen being emptied out but decided not to stop her. Amanda had a point, and turning down her help when we were finding it so hard to let go of this place felt silly.

Better her than us, I thought.

"And, um . . ." I put the couch cushion back in place, giving up my hunt for a charger for a moment to look at her. I fiddled with the hem of my shirt. "Did Noah . . ."

She shook her head.

"Oh. Right."

"He probably stayed at home last night," she said. "He's just . . . There's a lot on his mind right now, Elle, that's all."

I felt that old, familiar flare of jealousy over how close Amanda was with Noah, but this time with an intensity I hadn't felt since Thanksgiving. A lot on his mind? If he had a lot on his mind, why didn't I know about any of it? Did she just mean Levi? And why did *she* know but not me?

I swallowed the feeling back down far more easily this time.

Plus it helped a lot when she said, "He's not answering my calls or messages either. I'm kind of worried about him."

"He's done this before," I pointed out. "Usually when he's mad or thinks he's messed up or something."

"The Flynn brothers and their need to cool off," she joked with a roll of her eyes. "He'll probably be back later, though. I know you said he took off pretty quick yesterday, but he really does want to talk to you. I don't know about *what*, exactly, so you can get that look off your face right now, missy. He's been tight-lipped with me." Amanda mimed zipping her lips.

Whether or not he was still "cooling off" or just wanted some space or whatever it was, I felt my gut twist with the knowledge that something was going on. I needed to talk to him. I left Amanda to pack up the kitchen, fetching my keys off the table I'd dropped them on.

"I think I know where he is."

• • •

I breathed a small sigh of relief when I found Noah's motorcycle in the parking lot—but it wasn't a sensation that lasted for long.

I got out of the car and climbed up the hill, following the path Noah had shown me to the spot I knew he liked. Where he'd brought me last summer. Where we'd really *talked* about things and kissed beneath a fireworks show.

Where he'd come to mull things over and pull his head out of his ass after race day.

Where he'd come now.

The feeling in my gut twisted a little more. It made my palms prickle and sweat, made my lungs feel tight.

I spotted Noah at the top of the hill. His leather jacket was cast behind him, along with his keys and his phone. He'd changed his clothes since yesterday; he must have gone back home to his parents' house, like Amanda said. He sat hugging his knees, chin propped on them as he stared out at the view of the city.

He looked so small like that, so vulnerable, and so very not like Noah.

His head twitched at the sound of my arrival.

"Hi," I said quietly.

There was a beat before he replied, "Hey."

He unfurled his legs, stretching them out in front of him, his hands planted on either side of his hips. I sat down, mimicking his position, but turned my face toward his.

He needed a shave.

Or, well, maybe he didn't. The stubble was a good look on him. It made him look more mature, accentuated the squareness of his jaw. I resisted the urge to reach out and run my fingers over it.

Maybe I should've let Noah talk first, but with the silence stretching on between us, I couldn't stand it any longer. And besides, I had something to say, too.

"I wanted to say, you were right about Levi. All of you. You all tried to say something, and I didn't want to hear it. *Not* that that makes up for how you acted on race day or for going behind my back to talk to him about it, but . . ."

"Yeah," Noah sighed. "I probably could've handled things a little differently."

I shrugged. Maybe we both could've.

"What changed your mind?" he asked.

"He told me he liked me. And, um . . . he sort of, kind of . . . kissed me. A little. Like, a peck. Sort of . . . sort of more like a goodbye than anything else," I tried to explain, only realizing once I said it aloud that that had been *exactly* what it had felt like.

If I expected Noah to get angry about it, I was surprised. He just nodded.

I studied him for a few seconds. There was no tension in

any of his muscles. No tautness in his expression, nothing but an odd sense of calm about him that I really, really was not used to—especially after telling him that a guy who was *not* him had kissed me.

His calm demeanor only unnerved me. The feeling in my stomach worsened; my heart thudded hard in my chest.

"You're not gonna say anything? Not even 'I told you so'?"

Noah let out a soft, quiet sigh, still not looking at me. "Yesterday it would've been so easy to send that scrawny little shit sprawling on his ass. It's what I would've done before. But I didn't. Because I'm trying real hard not to be that guy anymore. Because even if he *did* deserve it, even a little, even if he did start it, he's your friend. But, thing is, Elle, you're a big part of why I'm trying not to be that guy anymore."

"Okay," I said gently, not sure where this was going—or why that sounded like it wasn't such a great thing.

"And I'm just not sure that's—" He broke off with another sigh, twisting now to look at me, a frown tugging between his eyebrows. "I shouldn't have to rely on *you* for me to be the guy I want to be for you."

It took a second to try to puzzle that one out in my head.

Noah went on. "I should just want to be that guy. Not because I think you deserve better. Not because he's your friend or I don't want to disappoint you or whatever. I should want that for *me*. And I . . . I do, but . . . you shouldn't be the reason why."

I kept staring at Noah. This time he gave me a few more seconds to take that in.

"Okay," I repeated, still unsure. "So . . . what does that mean?"

He held my gaze for a second, and there was something so *sad* in his lovely bright blue eyes that it hurt to look at them. Then Noah turned his head back out toward the view, his hand absently pulling at blades of grass.

"You always wanted to go to Berkeley. You and Lee. Always. As soon as you guys were old enough to know what college was, that was where you'd say you'd both be going one day. You had your heart set on it."

Noah paused for a second, and I watched him bite his lip, frowning deeper before speaking again.

"So why did you pick Harvard, Elle?"

Thrown by the question, it was all I could do to give him a straight answer. "We talked about this, remember? I guess I applied on a whim. You said something about how nice it would be to be in Boston together and—"

"You're going to spend four years at a school you applied to on a whim. A school you only applied to because of me. I don't want . . . I can't be responsible for you making a choice you might regret. Things already didn't work out between us once, and this summer . . . I know it's been hard. Not bad," he added hastily, looking back at me. "It's been great, obviously, but you said yourself, sometimes it's hard to love me. What if things don't work out, Elle? Just say.

And then you've moved to the other side of the country, given up on your dream of Berkeley, and for what?"

Now it was my turn to look away and be quiet for a minute.

"We sat here when you decided to accept your offer from Harvard. Do you remember? And you said you couldn't give it up. It was Harvard. You don't think that's the same for me?"

"Then I want you to be sure you're choosing it because it's Harvard, not because of me. You only applied because of me. Besides, I've seen how much this has driven a wedge between you and Lee, how hard you guys have been trying this summer to keep it together. You're always going to put each other first, and I don't blame you for that. I think it's kind of amazing, actually. I don't want to see you jeopardize that for . . ."

"For us?"

Noah slouched back. "Yeah."

There was a strange taste on my tongue and my throat was thick. I frowned out at the view, trying to breathe deep enough to fill my lungs. "So you think I should've turned down Harvard to go to college with Lee?"

Noah sighed, so quietly I almost didn't hear it. "You remember a couple of weeks ago, I said that sometimes you put everyone else first? You applied to Berkeley because of Lee, because our moms went there, because it's close enough that you can help your dad with taking care of Brad. All summer you've been so focused on spending time with me, or Lee, or Brad, or working so you've got money for bucket-list stuff with Lee, and I feel like you pick everybody else over yourself sometimes, Elle, and you shouldn't have to do that. And I guess . . ."

He trailed off, pulling up some grass in his fist, before finishing. "I guess I don't want to be someone else you put ahead of yourself."

And suddenly I heard everything he wasn't saying.

"So that's it? The fact that we love each other, that doesn't matter? That doesn't mean anything?"

"That's not what I mean, Elle. That means *everything*. But maybe . . . maybe it just isn't enough."

Forget the apprehension that had been twisting my stomach into knots: Noah's words were like a knife, driving right through me. I felt cold all over.

"No, you . . . you don't get to just *decide* for me. I made my choice, and I'm going to Harvard. I've already turned down Berkeley and accepted my offer there instead. You don't get to turn around now and tell me I'm not going. It's not up to you."

"You're right. But if you are going to Harvard, it's not going to be with me."

A quiet, broken gasp left my lips, a stilted rush of air.

He was breaking up with me.

"How long have you been thinking about this?"

Noah shook his head, his eyes pressing shut. "Please don't, Elle. It's not like I've been planning to do this all summer, drawing up lists of pros and cons or anything. But I can feel how distant things have gotten with us sometimes, even when you're right there next to me. And it's nothing to do with Levi or Amanda or Lee or anybody else. It's just . . ."

"Hard to love me sometimes?"

He gave a quiet chuckle, slumping back on his elbows now, lying almost flat, to peer up at me with that smirk I loved so much. "You're impossible not to love, Elle. But like I said, maybe that's not enough."

"So . . . that's it," I whispered.

"I . . . I guess so."

For a couple more moments, the two of us stayed there, the city sprawling out below us. Beyond the distant noise of traffic, the muffled sound of voices of other people around, I could hear Noah's breathing. Deep and slow and even.

Calm. So calm.

Meanwhile, I was holding my breath like it was the only thing keeping me together, and the second I let it go, I'd fall apart at the seams. My hands were trembling, and I balled them into fists. I felt like I should look away from him, that it might be easier to digest if I wasn't looking at him.

But it felt like . . . this was the last time I would get to see him, really *see him*, as my boyfriend. With the sunlight on his dark hair and shining in his blue eyes, clear and bright as the sky, that square jaw and crooked nose, those lips I'd kissed countless times.

We were breaking up. Boston, Harvard, Berkeley—none of it meant anything, not really. Noah and I had been fighting so hard to make things work after the mess of Thanksgiving. We had been working at it so hard.

And that had carried on into this summer, hadn't it? Even without race day or his almost-fight with Levi yesterday.

I'd asked myself when my relationships with Lee and Noah had become work, this job of spinning plates and balancing things.

It was easy to figure out the Lee part of that: it started when I chose Harvard.

But Noah . . .

That had always been a spinning plate.

Maybe he was right: maybe loving each other wasn't enough.

Maybe it was time to let that plate fall.

I reached out and cupped my hand over Noah's, giving it a last squeeze before standing up. I brushed off my pants, took a breath, and knew then that I didn't have anything else to say to him.

Because what would I say? Thanks for all the memories? We had a good run, it was great, see you at dinner later? I could fight for him, for us, of course I could. It was obvious that Noah had made up his mind, and nothing I said would change it.

I let out the breath I was holding back in a near-silent sigh and started down the hill.

I got a couple of feet away before I heard him scramble to his feet and call, "Elle!"

I turned just in time to see Noah running toward me, my heart leaping as I met his embrace, and he drew me in, his arms encircling me and my hands cupping his face as we shared one last kiss. His mouth moved desperately over mine, his tongue dragging over my lip, and I pulled myself closer. It was still there—that fire, like when we'd first kissed, like when we'd kissed every time since. One of my hands slipped to the back of his neck, my fingers toying with the ends of his hair, and one of his hands moved to the small of my back to pull me flush against him. There were no fireworks this time—just the quiet of the world seeming to stand still for us, before everything ended for good.

We broke apart suddenly, abruptly, both of us stepping back to put some distance between us.

He held my gaze for a second, on the verge of saying something, but I knew exactly what he meant and I nodded. He gave me a soft, warm smile in return, his dimple only just showing.

One last kiss.

One last time.

Chapter Thirty-Two

For a little while, I just drove around, replaying the whole conversation with Noah in my head. Tears kept pouring down my cheeks in a steady, quiet stream, in contrast to my loud, ugly sobbing the last time we'd broken up. My mind drifted to imagining what might have been: would things really have been any easier if we were together in Boston? Would we have fought less—or more—being under each other's feet all the time? Noah had obviously had doubts sometimes throughout this summer—enough, I guessed, that we'd ended up here.

I still couldn't believe how *mature* that conversation had been. How shockingly levelheaded Noah had been about everything, how much he'd obviously thought about this, and how *right* he was. I wasn't used to that.

I hadn't seen it coming, not in a million years.

And as for Harvard . . . I hated to admit that Noah did have a point. I'd only applied because of him, and I'd only accepted because, well, it was *Harvard*, and who turns that down? My dad was so damn proud. And it had meant being with Noah more.

I'd never really stopped to ask myself if *I* wanted to go there.

It was only when I started driving back toward the beach house that my mind turned toward Lee. I guessed maybe, if Noah and I weren't going to be an item anymore, I'd have a little more time to make sure my relationship with Lee didn't suffer because we lived on different coasts. And since Noah and I had ended on pretty civil terms, things should be a lot easier than the last time, and Lee wouldn't need to feel stuck in the middle.

Oh my God.

Lee.

The arcade!

I gasped audibly, letting go of the steering wheel to clap both hands to my face in absolute horror for a second before I grabbed the wheel again and jerked it around, hitting my turn signal at the last second to pull a U-turn.

I was the worst. I was the absolute worst.

Even though I was pushing the speed limit, it seemed to take forever to get to the boardwalk. Running down toward the arcade, I felt like I was running through syrup, like I was trying to run in a dream.

I couldn't believe I'd forgotten.

I couldn't believe I'd blown off the bucket list for my relationship *again*.

I was the worst.

By the time I reached the arcade, I knew it was too late. The sun was already low in the sky, a few lights shone outside buildings or along the boardwalk, and families were leaving. And Lee—

Lee was leaning against the railing, staring out at the water. The arcade doors behind him were closed, the lights inside all turned out.

Panting, I skidded to a stop a few feet away, enough to catch my breath and remind myself that yes, 100 percent, I was the worst. And then I crossed over to him.

My heart was in my throat and there was a shrill ringing in my ears.

"Lee, I'm . . ." My voice came out scratchy and thin. I cleared my throat and tried again. "I'm so, so sorry. I promise I'll . . . I'll make this up to you somehow. I'm so sorry."

He didn't look at me, but he did lift his head in some kind of half-hearted nod, and I heard the small breath of dry laughter he let out.

"Sure. That's what this whole summer was about, right? The bucket list. It was all about making it up to me. Well, forget it. Don't worry about me, Elle. I don't need it."

"Oh, come on, Lee. You know that's not what—"

"I don't have anything to say to you right now, Elle. I waited for you for two hours. But hey, you know, it's cool. I don't have to guess where you were."

My hand came up to squeeze his arm.

"I'm so sorry. My phone died at work, and then I went to find Noah and . . . well, he . . . we . . . um . . . Something came

327

up," I said. I knew if I told him now he'd think I was just looking for sympathy, and that totally wasn't the case. "Oh, come on. Please don't be mad. We still got to play a few days ago, right? And there's gotta be other *DDM* machines around somewhere, if you really want to play."

Lee's head snapped toward me, looking so furious that I fell back a step, my hand dropping from his arm as if he'd given me an electric shock.

"Is that what you think this is about? The *DDM* game? What, do you think I'm five years old?"

I don't know, you kind of act like it sometimes.

I bit my tongue. Right now was not the time for a snarky retort.

"It's not about the fucking game!" he cried. "It's about us! Our friendship! This whole summer, all the bucket-list stuff, I *know* it's all been about trying to make me feel a little less like second best after you picked Noah over me. I knew this was how things would turn out. Since you guys got together, you've been saying I still matter, that you're not putting him first, but the truth is, that was never going to last. At some point, it was going to be him. I just didn't think it'd happen this soon. And let's face it, Elle, if it wasn't Noah, it would've been college, or work, or Brad, or Levi, or whatever! It's been a long time coming, I guess."

I stared at Lee while he ranted at me and felt my anxiety over upsetting him vanish completely. By now, my blood was boiling, because how dare he?

Was he serious?

He had to be kidding me.

And I couldn't help but compare him, right now, to Noah. Noah, who didn't want to hold me back, didn't want me to put him first. And Lee, complaining that I didn't prioritize him *enough*.

"Second best? Oh my God, Lee. It's like you *are* five years old sometimes. You don't think I know it's not about the game? You think just because I had other priorities this summer that I care about you any less? School, college, work, Brad—you think I *choose* all that stuff over hanging out with you? You've never had to worry about anything like that. You've never had to stress over having money, or keeping up your grades, or looking after anybody else. You have had *everything* in life handed to you. So don't expect me to stand here and say sorry because I had to get a job just to keep up with the bucket-list stuff and earn some money for college or because I had to take care of my little brother."

Lee opened his mouth to argue back, but words seemed to fail him, which was just as well because I was still only mid-rant.

How dare he act so hurt over not being my sole priority? *Especially* when I'd been working so hard all summer to remind him how important he was to me.

And I couldn't expect him to understand, not really. I knew that Brad was just as much a part of Lee's family as he was mine, but he wasn't Lee's responsibility, and it wasn't as though Lee had ever *needed* to get a job. Maybe I should've let off some of this steam a little sooner or tried to explain it to him better, but right now, the dam had broken, and everything was flooding out.

"You're right," I snapped at him. "This summer was about making it up to you because I was planning to spend the next four years on the other side of the country, but it was so much more than that. This was supposed to be our best summer ever, but guess what? That was *never* going to happen. We wrote that bucket list when we were little kids, and we can't keep clinging to that! The arcade, the beach house, all those things that made our summers so great are going away, and we're never going to get them back. But that's life! That's what happens! Things go away, and *some of us* have to grow up! This summer, I was just trying to make sure we wouldn't have to grow apart!"

I stopped yelling at him just long enough to suck in another breath to say, "And for your information, Lee, you don't have to worry about me picking Noah over you anymore, because we broke up. For good this time. And part of the reason for that was because he could see how much he and Harvard were coming between me and you—but Noah's not out there being pissed at me for picking you sometimes or having a life outside of him. I'm sorry this summer didn't live up to your expectations and that I let you down today, Lee, I really am, but just . . . don't act like I'm sabotaging our friendship just because I have other things going on in my life. You're my best friend, and you mean everything to me, but jeez, Lee, my whole world doesn't revolve around you.

Maybe it used to, but we're not kids anymore, and you need to fucking *grow up* and realize that."

Lee stared at me while I caught my breath. I was shaking all over and was horribly tempted to just throw my arms around him and hug him tight and cry it out, but I knew I needed to give him some space right now to get his head around everything I'd just said. I could practically hear the gears churning in his brain as his eyes flitted between mine. Lee gulped, letting out a shaky sigh. A few times he started to say something but stopped himself.

Eventually, he just sighed and leaned back over the railing again.

I joined him.

Our arms pressed together. His head tipped onto my shoulder.

"This summer really went to shit, huh?"

"Just a little," I murmured back, resting my head against Lee's. "I'm sorry I missed our last dance at the arcade. It was a genuine mistake. Again."

"So you guys really broke up, huh?"

"Yep."

"Was it because of Levi?"

"Weirdly, no. For once it had nothing to do with him. It was actually . . . an okay conversation. Not like the last time. I think . . . I think we're done."

"And you're okay with that?"

"I . . ." I nuzzled my head against Lee's. "Not really. But I guess I'm gonna have to figure out a way to be."

"I'm sorry I yelled at you," he told me. "And I'm not just saying that because my brother broke up with you and I feel sorry for you. You're right. I have to grow up a little. I know I do. I'm just . . . finding it hard."

"You're forgiven."

"What, I don't get an 'I'm sorry' back?"

"You do not."

He considered it for a moment. "That's fair. But please never shout at me like that again, Shelly. It does *not* feel good. Even if I kind of maybe probably deserved it."

"I think you kind of maybe definitely deserved it. Honestly," I said, laying on the sarcasm now, "telling me I wasn't putting our friendship first and something was always going to get in the way of it. You're a literal five-year-old sometimes, you know that?"

"A literal five-year-old," he deadpanned. "Are you *sure* you got into Harvard?"

Chapter Thirty-Three

The next two weeks slipped by in the blink of an eye. Noah spent most nights back at home with his parents or slept on the sofa if he did stay at the beach house; he might've been able to stay in Lee's old bed, in Amanda's room, but Lee and I had kind of ruined the mattress in a bucket-list prank that had seen it in the ocean, with an unsuspecting Rachel napping on top of it.

Lee had also let up on the bucket-list frenzy now, so I took extra shifts at work. Levi kept his distance and ignored my messages when I tried to get in touch.

I was glad for the space from everyone, to be honest, especially from Noah. It was rough, being so close to him and not being *with* him. I cried myself to sleep in our bed a couple of times, but having more time to myself (even if I was working a lot) did help me to come to terms with the breakup a little more.

I *even* went home one evening to join Dad, Brad, and Linda for dinner. *And* I helped Linda with the dishes afterward and stuck around to play Uno with everyone. *And* I laughed at her lame jokes. *And* I apologized to her for yelling at her over Monopoly.

Like a mature adult.

Amanda and Noah spent a lot of time together, and Noah helped out with most of the handiwork that we'd been putting off around the beach house—or that we found out Lee had straight up canceled, whenever workmen were supposed to show up. Ashton and his girlfriend came to hang out a couple of days, and the guys came around for a few movie and game nights, although Levi didn't join us.

It was weird, how almost normal things felt.

It was a little delicate, but it was normal.

And I could finally breathe again.

Besides, Lee and I were down to about three things on Lee and Elle's Epic Summer Bucket List, none of which would be as big or crazy to pull off as race day, so we'd have no trouble ticking everything off. (Really, how hard could it be to set up a line of dominoes through every room in the beach house? We'd already ordered a massive set from Amazon.) Without all the stress, and now that Lee and I had *really* cleared the air between us, I could get excited about it.

Then June broke the news one morning.

Amanda was back to see her parents for the day; Rachel was down on the beach with some of the girls. Noah was supposed to be fixing the pool filter (again), but June told him it could wait and called him inside and told Lee and me to take a break from the dominoes. She made us all take a seat in the lounge, which was when I knew it was serious.

I half wondered if it was about Noah's and my breakup for a second, until—

"We've had an offer," she told us, "on the beach house. And we're planning to accept it."

The three of us were silent for a long while.

It was Noah who broke the silence. "So why am I wasting my time fixing the pool filter?"

"It's conditional on the fixing-up we said we're doing," June explained. "Obviously."

"Obviously," Lee muttered, and scoffed.

Sensing dissent in the ranks, June went into full army-general mode. She squared her shoulders, planted her legs firmly apart, set her jaw (I suddenly saw where Noah got it from), and placed her hands on her hips. A full-on Wonder Woman stance, with a stony look that lingered on each of us.

"We're planning to accept the offer, and we expect the sale to be complete within the next two weeks."

"Two weeks?" Lee and I cried.

"So I'm expecting this place to be spick-and-span. I'm going to need you guys to clear everything out and finish fixing things up. Okay?"

From the way Lee shuffled his whole body in his seat, grumbling quietly, and the scoff Noah let out, no, it was not okay.

My stomach sank with the news, too. We'd all been playing along with this stuff, letting contractors come in to fix the tiles on the roof, finishing some of the landscaping out back, but none of us had *really* been expecting this.

June cut us all another look. "Okay?"

"I've gotta finish working on the pool filter," Noah grumbled. He hauled himself off the sofa to storm outside, pulling the doors shut behind him and pressing play again on the portable speakers he'd taken out with him that morning.

"Guess I'd better go get some boxes to pack up our cherished childhood memories," Lee muttered, pushing himself up. He snatched his keys, kicked over some dominoes, and slammed the front door behind him.

June sighed, then looked at me.

"I suppose I should, um"—I ran a hand over the arm of the sofa before getting up—"get to work on the rumpus room. We never got very far."

I didn't get very far now, either, because June called after me as I got to the door.

"Elle, come sit down a minute."

Heading back toward her, I joined her in the kitchen and sat at the counter while she made us both some coffee.

Great. Whatever this was, it was a conversation that required a *coffee*.

"I was really sorry to hear about you and Noah," she told me once she'd filled two mugs and sat beside me. June put her hand over mine, giving me a soft smile, her strict demeanor all gone now. "He told me a couple weeks ago. I was kind of waiting for you to talk to me about it."

"Oh. Uh, I didn't . . ."

I'd just assumed Noah would tell her.

And honestly? I'd been trying to avoid this exact conversation.

"How are you doing, honey?"

"Oh, sure. I'm fine." I returned her smile to prove it. "Fine" was pushing it a little, but I was taking it better than when I broke up with him last year. "I guess maybe I should've seen it coming. Even without the distance, like this summer, it's not been smooth sailing all the time. But, yeah, I'm okay. Is Noah, um . . . is he . . . doing okay?"

June glanced away, looking through the doors at him. "He's hurting, but if you don't mind me saying, I think maybe it's for the best. For both of you. College is a huge change. And you guys . . ." She clicked her tongue. "I think it's fair to say things have gotten a little intense from time to time. I don't think it's a bad thing that you'll both have a little space to figure a few things out on your own."

Intense was putting it mildly.

But June seemed to know what she was talking about, and I didn't really have much reason to argue—especially since I hadn't fought against the breakup—so I just nodded.

"And obviously you know that, whatever happens, you're always part of the family, Elle."

"Yeah, I know. Thanks, June."

She squeezed my hand again, and I bumped my arm against hers gently.

"And, Elle."

Oh no. She was back in serious mode. What now?

"Do you mind if I ask you something?"

This had *really* better not be about Noah. I got the impression she was going to ask me anyway, but I nodded and said, "Sure, go ahead."

"Do you really want to go to Harvard?"

I let out a long breath, surprising myself when it turned into a laugh. "You want the honest answer? I really don't know. Noah made a pretty good point about me applying on a whim, and now I feel kind of bad about turning down Berkeley and Lee . . ."

"The thing is," June said slowly, cautiously, "all this time you've talked about college, I've never once heard you say what you actually want to study, or what it was about a school that made you want to go there. I know Berkeley has ties to me and your mom, and obviously Noah was the pull for Harvard, but I've gotta wonder if you only ever applied to the schools you did because that was what you thought other people wanted, instead of what you wanted for yourself. It's all well and good applying for schools because of the people you love, honey, but loving Lee and Noah has nothing to do with what you want to do with your life."

Berkeley had always been the dream school. It wasn't too far away and it was where our moms went, and like Noah had said, it was where Lee and I had said we wanted to go as soon as we were old enough to know what college was.

Harvard, on the other hand, was anybody's dream school. Shouldn't that have been enough?

"Noah said something kind of like that, too," I confessed.

She smiled, as if she wasn't too surprised to hear it, and I wondered if they'd talked about it—about me—together.

"Maybe it's time you start thinking about what *you* want, Elle. What *you* need. Figure out what you're passionate about and pick a school that suits *you*. Everything else . . . well, you can figure all that out afterward. If it's that important, it'll work itself out."

"You think?"

June gave me a wide, warm smile. "I know."

I had to look away from her, hunching over my coffee instead. How could she sound so confident? I'd spent weeks—*months*—agonizing over college applications. I'd gotten myself into such a frenzied crisis mode that Levi had had to come and talk me down from it. I *wanted* to go to college, I knew that much.

But June had a point, just like Noah. I hadn't applied to anywhere that I'd picked just for *me*.

Lee had already come to terms with going to college without me. Noah and I had broken up. Maybe it *was* about time I was really, properly selfish and picked something that suited me and the future I wanted and didn't take either of the Flynn brothers into consideration.

Except . . .

"That all sounds like really great advice," I told June, "but there's one little problem."

"What's that, honey?"

"I have no freaking idea what I'm passionate about."

June laughed, sipping her coffee. "Oh, you'll get there,

sweetie. I'm not saying you need to decide now what you want to do with your life—God knows your mother and I had *no* idea, and she applied to about thirty different jobs before she found one she liked the sound of. But it's worth thinking about what you might like to do. Working with kids, running a business, journalism . . ." June leaned back to squint thoughtfully at me. "I could see you doing something creative. Something *crazy.* Look at what you guys did with the kissing booth! The whole summer bucket-list thing! Just look at what you did with race day!"

It was my turn to laugh now.

"What, you think I'm going to make a career out of *Mario Kart*?"

"Well, hey. You never know. Stranger things have happened."

Chapter Thirty-Four

Our final days in the beach house were either miserably somber or we were almost manic in our mission to make the most of it. Everything from near-silent days as we moved around, packing things up, to a midnight feast our final night on the beach, which ended in Amanda going skinny-dipping and then immediately regretting it. She shrieked that she was "freezing her ass off" and raced all the way back to the house, butt naked.

On our last morning at the beach house, it was a somber kind of day again.

I'd been back in my old bed, sharing the room with Amanda, these last few days while Noah was back—it seemed silly to make him stay on the couch or for him to keep making the drive back and forth between the beach house and his parents' place. This morning, I crept out of bed before Amanda woke up and went to make myself some breakfast.

I stood in the kitchen, not tasting any of the Froot Loops I was slowly munching on, and surveyed the place.

It felt so *wrong*.

The cupboards were almost empty. Boxes sat piled up, half full and waiting to be closed. The couches looked so bare without the colorful assortment of old throw pillows and blankets. Noah had taken the TV home two days ago, leaving a gaping space against the wall. We'd scrubbed the floors to within an inch of their life, but I didn't think they'd ever looked so old and worn. And despite all our efforts to be careful, they were already sprinkled with sand again. All the walls had been repainted. They looked too clean, too bright.

The place practically sparkled in comparison to the start of the summer.

I'd never seen it in such good shape. I'd never seen it so *clean*.

Even with all the old, sagging furniture, it held a shiny appeal.

I hated it. It was wrong, all wrong.

Like the life and soul had been stripped right out of the place.

The sale was closing in three days. Today we would move out. Tomorrow, someone would come and take away the furniture. Then June and Matthew would be handing over the keys.

The soft, muted sound of footsteps creeping down the hallway pulled me out of my head. I looked up to see Rachel, already dressed, hair curling softly around her shoulders. She gave me a small wave and mumbled, "Hi."

"Hey."

I stepped out of her way as she got herself a drink.

"You're not having breakfast?"

Rachel shook her head. "No. I think I'm going to just head back home. Honestly, I don't have much of an appetite. I packed all my things yesterday and I'm taking some of these boxes back with me. There are so many of them."

I looked at her in surprise. "You're not going to stay and help pack the last of the stuff? Not that you should or we'd expect you to. I mean, it's not like this place is really your responsibility, and you've already been a huge help, and—"

She gave a quiet laugh, grinning at me, and shrugged one shoulder as she gestured out at all the boxes. "Everything is pretty much packed anyway. Besides, you're right. This place doesn't really have anything to do with me. You guys should have the chance to say a proper goodbye. I don't want to get in your way."

There had been times when "in the way" was exactly what Rachel was, as far as I'd been concerned. I'd wanted to spend time with Lee, but no, he was with Rachel. I'd thought we were hanging out, just me and the guys, but no, there was Rachel, and some of the girls along with her.

But over the last year and a bit that she'd been dating Lee, she'd really become a part of my life, too.

"You wouldn't be in the way."

She smiled, with so much emotion in her eyes that I wondered if she knew I wasn't just talking about today. "Thanks, Elle. But I think this is something you guys should really do by yourselves."

"Hear, hear."

We both jumped, startled, and found Amanda smiling at us. Her hair was frizzy on one side, flat on the other, where she'd slept with it wet after skinny-dipping. Her eyes were a little bloodshot. It was the closest to looking less than perfect I'd ever seen her.

Although how she managed to look cute in ratty old Harry Potter pajamas, the logo almost faded off completely, was beyond me.

"I'm with Rachel," she said. She began to clatter about the kitchen, examining the leftover food and then searching for utensils. "We were talking about this yesterday. Oh bugger, where's the icing sugar?"

"The what?"

"The . . . oh, you know . . . What do you call it? The powdered sugar!"

"I think we packed it in that bag."

"Everything to make French toast except the bloody icing sugar. Honestly." Amanda pottered over to the bag I'd just pointed to and rooted through it. "Anyway. Me and Rachel were talking about it yesterday. We think we should get out of your hair, let the three of you have some time to say goodbye to this place. We're not the ones who've been coming here every summer for our whole lives. Besides, my dad's flying back today. I said I'd go see him off before he goes to the airport. Oh, where's my phone?"

Dumping the powdered sugar, Amanda left to go collect her cell phone and Rachel turned to me again.

"I know we haven't had much chance to talk about the whole . . . you and Noah thing, but . . . are you okay?"

I'd be lying if I said it wasn't weird, being around him but not snuggling up to him, not kissing him. No casual touches, no lingering smiles. Both of us fighting hard not to fall into the easy way we bickered and flirted. I'd caught him looking at me a few times when he thought I wouldn't notice, but then, I was sure he'd caught me looking at him just the same.

Thinking about it now, though, I told Rachel honestly, "I've been worse."

"I'm sorry it didn't work out, Elle."

I gave a half-hearted shrug instead of an answer. I was sorry, too.

Rachel gave me a fierce hug, so suddenly and so forcefully it made me stumble backward. Laughing, I hugged her back. "What was that for? It's not like summer's over just yet. You'll still see me."

"I know," she said, and I was shocked to find tears in her eyes as she drew away. "It's just . . . I know I've only been here for this summer, but leaving this place, it really feels like it's all ending. Don't you think?"

My throat tightened. "Yeah. Yeah, I guess it does."

"I'll see you around, Elle."

I heard her pass Amanda in the hallway and the two of them said a brief goodbye.

"I'm heading back home the day after tomorrow," Amanda told me. "I fly back with my mum. Dad decided he couldn't so much as be in the same airport as her for a few hours, so . . ." She sighed, eyes watering. She blinked rapidly to clear the tears away. "It's fine. It really is. They'll get over themselves once they get this whole thing sorted out. The divorce, I mean. Is it bad that I'm glad I'll be at Harvard again next year and far away from all of it?"

"Sounds like exactly what you need," I told her. "I'm . . . I'm sorry it's so rough for you with them right now."

"It is what it is. It'll be fine. Eventually."

She set to making herself some cereal, the French toast apparently all forgotten. Maybe she'd lost her appetite, too.

"It looks so weird, don't you think? Without all your stuff in it."

I nodded. "I barely recognize the place."

We stood in silence. I rinsed my empty bowl and repacked the pots and whisk that Amanda had gotten out to make her French toast. She gave up on her cereal halfway through the bowl, too.

"I heard Rachel talking to you about you and Noah. Elle, I know it's really not my place to say and I don't know if this will help or not, but . . . I know how much he loved you. I know how hard that was for him, to let you go like that."

Let me go. Like he'd done some great, big, noble act. Like I'd needed him to do that for me.

Then I realized—maybe he hadn't done it for me. Or at least not only for me.

He'd done it for him.

Whatever retort I'd been about to bite back at Amanda, it

died on my tongue and I swallowed the words back down. "Yeah. Yeah, I know that. It was hard for me, too. But like he said—I guess loving each other isn't always enough."

"Guess not."

She squeezed my shoulder. "I know you're working tomorrow and you've got plans with your family, so I don't think I'll see you before I go to the airport. I know we had, um . . . Well, I think it's safe to say we didn't exactly get off on the best foot, but I've *really* loved getting to know you, especially this summer. And I think you're really bloody brilliant, Elle Evans, so even if things with you and Noah are a bit weird at the minute, please stay in touch. And we'll hang out next year, yeah? When you're at Harvard."

I gave an awkward smile and decided that was a conversation for another time. I was honestly touched by her little speech—and Amanda *was*, even after everything last Thanksgiving, a good friend.

"Next time I'm in Boston," I told her, "I'll look you up."

• • •

With the beach house stripped almost bare, Rachel was right: it did feel like it was all ending. The front door was open, and Lee and Noah were going back and forth loading up the cars with boxes—or trash bags, which we'd had to use to pack up all the bedding after we'd realized we didn't have any boxes left.

I left the rumpus room after giving it one final sweep to check we hadn't missed anything, not even a pen cap, and stood in the hallway with an empty box, surveying the wall of framed photographs.

My breath shuddered as my eyes roamed over the wall, drinking in each and every photo. I knew we weren't just tossing them out, but I also knew that June had no plans to re-create the gallery wall back at their house.

Our whole lives, right here on this wall.

I looked at each photograph, watching us grow up. Baby Brad, toddler Brad, all the way up to a ten-year-old Brad holding a jellyfish on the beach, beaming at the camera, Noah kneeling next to him and June with a stiff smile, looking warily down at the creature. My dad, standing with his arm around my mom, then without her, the lines quickly appearing on his face, then some of the grief on his shoulders disappearing as the years went on. Matthew and June, that one summer they were particularly frosty toward each other . . .

And each year, a photograph of me, Lee, and Noah. The three of us down on the beach. The start of summer, Fourth of July, the end of summer, some random day that meant nothing and everything—every summer of our lives, immortalized on this wall.

I blinked away the tears and sniffed.

Today I was determined not to cry.

(Lee had cried. Several times. Noah or I just handed him tissues each time—or toilet paper, when we discovered we'd packed the last box of Kleenex.)

At a noise in the doorway, I tore my gaze away from

the photographs to watch Noah stepping onto the porch. He stretched his arms over his head and cracked his neck. Long, strong limbs and a flash of the skin of his toned abs as his shirt rode up. His hair shone in the sunlight.

Lee was carrying one last box past him and paused to say something. Lee, with his mischievous, easy smile and dancing eyes, looking so like Noah and yet so *not*, his hair a mess and his nose red with sunburn.

Just like that. The blink of an eye, and they were all grown up. *We* were all grown up. With fall and college and new beginnings and new adventures on the horizon, this glorious, golden summer—it was ending.

"Hey," I yelled, and the Flynn brothers I'd loved so differently and so deeply both looked at me. "What do you guys say to one last photo?"

Chapter Thirty-Five

We still had time before summer was over, but not much.

With the beach house behind us, today felt like The Day for tying up loose ends. It was still pretty early when I got home. Two cars were in the driveway: Dad's and a shiny dark blue one I guessed was Linda's.

Inside, I found the three of them chattering in the lounge. Brad was jumping about as he told a story, a plate of half-eaten snacks and empty glasses on the table alongside a pack of cards, some game they'd abandoned.

"And then—*pchwwwww!*" Brad scrunched up his face, arms swinging. "He hit it right out of the park!"

Linda gasped. "Whoa! No way!"

Dad was laughing, and then spotted me in the doorway. "Elle! We weren't expecting you for another hour. Did you guys finish up early?"

I nodded.

His face fell. "Everything okay, bud?"

"Sure. Sure it is. Hi, Linda. Hi, Brad. Um, could I just . . . Dad, can I talk to you for a minute? In the kitchen?"

He got a look on his face, like he was bracing himself for bad news. My stomach fizzed, like a bath bomb that had been set off and wouldn't stop. I fidgeted with my hands, hearing my dad's sharp intake of breath as he followed me to the kitchen and closed the door.

"What's this all about?" he asked me gravely.

"It's about college." I took a deep breath. Today was a day for saying goodbye to things and looking forward. Today was a day to put everything right. Or as right as it could be. I closed my eyes for a second to compose myself, and then met Dad's serious, worried gaze before launching into the speech I'd prepared in the car.

"I've decided not to go to Harvard. I know you're going to be disappointed, but I've made my decision. I didn't pick it for the right reasons and I don't think I really even *want* to go there. And it was the same with Berkeley—I didn't pick it for the right reasons. But I've looked into it, and I've put in a late application to USC. I can start in the fall. Majoring in video game design. I know Berkeley and Harvard are great schools, but I really think this is what I want to do, and USC is the top school in the country for game development. Plus, I've already spoken to May and I can keep my job at Dunes while I'm studying, and I'll be around to help out here when you need, around my class schedule. I've got it all worked out."

There were several long, awful moments of silence when I finally stopped for breath. Dad blinked owlishly at me from behind his glasses, his mouth slack.

I bit my lip, shifting nervously from one foot to the other. "Dad? Dad, come on, please say something. I know it's not what you were expecting—"

"I'll say!" he interrupted with a burst of laughter that caught me completely off guard. He sighed, shaking his head. "Elle, the look on your face, acting so serious . . . I thought you were going to say you were pregnant! God!"

"Oh my God, *no*." My cheeks burned.

Placing his hands on my shoulders, he said, "Bud, listen. I'm proud of you for getting into Harvard, of course I am, but you go to college wherever you think is best for you. Hell, if you hadn't wanted to go to college . . . well, I wouldn't have been happy, but there's not much I can do, hmm? USC's a great school. And video game design . . . I mean . . . it does sound right up your alley."

"So . . . so you're not mad? You're not mad I turned down Harvard?"

"Absolutely not. Although this will be fun to explain in the office. I might have bragged. A lot."

I laughed, but felt my body sag with relief. Ever since my conversation with June, she'd gotten me thinking—and after she'd planted the ridiculous idea in my head that I could make a career out of *Mario Kart*, I hadn't been able to let go of the idea. It made me excited for college in a way I hadn't been yet.

Lee would love it. Especially since it'd mean we'd both be in California and it'd be so much easier to hang out.

"This isn't just because Noah and I broke up," I told my dad. "I don't think I was ever *really* a fan of leaving you guys to fend for yourselves. I know you've got Linda now, but . . ."

"Oh, bud. Come here." He pulled me in for a bear hug and laughed again. "We're perfectly capable of 'fending for ourselves,' but it'll be nice to have you around from time to time. I'm really proud of you, you know that?"

"Even though I turned down Harvard?"

"*Especially* because you turned down Harvard."

• • •

Levi still wasn't answering my calls, so I pulled out the big guns and called his landline. His dad answered with a cheerful, "Elle! We haven't heard from you in a while! How's everything?"

He told me Levi was at work, so after dinner with my family and Linda, I got in the car and headed out to the 7-Eleven.

There he was, behind the counter, slouched over his phone, not even looking up at the sound of someone coming in.

I grabbed the nearest bag of candy and walked up to the cash register. I slid the candy across the counter and cleared my throat. Levi glanced up and did a double take, his eyes bugging wide.

"I come in peace," I said.

"Elle. I . . . I didn't . . . What're you doing here?"

"Visiting one of my best friends, because he's been ghosting me for the last, like, month?"

He flushed, ears turning red, and glanced away. "I'm sorry. I thought . . ."

"Oh, you messed up big-time," I told him with a smile and a nod. "But you're still my friend, and I still care about you. Even if you're a big idiot."

"I heard you and Noah broke up," he mumbled.

"That is *so* not why I'm here." I heard how harsh I sounded and winced. "Sorry. Didn't mean to burst your bubble or whatever."

"No! No, I just meant . . . I hope it wasn't because of me. That's kind of why I've been avoiding you. I thought you'd hate me, because . . . if I messed things up and caused any trouble between you guys . . ."

"You didn't," I reassured him. "I think it was always going to end like that, you know. Me and Noah. It's okay."

(It wasn't, really, but it was getting there.)

Levi nodded slowly, uncertainly.

We hadn't spoken in weeks, so I decided not to waste time being delicate or beating around the bush. "Do you still have a crush on me?"

Levi cracked a smile. It was small, and tired, and lopsided. "I think I'm always gonna have a little crush on you, Elle."

"Well, if you can keep a lid on it and not kiss me again, I'd really, really like it if we could go back to being friends. I *miss* you. But I get it if it's, like, too hard for you to—"

"To be around you?" Levi beamed, throwing his head back in laughter. "I said I have a crush on you. I didn't say that your womanly wiles are so irresistible I'm putty in your hands and will kiss the ground you walk on. I've been your friend for the past year. I miss you, too."

"My womanly wiles?" I echoed, trying hard not to laugh.

Levi pulled a face, head wobbling side to side as he pretended to consider it. "They're not that great, sorry to break it to ya."

I clutched a hand to my heart. "How will I ever recover from such an insult?"

"Oh, I'm sure you'll find plenty of distractions in Boston to take your mind off it."

"Actually, I'm not going there anymore."

I explained the whole thing to Levi, stopping a few times when an actual customer came in and needed serving. His manager came over at one point to tell him to socialize on his own time. I left him not long after that, but only once we'd made plans to hang out in a couple of days when we were both free.

I really *had* missed Levi these last few weeks, and I was glad to have finally cleared the air. It would've sucked to lose him as a friend, especially when I would be staying in California for college.

I'd break the news to Lee soon. He'd need a little cheering up once the beach house sale went through, and this was sure to do the trick. As for Noah, he'd understand, and I didn't think he'd blame himself. He was too smart for that.

Last year the distance between us had been awful; I had a feeling that this time, it was exactly what we both needed.

I knew that I should've felt worse. I should've been disappointed and sad and had that hollow feeling in my chest because everything was ending. But at some point today, it had stopped feeling like that. If anything, it finally felt like it was all falling into place.

Chapter Thirty-Six

"You're here!" Lee cried.

He dropped the duffel bag, raced across the street, and threw himself at me, his arms engulfing me in a hug that lifted me clean off my feet. I laughed as he set me back down. I pushed some of the hair out of his face.

"You didn't think I'd let you get away without saying goodbye, did you?"

He beamed at me, blue eyes sparkling. "I thought you were at work!"

"Yeah, well, May let me go early so I could see you off. *And* she asked me to give you this. . . ."

I opened my purse and reached in to give him the crisp sheet of paper. A printed certificate with the Dunes logo on it, signed by May, declaring Lee Flynn—

"Employee of the Month!" he read aloud, and hooted with laughter. "Aw, man. Give her a hug from me, will you? And tell her this will be granted pride of place on my wall at college. I want everybody to know."

"She's so excited you'll finally be out from under her feet. The employee who never was."

"The best non-employee she's ever had," he agreed. He'd been spending so much time with me lately that a lot of it had been at work—and while Levi's manager was never happy to see me, May just rolled her eyes and threw her hands in the air whenever Lee came to the restaurant, where he'd inevitably get stuck with helping the rest of us out.

We started walking back to his parents' car, which was piled high with boxes and bags, ready for Lee to move into his new dorm room. Noah had flown back to Boston a couple of days ago. "So you're all set?"

"All set," he confirmed. "I mean, I'm planning to come back next weekend. Pick up my car and anything else I've forgotten. Hey! You could always drive up to bring me back? I could show you the place, introduce you to whatever people I meet this week."

I grinned at him. "I'd love that."

For a second we just stood there, smiling at each other, before Lee sighed, his expression crumpling. He took my hands in his. "It feels so weird to be leaving without you."

It was weird for me, too. I knew it was stupid because it wasn't like he was *that* far away, and we'd see each other plenty, but we'd barely spent more than a couple of days apart before.

Lee had been emotional enough for all three of us when

we'd cleared out the beach house. I'd been determined not to cry that day, and I was determined today, too.

But my resolve broke, and tears filled my eyes. My voice cracked.

"I'm going to miss you so damn much, Lee Flynn. You have to promise to call every day."

"Cross my heart."

"And you'll FaceTime me after you've unpacked, to show me your room?"

"Absolutely."

I sniffed, trying to take a few breaths. A rogue tear slipped down Lee's cheek and I grabbed him into one last hug. "I love you."

"Love you, too, Shelly."

We broke apart and Lee cleared his throat gruffly, puffing out his chest and shaking his head.

His mom, over by the trunk of the car, yelled, "Lee! Did you pack the box with all the cleaning products? I haven't seen it yet."

"Damn, I was hoping she wouldn't notice." He winked at me and said, "I've gotta run back inside for it. Promise you'll stay to wave me off?"

"You couldn't get rid of me if you tried."

We'd considered me joining Lee, getting in the car with them to drop him off at college. I'd have been welcome, and we'd have said our tearful goodbyes in his dorm room, but in the end, we'd decided it was better this way. Lee and I had driven up to Berkeley last week together, going to a few spots Ashton had suggested we check out, and that had been enough.

Going to Berkeley wasn't our thing anymore. It was Lee's. Today was just for him.

He disappeared back inside, and June stepped over to me after giving Matthew strict instructions on how to re-pack some things in the car.

"Hey, sweetie. How're you doing?"

She wrapped me in a brief but warm hug, then held me at arm's length, scrutinizing me.

"I'll be okay," I settled on saying. Because, really, I was getting there.

She nodded, smiling and dropping her arms. "All of you, so grown up. He made me promise not to cry, you know, but I think we all know I will. And you know if you want a hand doing any shopping or help moving in—just yell. We're around. Matthew and I are happy to help out."

"Thanks. I know. But it's okay—my dad and I have got it in hand. And Linda is going to come with us tomorrow to go shopping."

Linda joining us had actually been my idea. She wasn't so bad, I guessed. And she did have really good taste (and a penchant for coupons). Besides, I could see how much of an effort she was making for me; it was probably about time I returned the favor.

"Oh! And I meant to tell you—we finally got everything sorted. All the paperwork and everything. Had to pay the buyers back for all their fees, but it's done now. The beach house is officially remaining in the Flynn name."

I gasped, beaming at her. "That's amazing news. Thank you, June."

"And all because of you. Don't thank me. I was sorry to see that place go, too, but . . . turned out I just needed a little nudge in the right direction. Like someone else, huh?"

The day after we'd left the beach house, I'd taken the photograph of me, Noah, and Lee down on the beach—one final picture of the three of us and a summer at the beach house—and gotten it professionally printed and framed before taking it to June and Matthew that same day.

Matthew had started tearing up and left the room.

June had looked at me, then the box full of the photos from the beach house and the new one I'd had made for them, and she'd grabbed her phone, calling the movers to tell them to stop.

It hadn't been easy, but they'd managed to cancel the sale and keep the beach house.

I knew we all had to let go and grow up and move on—but I was so, so glad we didn't have to lose the beach house to do all that.

I helped the three of them finish packing up the car.

Lee rolled down his window, the back seat piled up with pillows and a comforter beside him, and his backpack.

"Just as well you didn't come with us. There's no room for you."

"Just as well," I echoed. "Call me later, okay?"

"Yeah, I know. I promised, didn't I?" He grinned. "And hey! When you get home, check your garage. I got you a little going-away gift."

"In the garage?"

He grinned and reached out to tweak my nose. I stepped back and blew him a kiss, then watched the car drive off, taking him to Berkeley.

Just because we were growing up didn't mean we had to grow apart. My relationship with Noah might have ended, but my friendship with Lee would last forever, whatever happened, wherever life took us.

If there was one thing in life I could count on, it was that. It was him.

Once they were out of sight, I walked home.

How many thousands of times over the years had I walked to Lee's house? I could walk this route blindfolded.

I wondered when I'd walk it next.

Back at home, the house was empty. I went inside to find the keys for the garage and hauled the door open.

And right there, in the middle of the garage floor, taking up so much space and standing proudly, in all its bright pink-and-blue glory, speckled with rust and starting to fall apart, was our *DDM* machine from the arcade.

"He didn't," I whispered, stepping inside slowly, reverently. "Oh, Lee, you didn't."

A note was taped to the screen, and I pulled it off to read it.

Shelly—Until our next dance. Your best friend forever—Lee.

I clutched the note to my chest, tearing up all over again and running a hand over the old game.

Classic Lee.

Epilogue

Laughter filled the air and chatter bubbled all around us. Electronic *ding*s and *schwoop*s sounded every so often. A ball collided hard with a wooden target board, followed by a splash and a chorus of cheers as a teacher plummeted into a dunk tank. Grass was trampled into the mud by hundreds of feet and the sun beat down on us. Music was being pumped out of speakers nearby, but you could barely hear it over the sound of everything else.

A hand clutched my arm, turning me around, and a face I knew better than my own beamed at me. "There you are!"

"Hey, you guys!" I took turns hugging Lee and then Rachel, like I hadn't just seen them a couple of days ago, or video-called them just last night to make sure we were still on for the day.

Rachel looked around, awestruck. "I can't believe how . . . I thought it would've changed a lot more."

"It has," I told her. "They got a brand-new moonwalk this year."

But I knew exactly what she meant. I'd felt it, too. Coming here today had been like stepping into a dream.

The annual Spring Carnival. Our school was still running it, after all these years. This year, they were raising money for a climate-change organization. A lot of the booths were the same ones we'd known; kids were still hooking the exact same rubber ducks from a pool that we had used.

It had been six years since we graduated high school. Six years since we'd all been back here together.

I'd been back a couple of times. Parent–teacher conferences for Brad that Dad and Linda couldn't make it to that I'd filled in on. Those had been weird as hell—but being at the carnival today was something else entirely.

Six years, and Lee and Rachel had stuck it out together all this time. Rachel had moved back home after graduating from Brown. She and Lee had gotten an apartment together. He'd proposed at New Year's.

I didn't have an engagement ring (or a boyfriend at all, for that matter), but I did have an apartment of my own, just downtown from them. Near my family, not too far from Lee, and within walking distance of work.

"So where's Brad?"

"Probably stuffing his face with cotton candy." I rolled my eyes. "That kid's a dentist's dream. Or nightmare, depending on which way you look at it. He's gotta get *another* filling, you know."

"Living his best life," Lee declared.

Rachel swatted a hand across his chest before I could do exactly that. "Don't encourage it."

"Good luck when you guys have kids," I told her. "He's going to be a handful. Especially on Halloween. Can you imagine? Although, that said, he'll probably eat all their Halloween candy before they get a look at it. Oh my God, that's weird, isn't it? *Kids*. You guys might have *kids* one day. I swear *we* were just kids."

"We were," Lee told me in a flat voice. "So please don't, because I came here to have fun and relive my childhood, not have an existential crisis."

"You're twenty-four," Rachel scoffed.

"Exactly. I'm a grown-up now. And I can have an existential crisis any time I want, thank you very much."

"Lee, you had cake for breakfast."

"Well, you shouldn't have bought a whole cake, then, should you? Then there wouldn't have been cake for me to eat for breakfast."

I laughed, looping my arm through Lee's. Some things never changed.

The three of us set off to explore more of the carnival, and speaking of things that never changed . . .

"Oh my God," I blurted, stopping in my tracks.

Lee stopped too. "No way."

It couldn't be.

Just as we'd turned a corner, we saw a crowd around one of the booths. One we recognized all too well. The paint was a little faded now. Looking at it, I could still feel the wet splash of paint on my skin when Lee had flicked some at me while we'd been working on the booth. I could hear his laughter from that afternoon ringing in my ears.

"Whoa," he breathed, and clutched my arm. I grabbed him right back.

Because right there in front of us, seven years later, was the kissing booth.

As we watched, a guy walked up to the booth. He said something to the girl there and she blushed furiously, looking nervous before leaning in for a kiss.

My stomach swooped and, just for a second, it was me sitting in that booth, with Noah sliding across two dollar bills and my heart hammering in my chest as he told me, "I didn't pay to talk to you, you know. I paid to get a kiss."

I could feel my lips tingling.

The couple in the booth broke apart. The guy said something and the girl laughed, tucking her hair behind her ear and nodding at him. They kissed again, and the crowd cheered.

I'd never forgotten my first kiss. How could I? I could still remember the way Noah's lips had felt against mine, the way he'd tasted.

Even after six years, it was impossible to forget Noah Flynn.

He didn't come home that first Thanksgiving after we broke up: he spent it in Boston with Amanda. But he did bring her back for Christmas, because she was still having a hard time being around her parents while they fought out a bitter divorce. It had been weird, but not horrible.

We'd stayed friends. Maybe not *good* friends, but it wasn't as though we could really stay out of each other's lives. We were friendly, at the very least.

And I'd dated other guys since. I'd had other boyfriends. Just like Noah had had other girlfriends.

But even so.

Noah was . . . something else.

I looked away from the couple in the booth—and my eyes landed on a tall figure moving through the crowds toward us. Piercing blue eyes, his dark hair cut short, a simple gray shirt and jeans that didn't have a single loose thread for a change.

"You made it!" Rachel enthused, hugging Noah hello while Lee and I exchanged a baffled look.

"I made it," he confirmed, cracking a smile and gesturing at himself. He smiled so much easier now. It was nice to see. He caught my eye, just for a second, then hugged Lee. "All right, buddy? Long time no see. And, hey, now I can say it properly, face to face: congrats on the engagement."

"Uh, y-yeah, thanks."

"Come on," Rachel said, tugging on Lee's arm. "You can buy me some cotton candy."

"But—"

She hissed something at Lee and he shut up. I cast him

a brief, somewhat desperate look before they disappeared around the corner.

Leaving me and Noah alone together for the first time in years.

"Been a long time, Shelly."

I laughed. "Oh, please. I thought I dropped that nickname ages ago. I, um . . . I didn't know you were back in town."

"Thought I'd surprise you guys."

"Are you just back to see your parents?"

His head wobbled. "Actually, uh . . . it's kind of for work. My company is opening a new branch in the city and they're looking for a new manager. I've been hoping for a promotion, so . . ." He shrugged, lifting his hands, palms out. "Looks like I'm moving back."

"Wow. Wow. A promotion. Manager! That's . . ."

He was moving back.

And he was looking at me like . . .

Like he did that day at the kissing booth.

"That's great, Noah. I'm really pleased for you. Congratulations."

"And to you," he said. "Lee told me you started at a new company a couple weeks ago. Better money, better job . . . He said you're actually designing games now."

"Yeah! It's amazing. It's a pretty small company, but they've got some serious investment behind them, and I get so much more creative freedom in this role, and I'm going to start babbling about how much I love the coffee machine in the office if you don't stop me," I said with a laugh. I loved the place I was working now—and since it all still felt like kind of a novelty to me, I kept falling into the trap of gushing about how great it was to anybody who'd listen.

Noah smiled at me. Soft and slow, just hinting at the dimple in his cheek, his eyes crinkling around the corners.

That smile sent my heart racing.

How did he still manage to have this effect on me? After all this time?

I was being ridiculous. It was just seeing the kissing booth again, sending all those memories flooding back. I was nostalgic, and as far as Noah was concerned, I was just some girl he dated once, back to being his kid brother's best friend.

But the way he was looking at me . . .

I used to know Noah so well. And he hadn't changed so much in these last few years that I didn't know that look.

"Maybe we could go grab dinner after this, if you're free. You can tell me all about that coffee machine."

After seven years, after two breakups, after moving on with our lives and forging our own paths, here we were. Right back at the Spring Carnival, standing by the kissing booth.

My heart fluttered, and I smiled back at him.

"I'd like that."

A faint blush colored Noah's cheeks, and I could see him fighting not to smile too much wider. He settled on smirking at me instead.

"Then it's a date."

Acknowledgments

Whoa. Well, I guess . . . we're here. Five books and three movies, ten years from where it all started. To think back to being fifteen, in the middle of exams at school, working away on Elle's story at night and secretly uploading it to Wattpad, to . . . *this,* is a wild journey.

So firstly: thanks to you, for being a part of it.

There's a lot of people to thank for this book—for the whole TKB series—but I'll do my best.

A massive thank-you to everyone at the Darley Anderson Agency. Clare, for being such a rock star of an agent; Sheila, for all your work behind the scenes with the movie adaptations; Kristina, Georgia, and Mary in the Rights team. I couldn't have asked for a better team championing my books.

And speaking of everyone behind the scenes—thanks to Naomi, Sara, and Shreeta for all your help in editing this, and the rest of the team at Penguin Random House, as well as Kelsey, Beverly, Colleen, and the rest of the team in the States. And thanks to everyone at Wattpad, for giving me a platform to share Elle's story all the way back in 2011.

Next up: the gang behind the movie! I've always known how Elle and Noah's story would end. I remember discussing it with Vince Marcello, our wonderful scriptwriter and director, back when we were just talking about his vision for the first film. It was a unique sort of challenge to write the novelization of the movie based on my books, but it was made all the more exciting (and easy!) by Vince capturing my characters so well. So thank you to Vince for taking such good care of Elle, Lee, and Noah, and to the team at Komixx and Netflix for creating such incredible movies of my books—and to the cast for bringing everyone to life so beautifully.

My family are obviously on the list to thank, so they're up next. Thanks to Mum and Dad, who had no idea how big this was going to be when I casually mentioned I was uploading a book online in the middle of my GCSE exams—for indulging all my FaceTime calls to share whatever weird and wonderful book news I had . . . or coming out to Cape Town to watch it come to life with me (thanks, Dad!). Thanks to Kat, for keeping me grounded and being such a brilliant sister. Thanks to Auntie Sally and Uncle Jason for the laughs—and Ruby for the cuddles. Thanks always to Gransha, for being my absolute biggest fan.

My friends most *definitely* need a massive thank-you, too. I wrote this book in under five weeks, late 2019, and you guys couldn't have been more supportive. Thanks to Amy and Katie for coming along to fun nights out in London during that time, and helping keep me afloat. Thanks,

Haz, for always being happy for his lab buddy's successes, and Emily and Jack, too. To Lauren and Jen, to Hannah and Ellie, for keeping me smiling and keeping me sane; and as always, to Aimee, who's known me since I was the awkward, introverted teenager writing in secret and always has a great story of her own to share.

Also, thanks to me. (Because you know what, these are my acknowledgments, and I'd like to acknowledge that past me deserves a pat on the back.) Thanks to me, for being such a weird fifteen-year-old who chose to spend so much time in her room instead of going out, spending hours getting lost in a Word document and being brave enough to share some of those stories online, and finding a community in Wattpad that helped all this happen now.

Which, I guess . . . leads me back to you. My lovely readers.

Whether you've been following the Kissing Booth since its early days on Wattpad, whether you're just discovering the books now because of the movies . . . You're here, and thank you for that. I hope this took you back to the joys and dramas of first love—or gave you a spark of hopeless romanticism for it, or reminded you of you and your best friend, goofing around in the back of a classroom. And if you're a teenager with a story to tell . . . hey, go for it. Who knows what could happen?

All this happened because of *The Kissing Booth.*

ABOUT THE AUTHOR

Beth Reekles is the author of the Kissing Booth series, which inspired the Netflix films. She first published *The Kissing Booth* on Wattpad in 2010, at age fifteen, and it accumulated almost 20 million reads before it was published by in 2012 by Random House Children's Books. Two more novels, *Rolling Dice* and *Out of Tune*, followed. She has also published a short story with Accent Press called "Cwtch Me If You Can." She was named one of *Time*'s 16 Most Influential Teenagers in late 2013, and has been shortlisted for several awards, including the 2014 Queen of Teen Award. Beth now works in IT while maintaining her career as an author and runs a blog where she talks about life as a twentysomething and offers writing advice.

authorbethreekles.com

🐦 📷

DON'T MISS THE BOOKS THAT STARTED IT ALL!

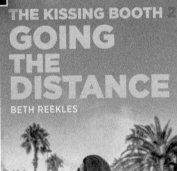